We are just beginning to realize that space power lies within our grasp, if we can only fend off those who would rather we were still living in caves, chanting to gods who behave like spoiled children. We've grown beyond that. We can and will achieve the final frontier of space with the power of the gods in our hands and under control.

The pessimism that seems to grip our age is unfounded. It is not the first time in history that this spirit has taken hold of us. But now we know what to do about it . . .

SPACE POWER

It's time to stop talking about it.

It's time to make it *happen*.

IN MEMORY OF

Dandridge MacFarlan Cole
1921–1965

He understood space power.

SPACE POWER

G. HARRY STINE

SF
ace books
A Division of Charter Communications Inc.
A GROSSET & DUNLAP COMPANY
51 Madison Avenue
New York, New York 10010

SPACE POWER

Copyright © 1981 by G. Harry Stine

An ACE Book

First Ace printing: September 1981
Published simultaneously in Canada

2 4 6 8 0 9 7 5 3 1
Manufactured in the United States of America

FOREWORD

Like most books, this one is a synthesis of the concepts, ideas, experiments, research, study, and work of many people. Some of their names are lost in antiquity because they developed early sources of energy and power long before the verbal or written records called "history" were kept. This should give one some notion of the scope of this book. It rests on foundations that are eons old, and describes power that is well within our technical grasp. Centuries of human effort seem to have been working toward this one ultimate concept: *space power*. As we will see, space power is the ultimate power for Planet Earth.

The concept of space power could not arise until human beings had actually broached the space frontier above the Earth's atmosphere. Thirty years ago, the subject was mentioned by Robert A. Heinlein in his script for the classic motion picture, *Destination Moon,* and in his book, *The Man Who Sold the Moon* (Shasta Publishers, Chicago, 1950). Twenty-five years ago, at the opening of the Space Age, some of us began to grasp the full significance of space power. But it was not until brilliant people like Dr. Krafft A. Ehricke, Dr. Peter E. Glaser, and Dr. Gerard K. O'Neill began to explore some of the uses of space for harnessing natural energy and for converting this into power that the full impact of what was happening began to dawn upon some of us.

Because this book is a synthesis, I must acknowledge the contributions of many people whose recent work has provided data, framework, and foundation for its development. I've already cited the pioneering work of Ehricke, Glaser, and O'Neill. But other, more recent, sources have contributed, especially in connection with the United States De-

1

partment of Energy (DOE) Satellite Power Systems Concept Development and Evaluation Program. This important study, conducted jointly with the National Aeronautics and Space Administration (NASA) was carried out by a large number of independent subcontractor firms and individual consultants between the fall of 1977 and the summer of 1980. The "DOE Study" developed the "baseline SPS" and a series of white papers on various technical, social, political, financial, management, and military aspects.

In addition to Ehricke, Glaser, and O'Neill, I'm indebted to colleagues with whom I participated in the preparation of white papers and further studies for DOE. These include Dr. J. Peter Vajk, Robert Salkeld, Gerald W. Driggers, and Richard D. Stutzke.

Last but not least, one should applaud James Patrick Baen and Susan Allison, editors at Ace Books, who've had the courage to look ahead with the author, grasp the concepts of space power, and encourage the writing and publication of space power concepts which are not "far-out Buck Rogers stuff" at all, but the sorts of things that will affect our lives and those of our children starting *now* and continuing into the foreseeable future.

If we proceed with space power, we will be able to solve a lot of problems.

If we understand the concepts of space power and their various implications, we stand a much better chance of preventing its mis-use.

G. Harry Stine
Phoenix, Arizona
November 1980

CHAPTER ONE

Energy.

It's the cornerstone of the universe, life, our individual existence, and our civilization.

We're being told by demagogues that we're running out of energy.

Nothing could be further from the truth.

An outstanding scientist and inventor, Dr. Henri M. Coanda, once told the author, "We are surrounded by energy; we must only learn how to use it."

We've done so in the past, and we'll continue to do so in the future, because the development of the human race from an animal-like existence to a condition where *some* of the members of the species are reasonably civilized is inexorably linked to the increasing use of energy.

According to anthropologist Carleton S. Coon:

"Man has been converting energy into social structure at an ever-increasing pace. As he has drawn more and more energy from the earth's storehouse, he has organized himself into institutions of increasing size and complexity."

This process perhaps began when early people learned how to use the energy of fire to heat their living spaces, cook their food, and fire-harden the points on their wooden hunting spears, and therefore operate more efficiently together in larger groups or "institutions" beginning with the tribal family. It has progressed to the point where today we have developed a wide variety of local, regional, national, and international institutions ranging from clubs to international associations. These have been made possible *only* because we've had the energy available for activities above and beyond the mundane task of surviving on a meal-to-meal and day-to-day basis.

Worldwide social organizations have recently evolved to

serve a totally new function in the annals of history: to keep people from destroying the world using the massive amounts of energy available from nuclear fission and fusion.

Again, the operation and maintenance of these large, far-flung, sophisticated, and highly complex institutions require a large amount of energy. Being the newest, most fragile, and most energy-intensive human institutions, they are also likely to be the first to fail if we do indeed face an energy shortage.

But as the professor states in the initial lecture at the beginning of the course, "Let us define our terms." This must be done to insure that the reader or student has the same basic referents as the author or teacher.

What is "energy"?

What is "power"?

Scientists have come up with various explanations for the concept of energy. When these are sorted out, the best paraphrase of their deliberations might be that "energy is a characteristic of the universe which causes things to change." Without energy, there can be no change.

Force, work, and power are concepts that grow out of the concept of energy. We'll be discussing all of these, but the two concepts of primary interest are *energy* and *power*.

We've already defined energy as best we can. Some scientists may argue with our initial definition, but it will serve as well as any other definition of energy, at least for the purpose of this book.

Power, on the other hand, is the time rate of application of energy to cause change. In other words, the quantity of energy applied or used or otherwise manipulated over a certain period of time—energy units per second, for example.

That's what we'll be talking about when we speak of space power: the continuing use of energy from a new source in order to produce power.

There are different forms of power:

Power includes the concepts of (a) power over the universe to make it do predictable things for personal or social benefit;

and (b) power over people to coerce them, willingly or otherwise, to do predictable things for their leaders, for themselves, or for joint benefit.

The latter is made possible by the former.

The nuclear physicists and engineers at Los Alamos Scientific Laboratory and other facilities of the U.S. Army Corps of Engineers Manhattan District learned this in 1942–1945.

Those of us involved in astronautics or cosmonautics ("star-sailing" in the United States, or "universe-sailing" in the Soviet Union) have been well aware of this since Dr. Wernher von Braun went to work for the Waffenprufamt of the German Wehrmacht on October 1, 1933. Military rationales, justification, and funding were the foundations for the development of large rockets which made possible the initial exploration of space and the discovery of space power.

This is still the case. The military potential of space power is as real today as it was to General Professor Becker, Captain von Horstig, and Captain Dr. Ing. Dornberger of the Waffenpruftamt of the German Wehrmacht in 1929–1930. The promise of power over people has provided the incentive for the development of data and techniques having to do with power over the universe.

This relationship is unlikely to change in the future, because human beings are basically lazy people. They unconsciously obey the Biological Law of Least Effort: Once they discover some technique that works, they stick with it until a technique that requires less effort comes along. Engineers and statesmen are no different in this regard. Both are highly conservative and reluctant to tamper with a working system or to try radical new methods unless they do so one step at a time. There's much to be said for the truism: "If it's working, don't fix it." However, blind adherence to this rule of thumb is incredibly presumptuous; it signifies the devout belief in the tenet of materialism that claims, "We know everything there is to know about the universe." Sure: if it's working, don't fix it. But this doesn't mean that one cannot or should not try to *improve* it a step at a time.

That's one reason for this book. The potential of space

power is so large that we cannot and should not merely plug it into the existing way of doing things without trying to make some improvements while doing so. Otherwise, the solution is worse than the problem.

Time for another definition:

Space power is the utilization of energy obtained in space from the Sun and other sources for application to *both* peaceful and military activities on Earth *and* in space.

Many space planners have long dreamed of the peacful use of outer space. The United Nations has drafted several treaties in this regard to which the United States and over fifty other nations are signatories. There is even a United Nations Committee on the Peaceful Uses of Outer Space.

But we cannot neatly separate the peaceful and military uses of outer space or of space power. Nor can we consider one without thinking of the other and taking both into account. *Every* technology and *every* form of power has both peaceful and military implications and applications.

Even the simple hunting spear with its fire-hardened point can be used for the peaceful purpose of hunting and therefore feeding one's self and others. It can also be used for threatening, coercing, harming, or killing other human beings. As our remote ancestors were concerned, this dichotomy was no reason to outlaw the spear. Our remote ancestors depended on spear technology and were not willing to forego it just because it was murderous in the hands of some of their colleagues.

Space power and its technologies are no different. Since space power offers such outstanding solutions to the many problems facing the human race on Planet Earth today, we cannot turn our backs on it because of its potential military implications or applications. In a like manner, we cannot forge blindly ahead in the development of space power and its technologies without knowing full well that there will be military implications and applications . . . and without trying to do something about these military aspects in the process.

The reason is simple:

There is so much energy available in space, and this almost limitless source of renewable energy can be made available with known technology so soon, that *some* segment of the human race will tap this energy to create space power.

It *will* be done because it *has* to be done. The alternatives to doing it are far worse than the consequences of not doing it at all:

Without using this large renewable energy resource in space, the human race is faced with a sure future in which the limited stores of natural energy on and in the Earth will be depleted. This may come in fifty years. It may come in a hundred years. It may not come for a thousand years. But it will surely happen even though we tap geothermal, tidal, wind, and other natural terrestrial sources. When it does happen, there will be less and less surplus energy available to support our most delicately balanced institutions: for example, the worldwide international ones that are presently keeping itchy trigger fingers from unleashing the thermonuclear holocaust. Without space power, the world will not die with a whimper; it may die in one hell of a bang.

This bang-up ending may also occur if we *do* exploit space power, but space power strangely contains within its military potential the seeds of universal terrestrial strategic disarmament as well as a final demise of the current balance of terror emobodied in the doctrine of MAD (Mutually Assured Destruction).

(This is not to say that MAD is bad. It works; it worked in October 1961 when it was put to its first test. Since it works, don't fix it . . . but *replace* it with something better called space power. After all, it *is* a MAD doctrine and should be replaced with something better lest it someday fail to work . . . as everything eventually does.)

But the Free World—the United States, Western Europe, and Japan are the primary Free World space-faring nations at the moment—now has the opportunity to exploit space power and to make it happen as we've been discussing: with the long-range goal of the peaceful solution to the world's energy problem uppermost in mind *and* with the intent of using the military implications of space power to hold in check others in the world who would use military space power as Atilla, Tamerlane, Napoleon, Hitler, and other "men on horseback" of the past have used military earth power.

If the Free World doesn't accept this responsibility and take on this task, then others will most certainly do so. Space power is an inevitable consequence of the utilization of space.

The utilization of space—the Third Industrial Revolution or the Space Enterprise—isn't a far-off dream. It's real. It's happening now. It's been happening on an increasing scale since 1962. It's happening because services and products of value can be obtained from space. In the realm of communications alone, more than half the world's communications traffic now uses satellites and the revenues from this use of space alone amount to more than a billion dollars per year.

The use of space includes not only the communications industry—which will grow exponentially in the last two decades of the twentieth century—but also the industries involved with producing new and unusual products in space, the use of raw materials from other sources in the Solar System, and the harnessing of the energy of the Sun in space both for use in space and for transmission back to Earth.

The products segment of space industrialization is now getting under way. The initial experiments have been carried out. It appears that a wide range of new products can be made in space because of the absence of gravity in the weightlessness of orbit and because of the high vacuum that can easily be obtained in space. Among these products are new metal alloys, improved glass, new and high-purity pharmaceuticals, and greatly improved crystals for advanced microelectronic integrated circuits.

In the United States, experiments are being conducted in small sounding rockets while experimenters wait for payload assignments on the NASA space shuttle flights. Space shuttle flights are now booked through 1985. The current "traffic model" eventually calls for one flight per week into orbit using one of four available space shuttle orbiters through the year 1991. Many firms are looking carefully at space products. Rockwell International has already stated that it intends to be the first company to make a profit from a product made in space.

The Japanese and the Western Europeans are not far behind. The government of the Federal Republic of Germany (West Germany) has already made a commitment to provide incentives to companies engaged in space product research, development, and production. The Japanese have made a similar commitment. Although the Europeans will use both the SpaceLab that fits into the American space shuttle payload bay and their own rocket booster, the *Ariane,* the Japanese have their own stable of space launch vehicles with which to carry out this work. And the Japanese have hosted some rumors about buying American space shuttles for their own use.

The People's Republic of China is a space power. Their two-staged CSS-X-4 ICBM is comparable to the American Titan-II. As the FB-1 space launch vehicle, this Chinese rocket is capable of placing 2,645 pounds in orbit around the Earth and has done so with *five* Chinese satellites to date. They are now working on an up-rated version of the FB-1 that would permit them to place a ton of payload in the important geosynchronous orbit 22,400 miles above the Earth. The FB-1/CSS-X-4 isn't a Chinese copy of anything; they designed, built, and tested it themselves.

Meanwhile, back in orbit, the Soviet Union has quietly been stealing the show when it comes to extended space operations and to the important area of space products.

The Soviet Union opted out of the race to the Moon with the United States in December 1968 . . . in spite of the fact that the official line from Moscow said the Soviets weren't in the race at all. This is twisting history because the historical archives are full of the public statements of Soviet scientists, engineers, politicians, bureaucrats, and cosmonauts discussing Soviet lunar landing goals and plans. I have the newspaper clipping from the New York *Times* dated December 18, 1968 by United Press International out of Moscow, reporting that Soviet officials had called off their planned manned circumlunar mission; they did it in the face of the risk that the United States would indeed up-stage a Soviet circumlunar flight with Apollo-8, which would orbit the Moon rather than just fly out and around the Moon and back.

But the Soviets did *not* drop their space program. They changed its goals. They opted to develop a capability for long-duration manned earth orbital operations for both military and industrial purposes.

They had a highly reliable manned launch vehicle, the Korolev R-7 "Semyorka" first-generation ICBM up-rated with upper stages; this vehicle was in production and they kept it in production because, unlike Americans, the Soviets don't change models every year. Once they've got something that works, they keep on making it because it provides secure jobs.

They had a heavy-lift launch vehicle of the Saturn-I class, the so-called "Proton" or "Type D" launch vehicle, the SL-9. They've had continual troubles with the guidance and control systems of this vehicle, to the extent they've decided not to man-rate it. Instead, the Soviets have used it as the launch vehicle for developing MIRV warheads and high-velocity re-entry bodies, boosting their *Salyut* space stations into orbit, and testing their manned, reusable winged space shuttle. Currently, they produce five of these Proton or SL-9 vehicles annually.

In 1970–1971, the Soviets shelved the development of a *real* heavy-lift launch vehicle that's bigger than the American Saturn 5. This Soviet monster has a liftoff thrust of 14 million pounds and can place an estimated 250,000 pounds in Earth orbit. The first one blew up on the launch pad in July 1969, killing a cosmonaut and several top engineers of the Soviet space program. The second and third attempts to launch what has been called "Webb's Giant," "the G-Class launch vehicle," and "the Lenin booster" ended in failure with mid-air explosions after launching. As of mid-1980, there were indications that the Soviets had commenced work on this vehicle again because they apparently need it to launch a space station larger than the *Salyut*.

The Soviets are also developing a winged, manned, reusable space shuttle. It's smaller than the NASA space shuttle, and will probably be put into operational use with an expendable booster. The Soviet Union has already made test flights of their shuttle, lofting two test shuttles at one time atop a Proton D-class launch vehicle on each flight. Since only five of these Proton vehicles are available per year, the Soviets are thus getting two tests for the price of one launch vehicle. The Soviet space shuttle does not involve as much highly advanced technology as the American space shuttle, but this has been typical of the Soviet approach to space for a quarter of a century. This philosophy of "keep it simple" and "overdesign to achieve reliability" has been abundantly apparent for more than fifty years in their aeronautical technology. Having ridden in Soviet-designed aircraft, I can attest to the fact that their aircraft are built with very rugged construction and very simple aerodynamics. Since their space engineers come out of aeronautical training schools and military aviation academies, one would certainly expect that the same design and operational philosophy would prevail in the Soviet space program. And it has, as Americans rediscovered in the exchange of information preceding and during the Apollo-Soyuz political flight in 1975.

At this time, the Soviet Union has achieved what the United States has not: the technology and the space transportation system to permit a continuous manned presence in space with a capability to automatically re-supply a space station using unmanned cargo vehicles. The Soviets have amassed an incredible record of long-duration space flights. In August 1980, cosmonaut Valery Ryumin celebrated his 41st birthday aboard the *Salyut-6*, the second straight year he celebrated his birthday in space; all told, Ryumin has spent more than a year in space on two different missions in *Salyut-6*.

The Soviets are regularly re-supplying *Salyut-6* using

Prognoz unmanned cargo ships and are capable of sending up additional 2-man *Soyuz* manned vehicles at regular intervals. Unlike the American SkyLab space station, *Salyut-6* has been refurbished, resupplied, and remanned almost constantly since it was launched in September 1977.

Salyut-6 has been more than just an experimental space station. The Soviets have used it as a space factory to produce new alloys and other products they're not talking very much about.

As an example of the propaganda use of space power, the Soviets have started to point to their *Salyut-6* achievements in direct contrast to the American lack of manned space flight activity because of delays in the NASA space shuttle. "The United States used its last Apollo for the Apollo-Soyuz test project, then switched over to the design of the space shuttle, due to which it has not conducted a single manned space flight for the past five years," a Soviet source said in August 1980. "The point is that the strategy chosen by the U.S. leadership has led to a long break in the implementation of the national program and to the postponement of the programs of international cooperation for those countries which have linked their fate with the shuttle." The Soviets pointed out how the joint Soyuz flights to Salyut-6 using cosmonauts from Eastern European countries and Viet Nam have expanded their international cooperation activities. Two cosmonauts from France are currently undergoing training at Star City, USSR, the space training center for the Soviet space program. "It is difficult to say," the Soviet spokesmen go on, "who will suffer most as a result of the course taken of late by the United States."

To some extent, the Soviets are, as of 1980, quite correct in their assessment of the situation.

At this writing, the Soviet Union is five years ahead of the rest of the world in space technology and in the important industrial area of space manufacturing. While the United States dismantled its space program, the Soviet Union increased its space effort, knowing full well the implications of space power. In the usual historical fashion, the United States leaders are very slow to learn the realities of world politics, and, in particular, how to wage technological warfare. This is because the political, bureaucratic, and administrative leadership changes completely in the United States on the average of once every six years, resulting in severe dislocations in *any* long-range technology program. In fact, if it hadn't been for President John F. Kennedy's concise statement of the lunar landing goal and the fact that the goal was originally determined by President Lyndon B. Johnson when he was Kennedy's Vice President and Chairman of the National Aeronautics and Space Council, it's extremely doubtful that the Apollo Program would have survived the attacks of the growing anti-technology movement in the United States during the late 1960's.

That U.S. anti-technology movement is still around; it is strong, and it is well-entrenched in the Washington bureaucracy that writes and enforces the federal regulations having to do with energy, environmental safety, product safety, consumer safety, etc.

The United States has another problem compared to the Soviet Union's space program: the attempted separation of U.S. civilian and military space programs. The United States has assiduously attempted to maintain a sharp line of demarcation between civilian and military space programs since President Dwight D. Eisenhower announced this American policy in 1955. However, the fine line between civilian and military space programs has always been drawn with a broad brush rather than a fine-tipped pen. With the space shuttle program, the military and civilian space programs of the USA merged again because the space shuttle design was strongly influenced by performance requirements of the United States Air Force, which had been told to use the Space Shuttle with military crews to place military satellites in orbit. The Air Force didn't like this order then because they'd developed several highly reliable expendable launch systems such as the Titan-III series. As the dividing line between military and civilian space programs has slowly vanished in the USA, it has been accompanied by an increasing amount

of squabbling between the civilian segment headquartered in
NASA and the military segment lodged in the United States
Air Force. The most recent change of heart in the Department
of Defense has the United States Air Force fantasizing about
the "Blue Shuttle"—the U.S. Air Force taking over the
entire NASA space shuttle program in the interests of national defense.

This is not to say that there isn't a significant American
military space program or military presence in space without
the space shuttle. There is a great deal more to it than the
American public knows. (In fact, the Kremlin undoubtedly
knows more than the American people do, which naturally
leads one to wonder who's really being denied information
and why.)

There's no such division between military and civilian
space programs in the Soviet Union, and there never has
been. There's also no comparison between American security measures and the intense secrecy of the Soviets. ("The
Devil's Dictionary" by Ambrose Bierce defines a Russian as
"a person with a Caucasian body and a Mongolian soul.")
It's true that in the past we have seen a slackening of the
Soviet scientific space program during periods when their
limited cadre of space engineers and technicians have had to
shift their efforts over to new military strategic rocket systems. This is rapidly changing, however, because the Soviets
have educated and trained a very large corps of rocket and
space scientists, researchers, engineers, technicians, and
military troops. We can no longer count on the "short blanket
nature of the Soviet economy" (When the shoulders get the
blanket, the feet get cold) to place an occasional brake on the
Soviet space program.

Therefore, the concept of space power isn't an exclusive
American space doctrine. If a private citizen such as myself
can dig out the facts and come to some conclusions regarding
space power, other people in other countries and cultures can
do the same. I have no military security clearance; all my
information comes from open, unclassified sources in the
public domain. Nobody leaks information to me, either. I am

but one of a group of space intelligence gatherers with access only to public data, but I can assure you that members of this group are in almost constant touch with one another for the purpose of exchanging information.

In two separate books—*The Third Industrial Revolution* (Ace, 1979) and *The Space Enterprise* (Ace, 1980)—I've pointed out in some detail what can be done in space and how to make it profitable. Basically, there's a buck to be made in space, and a company called Comsat has been doing so for more than a decade. But there's another aspect that was only briefly touched upon in *The Space Enterprise*: There are military consequences to our human activities in space, and there are matters of defense and survival that demand great attention because of the implications of an outgrowth of the space enterprise, space power.

In other words, if our space enterprise isn't done properly, somebody can come and take it all away with space power they've developed from their own space industrialization activities.

Right now, space power is slipping through the fingers of the people of the United States—you and I who own and work for the companies, big and small, that make up the basic economy and form the basic strength of the United States of America. It's not too late yet to re-acquire American space power, but it will take a quarter of a century or more to regain it and constant attention thereafter in order to maintain it.

Like it or not, we have a tiger by the tail. In that situation, the only thing possible is to swarm aboard and ride that tiger.

CHAPTER TWO

Space power comes from space energy.

The major source of energy in the Solar System is the Sun.

The Sun probably formed long before the planets, planetary satellites, planetoids, and other celestial bodies in the Solar System. The forces of gravity and magnetohydrodynamics caused the matter at the core of the proto-Sun to be squeezed hard enough to ignite the thermonuclear fires that are still burning and will continue to burn for millennia, radiating their energies outward into the Solar System and interstellar space as the nuclear particles of the solar wind and as electromagnetic radiation—radio waves, microwaves, infra-red, visible light, ultra-violet, X-rays, and gamma rays.

The manner in which the Sun and our Solar System were born is of little consequence for the purposes of this discussion. The fact that the Sun is there and providing energy *right now* is of prime consideration.

The Sun is the only operating nuclear fusion reactor known at the time of this writing.

The Sun is a star, and only an average, middle-aged star at that. Although we're learning more about it every day because of space science research, the following general data are of interest.

The Sun has a mean or average visual diameter of approximately 1,393,000 kilometers. It has a volume 1,300,000 times that of the Earth and a mass 330,000 times the Earth's. It contains most of the mass in the Solar System. In fact, an extraterrestrial astronomer looking at the Solar System from a distance of five light years would conclude that it consisted only of the Sun and the planet Jupiter, which in itself contains 72% of the *planetary* mass of the Solar System.

But the important thing about the Sun is the enormous amount of energy produced by the thermonuclear fusion that goes on within it. The Sun "burns" hydrogen into helium by nuclear fusion processes, consuming 657,000,000 tons of hydrogen every second. Its core temperatures run into the millions of degrees, but the temperature of the photosphere which we see is only about 6000° Celsius. Each square meter of its surface radiates energy at the rate of 80,000 horsepower continuously. At a distance of the orbit of the Earth, this energy amounts to 1.94 calories per square centimeter per minute. This quantity is known as the *solar constant*. It's not truly "constant" because modern astronomers have found small changes in the solar output from time to time for reasons as yet unknown. However, for all intents and purposes, we can use the number 1.94 cal/cm²/min as a "constant."

Geothermal energy—or more properly "planetothermal energy"—is the only energy in the solar system that doesn't originate in the Sun. Planetothermal energy comes from the gravitational squeezing of matter in planetary cores. It's the same sort of energy that lit the fires of the Sun eons ago. It didn't light the thermonuclear fires of Earth because Earth is too small to create enough squeezing to accomplish the thermonuclear light-off. However, the planet Jupiter is apparently right on the edge of being a proto-star, being just a little bit too small to generate enough thermonuclear energy by gravitational squeeze to become a star.

All the remaining energy in the solar system comes from or came at one time from the Sun.

This is also true of the planet Earth. Coal represents solar energy converted to organic matter by plants millions of years ago and stored up within the Earth. The same can be said for petroleum. Tidal forces are caused by the combined gravitational fields of the Moon and the Sun. Wind forces are caused by unequal heating of the Earth and its atmosphere by the radiation from the Sun. Wood and other organic fuels are of solar origin; the trees that produced the wood could not have grown without the process of photosynthesis within them producing cellulose and other carbohydrates with solar radiation as the energy to drive this complex system.

For the past several millennia, the human race has been using that vast quantity of converted solar energy stored within plants from season to season and stored for eons underground in the form of coal and petroleum. The human race has also tapped wind power and tidal power, but most of our energy has come from the "fossil fuels": coal, petroleum, and natural gas.

In accordance with Coon's energy thesis, we've been converting more and more of this natural energy of the Earth into social structure at an ever-increasing rate. Depending upon which futurist you talk to and the particular computer program he's developed to provide a mathematical model of the world, you'll be told that we'll use up all the fossil fuel reserves in anywhere from twenty years to five hundred years.

According to the best current data I can get my hands on, we have enough fossil fuel to last well into the twenty-first century.

The amount of coal in the United States alone would last this country more than 2,000,000 years at our current rate of consumption. The entire known world reserve of coal amounts to 560,000,000,000,000 tons, enough to last the whole world for at least 250 years at current consumption rates.

In the case of petroleum, there have been twenty-five serious forecasts of world petroleum reserves made since 1942. By 1980, *six* of these estimates had already been exceeded by known, proven, and producing petroleum fields discovered since the forecasts were made. It's currently estimated that the world has 4,000,000,000,000 barrels of petroleum, a ten-fold increase in forecast reserves over the last thirty-five years. At the current rate of consumption, this currently estimated reserve will last until 2150 A.D.

The United States alone has 11,900,000,000,000 cubic feet of natural gas in reserve, enough to last at current consumption rates for another 196 years.

However, the current rate of fossil fuel consumption is increasing in perfect agreement with Coon's energy thesis.

Even though this increase in consumption rate means a quicker end to the Earth's fossil fuel reserves, we can forget about running out of fossil fuels because over the next fifty to seventy-five years the human race will not be using coal, petroleum, or natural gas for fuel. People will be conserving and recycling these precious non-renewable resources for chemical feedstocks that can be used over and over again.

Where will we get the energy we need if not from these fossil fuels?

From where that fossil energy came from in the first place.

We will get the energy from the Sun.

And we will get that solar energy in space.

We will have to get it in space because of the manifold problems of getting enough of it here on the surface of the Earth.

With a solar constant of 1.94 calories per square centimeter per minute, solar energy is diffuse. It takes a large solar collector to bring together enough energy to be of either domestic or industrial use. An increasing number of buildings in the United States are being heated or cooled by solar energy, and this requires that they have a very large area of solar collectors. These large collectors are expensive because they require structural bracing and support against Earth's gravity. In addition, because human beings have voluntarily crowded themselves together in densely-populated centers called "cities," there isn't very much surface area available for these large collectors near the place where the solar energy is to be used.

One other major problem faces earthbound solar energy technology: the sun doesn't shine all the time on a given location in the densely-populated temperate zones. Therefore, some manner of energy storage must be used to make the solar energy collected during daylight hours available when it's needed at night. This in turn means larger solar collectors because the collectors must bring together 100% more energy beyond immediate demand during the day so that this excess can be stored for nighttime use. Probably the best widely-available heat storage material is water, which creates another problem because sunlight is most abundantly available in locations where water usually isn't: the deserts of the world.

These many problems of harnessing solar energy on the Earth's surface are engineering problems, and they will be solved. They require the development of known technology, not the invention of new technology. However, because of the Earth's gravity which places limitations on very large structures and because of the Earth's rotation which creates the day-night cycle, solar energy usage on Earth in the foreseeable future is likely to be confined to small, decentralized, local applications. In this regard, terrestrial solar power offers some promise in the area of decentralization, which is certainly an admirable goal. It is particularly useful in the Third World nations whose energy needs may be too small to justify the large decentralized energy collection, generation, and distribution systems. Decentralized terrestrial solar energy technology will be useful in the isolated regions of the most highly developed countries, too.

Decentralized terrestrial solar energy technology can't provide us with enough energy to satisfy the demands of our growing planetary culture and its social institutions, however. In order to meet the 1978 demand for heat energy obtained from coal and petroleum alone, one would need to cover over a thousand square miles of the Earth's surface with solar collectors at various points in order to cover the contingencies of bad weather plus the day-night cycle of solar energy. We need that land for other purposes: people, animals, plants, and water storage.

Although terrestrial-based solar energy collection can't do the job all by itself, there's a possibility that it can be augmented or assisted by the use of devices located in space around the Earth.

The simplest apparent approach to this is the use of mirrors.

For many years, one of the pioneer space thinkers and planners, Dr. Krafft A. Ehricke, has been considering (among other things) a system called "Soletta" or "little sun.'' A soletta unit is a collection of large mirrors built in orbit and reflecting the raw sunlight of space to the surface of the Earth below. A soletta unit would be large. In order to reflect to Earth 50% of the daytime solar intensity, it would be approximately 650 meters in diameter. A cluster of three soletta units would be required in order to reflect 50% daytime illumination onto an area of approximately 2700 square kilometers (1047 square miles) on the Earth.

The soletta illumination could be used for photosynthesis enhancement—providing an environment of constant sunlight in which plants would grow, thus theoretically increasing crop yields. Soletta illumination would also provide a means for operating solar collectors on an around-the-clock schedule to provide a constant source of heat or electrical power derived from photovoltaic cells (solar cells). The problem is the cost of doing this—approximately 80 billion 1980 dollars per soletta system. This cost is high when compared to other space power systems.

Another alternate space power system that has been considered is the location of fast breeder nuclear reactors in orbit to eliminate any possible safety hazard of operating them on Earth.

But by far the most promising space power system under consideration in 1981 is the Solar Power Satellite (SPS) invented and patented in 1968 by Dr. Peter E. Glaser of Arthur D. Little, Inc., Cambridge, Massachusetts.

The SPS offers an elegant solution to the problem of getting diffuse solar energy from space to the Earth's surface with an energy density high enough to be economical.

As we've seen, solar energy is diffuse—1.94 calories per square centimeter at the Earth's orbit. Furthermore, on the Earth's surface the sun doesn't shine constantly. The SPS takes advantage of the fact that the sun shines continuously in Earth orbit—except for brief occasions when an SPS would be momentarily in the Earth's shadow. And the SPS concept offers at least two ''buckets'' for getting the solar energy down to Earth in a concentration that's economical.

The orbital segment of an SPS system is the powersat

itself. It would be located in "geosynchronous orbit" (GSO
or GEO), an orbit 22,400 miles above the Earth's equator
where a satellite goes around the Earth once every 24 hours,
thus appearing to stand still in the sky when seen from the
Earth below. Many communications and weather satellites
are currently positioned in "geosynch" orbit.

The advantages of locating a powersat in geosynch orbit
should be obvious; since the powersat appears to stand still in
the sky, a ground antenna working with the satellite can be
positioned and locked into alignment without having all the
technical problems involved with tracking the satellite across
the sky.

The type of powersat that appears to be most economical
and most technically feasible at this time would be made up
mostly of huge arrays of photovoltaic cells or "solar batteries" that are very similar to the type you can buy for
experimental purposes in most radio/electronic stores.

The photovoltaic powersat converts sunlight directly to
electricity by the use of solar cells made either from silicon or
from gallium arsenide—two possibilities for use of different
solar cells types exist with this design.

Another type of powersat that has been studied would
concentrate solar energy by means of huge mirror arrays to
boil a working fluid. The thermal cycle powersat—so-named
because it uses a thermodynamic cycle in the making of
electricity from heat—would require the use of turboelectric
generators to convert heat energy into electric energy in a
manner similar to the way it's done at most coal-fired or
oil-fired electric plants on Earth. However, the thermal cycle
is a closed system that recycles the working fluid rather than
exhausting it into the environment as is done on Earth.

A photovoltaic or thermal cycle powersat will be big. The
Baseline Reference System used by the U.S. Department of
Energy in its 1978–1980 SPS design study would produce
5,000,000,000 watts of electricity—that's five billion watts
or, in technical shorthand, "five gigawatts." For comparison, Hoover Dam on the Colorado River can produce a
maximum of 1.835 gigawatts (Gw) of electricity.

A five gigawatt SPS powersat would have a solar collection array 10.5 kilometers (6.5 miles) long and 5.25 kilometers (3.42 miles) wide having an area of 55.125 square kilometers (22.23 square miles). The thickness of this structure would be only about 500 meters (310 feet), making its thickness to area ratio thinner than the sheet of paper of this page. It can be constructed and it can maintain its structural integrity because it will be in the weightless condition of orbit.

The structure would be fabricated of graphite-reinforced composite plastic beams and girders formed in space by a ''beam builder'' device using raw materials brought up from Earth by Earth-to-orbit cargo rockets.

On one end of the array—in the middle of some designs other than the DOE baseline design—is the power transmitter. Two methods are under consideration for the transmission of electric power from the powersat array to the ground. One method would convert the array-generated electricity of the powersat into a high-energy laser beam. The other method which is considered as part of the DOE baseline system would convert the electricity into a radio beam. The radio frequency selected by DOE (but not yet approved by international treaties which allocate the electromagnetic frequency spectrum) is 2.45 gigaHertz up in the electromagnetic frequencies utilized by radars.

Either the laser beam or the radio beam would be aimed toward a ground-based receiving unit. In the case of the radio beam power transmission method, this is a rectifying antenna called a ''rectenna.''

If the rectenna were located at the Earth's equator directly under the powersat whose power beam it was receiving, a rectenna would be approximately 10 kilometers (6.2 miles) in diameter.

The size of the ground rectenna is based upon (a) the acceptable level of radio energy required to insure the safety and health of living organisms on the ground around and under the rectenna, and (b) an acceptable level of energy density in the power beam that will not cause beam/atmosphere interactions or radio-frequency interference. The bigger the rectenna, the more diffuse the radio frequency (r-f) energy in the power beam. The design guidelines for the rectenna were set by DOE at 23 milliwatts per square centimeter at the center of the rectenna and one milliwatt per square centimeter at the edge.

The energy in the middle of the radio power beam at the surface of the Earth is orders of magnitude below anything that will cause harm to living beings or the environment. This statement is based upon proven fact.

The accepted United States standard for r-f energy safety for human beings is 10 milliwatts per square centimeter, a figure that was arrived at with great care as a result of data accumulated for nearly half a century. However, some recent experimentation indicates that the beam energy density at the center of the rectenna could be safely increased to as much as 40 milliwatts per square centimeter without incurring either safety hazards or ecological damage.

The "spill-over" radio energy from the edge of the rectenna will be concentrated in "side lobes," but the energy density in the first and most powerful side lobe located approximately 8 kilometers (5 miles) from the center of the rectenna has an energy density of less than 0.8 milliwatts per square centimeter—more than a hundred times less than the U.S. safety standard.

A small prototype of the rectenna was tested at the Jet Propulsion Laboratory (JPL) of NASA in 1975. Tests conducted with the Arricebo radio telescope in Puerto Rico have shown that there would be no significant affects on the Earth's atmosphere—non-linear self-focusing instabilities and thermal runaway conditions—caused by the passage of a radio power beam of the size and energy level planned for a powersat.

The energy density in the power beam for rectennas not located on the Earth's equator is going to be less because in the temperate zones at, say, 35-degrees North latitude, the rectenna is tipped with respect to the beam and therefore occupies a larger area because the circular power beam has an elliptical footprint on the Earth's surface at these higher latitudes. Thus, a rectenna built in the southwestern United States would have an elliptical ground dimension of, say, 10 kilometers (6.2 miles) wide east-to-west by 17.4 kilometers (10.8 miles) long north-to-south.

The reason why radio power beams are being considered over laser power beams is the greater efficiency of the radio power beam transmission concept. Laser power transmission suffers from losses due to distances and to interferences with the Earth's atmosphere because the laser frequency will, of necessity, have to be in the infra-red portion of the spectrum rather than in the visible light portion, the power beam must be able to get through to the rectenna even if there's a cloud cover over the rectenna, and the power beam must *not* interact with this atmospheric moisture.

The feature of the r-f power beam that permits it to be closely controlled, directed, and concentrated is the ability to "phase-lock" the beam. This is a technical term meaning that all the transmission elements radiate r-f in a precise split-second sequence from the powersat. The phase-locked power beam can thus be directed to the rectenna 22,400 miles or more away with the greatest precision. It assures not only the maximum efficiency and least degree of loss within the power beam, but also permits the direction of the beam to be controlled.

The power beam would be further controlled by a "pilot beam" transmitted up from the rectenna. This pilot beam is a coded radio signal to the powersat telling the control circuits in the powersat beam transmitter where to direct the beam and how to control the phase-locking. If the power beam wanders slightly away from the rectenna, radio frequency sensors would detect this, tell the pilot beam control circuits, and thus cause the power beam to be directed back into confluence with the rectenna. All of this happens within microseconds.

If the pilot beam fails, circuitry in the powersat "defocuses" the power beam or turns it off, thus rendering it harmless by spreading its energy out over a very large area with a power beam density many orders of magnitude below the safety limit.

The rectenna itself would be a collection of structures that would look like roofed sheds with an open steel mesh mounted horizontally on steel framing structures supported by steel columns on concrete footings. Solid-state diode rectifier elements would be mounted directly on the rectenna elements, and DC electricity collected from the rectenna diodes would be carried to a central point where the electrical energy could be converted from DC to whatever the local electrical power grid standard happens to be—in the United States, 22,000 to 330,000 volts at 60 Hertz.

Each powersat in orbit would have its dedicated rectenna which would in turn have a coded pilot beam that would be recognized only by the proper powersat.

The overall efficiency of the SPS system is about 7%, and this is almost totally determined by the efficiency of the solar cells used in the powersat. The radio power beam transmission system has an efficiency of 63% from the point where the electricity is taken off the bus bars of the powersat solar array to the point where the electricity is delivered to the local electric power grid at the rectenna output.

It's a very good bet that more highly efficient solar cells will be developed in the future, thereby permitting a significant increase in the efficiency of the overall SPS system.

Even at an overall system efficiency of 7%, the SPS system doesn't fare badly in comparison with other electrical energy generation systems currently used on Earth.

The DOE Baseline SPS System was predicated on 1990 technology, which means that there are still a few technical items that haven't been tested yet. But there is no deep secret of nature that needs to be uncovered before an SPS system can work. We need only to test and develop portions of the system that are new to determine the best way to make them or operate them most efficiently.

The rectenna system element based on Earth is simple. Most of it can be prefabricated. It can be assembled, erected, and put on-line with relatively unskilled labor.

The powersat itself requires high technology, new elements, and the construction and operation of a large space transportation system in order to lift the materials from Earth to orbit, fabricate them in orbit, and assemble the powersat.

The first pilot powersat will be the biggest engineering job attempted in space thus far and the construction of the SPS system will rank with the greatest engineering tasks of all time.

The first SPS unit will be the most difficult to build and the most expensive, because that's where all the mistakes will be made. Once the first one is on line, it will be possible with the space transportation system in place and the facilities available to construct two 10-gigawatt powersats per year in Earth orbit.

Big numbers impress only small people, and engineers deal with big numbers in their everyday work. Therefore, it will come as a surprise to most non-technical people to learn that a single 10-gigawatt powersat will weigh more than 38,000,000 kilograms (83,800,000 pounds or about 42 thousand tons). This isn't even as heavy as one of today's oil tankers and less than a Great Lakes ore carrier ship. It will come as a surprise to non-technical readers who are still amazed and astounded at the engineers' ability to put a one-ton satellite in orbit. Many readers may remember the dark days of 1958 when the launching of the 38-pound *Explorer-I* was hailed with delight as the first U.S. earth satellite. Well, things have come a little ways since that day . . .

To lift all of this mass into geosynch orbit will require a very large space transportation system, and that's one of the great spinoff benefits of building an SPS system. We'll get more than an answer to our energy needs; we'll also open the door to the solar system in the process.

CHAPTER THREE

A *big* space transportation system will be necessary to lift the millions of tons of material into geosynch orbit required to build a powersat.

Because of all the publicity that was given to space launch costs by the news media during the Apollo manned lunar landing missions in the 1968–1972 time period, there is a stigma of "exorbitant cost" associated with every space mission.

Therefore, the difference between the Apollo flights and the SPS transportation system operation needs to be firmly established right at the start.

The Apollo Program was a politically-motivated project, funded by the government with cost a secondary concern to the primary goal of getting to the Moon before the Soviet Union. We know the Soviets had a manned lunar program; we also know now (and may have known at that time through intelligence sources) that the Soviets had the capability of sending a single cosmonaut on a circumlunar mission in December 1968, but that they apparently did *not* have the capability to land even a single cosmonaut on the Moon and return him to Earth alive. Even if we'd had this knowledge of the Soviet lunar capabilities in 1968–1970, we would have certainly gone ahead with Apollo anyway because the program was so large and so near completion that its very momentum would have carried it through. As a matter of fact, that is exactly what happened. The program's sheer size meant that it couldn't be stopped immediately, but it was brought to a halt in December 1972 with the return of Apollo-17.

National prestige was the primary driver behind Apollo. "Hang the cost! Hire another acre of engineers and print another billion dollars!" We *had* to beat the Soviets to the

Moon . . . and we did. Once we'd done so, the whole space program was wound down because its function as an instrument of national prestige—*not* of scientific exploration and *not* as the exploitation of a new frontier—had been completed.

On the side, a lot of people made a lot of money as a result of Apollo, and they couldn't let it be stopped or fail. One of these was Lyndon Baines Johnson who "happened" to have some interest in some swampy land south of Houston and northeast of New Orleans . . . There were others, but that example serves the purpose here.

The space transportation system for the SPS program is not the same sort of animal. It is to the Apollo program as a transcontinental airline is to a single person flying a single-engined airplane across the country. Charles A. Lingbergh certainly pioneered transcontinental air transportation with his "Spirit of St. Louis" and other aircraft, but when United Airlines, American Airlines, and Transcontinental and Western Air (TWA) were in business ten years later, their operation and philosophy was greatly different . . . and so were their cost structures.

The SPS space transportation system depends upon other factors than have been paramount in the governmental space program to date: low cost, high reliability, ease of operation, inherent safety, and the capability for a high level of use. Without these factors, the SPS program cannot be carried out at all. *Something* must transport tons of material and hundreds of people into space at the lowest possible cost because investors can't afford a "cost be damned" program; with the highest reliability because project managers will count on each flight; with ease of operation because of the large number of flights required; with safety because human beings will be using the system; and with versatility because of the wide variety of different types of cargoes that will have to be lifted to space in the SPS project.

If this sounds like a tall order in light of the history of space transportation thus far, it isn't.

As a matter of fact, such a space transportation system is

on the drawing boards of at least *three* aerospace companies as of 1981.

An SPS space transportation system can be built starting today with technology that is either in existence or that can reasonably be expected to be in hand by 1990.

First of all, we must define what we mean by the term, "space transportation system." It is usually thought of as being rocket-propelled spacecraft. But a space transportation system is more than vehicles. This is true of *any* transportation system. This statement will be readily admitted by anyone who's worked in the transportation industry on Earth or who's engaged in the hobby of modeling transportation systems such as railroads. Some model railroad fans are interested in motive power—the locomotives. Others find their greatest interest in rolling stock. Still others enjoy track work while others delight in making realistic scenery. And yet another category of rail modeler enjoys the operation of the model system itself. Like a space transportation system, a rail transportation system is nothing if you've just got motive power and nowhere to go with it, no way to load or unload payload, no terminals, no maintenance shops, and no control systems.

So our discussion of a space transportation system will have to include these additional support elements as well.

The DOE Reference SPS System or "Baseline System" that's being used as an example of how to get started in space power goes into considerable detail regarding space transportation. But, the space transportation system that we'll discuss here is a synthesis or amalgamation of the DOE study and the systems proposed by Rockwell International and Boeing Aerospace, combining systems to achieve the greatest ease of operation and the greatest possible versatility. The number of "throw-away" elements is minimized, thus reducing costs. Specialized vehicles have been replaced by spacecraft with a greater versatility in the sort of cargoes they can carry.

At this stage in the development of space transportation, it's simply not possible to place very large payloads at geosynch orbit 22,400 miles above the Earth's surface with a *single* launch vehicle having any reasonable size. It's like sending a cargo by ship from Liverpool, England to Pittsburgh, Pennsylvania. One sort of ship is required for the transatlantic portion of the trip—i.e.: a large ship can be used to cross the Atlantic Ocean, thus reducing costs. But to navigate up the Mississippi and Ohio rivers from New Orleans to Pittsburgh requires smaller ships with different characteristics. The analogy holds true for sending cargoes to geosynch orbit. It will have to be done in two steps.

The first step involves lifting payloads of cargo and people from the Earth's surface into low Earth orbit (LEO) about 150 miles up.

The second step lifts payloads from LEO to geosynchronous Earth orbit (GEO or GSO).

Two different types of space vehicles are required for the different steps.

The Earth-to-orbit step requires a lot of rocket thrust because the space vehicle or ship goes from the bottom of a very deep well—the Earth's gravity well—surrounded by the Earth's atmosphere up to the weightlessness and vacuum of LEO. To be reusable, the ship must be capable of repeatedly withstanding the very high temperatures associated with ramming back into the Earth's atmosphere, it must possess some way of being guided and controlled in the atmosphere, and it must be capable of safely landing on the Earth's surface in a condition that permits it to be used again with a minimum amount of time, money, and materials expended. To achieve the least costs, an Earth-to-orbit ship should be as large as it's practical to make it because, as its size goes up, the ratio between its structural weight and its loaded weight decreases. More of its gross weight can then be devoted to its payload: rocket propellants and cargo. For convenience, we'll call the Earth-to-orbit-and-return ship a "shuttle" even though it may not resemble the current NASA space shuttle. "Shuttle" will be a generic term for the sort of ship that operates between the Earth's surface and space.

For the second step in the trip, LEO to GEO, an entirely different ship is required, one that *always* operates in the vacuum of space and therefore does not need any aerodynamic shaping. This "deep space" ship also operates always in the weightlessness of orbit or under the accelerations imparted to it only by its own rocket engines. Therefore, the deep space ship can be designed and built quite differently to maximize the efficiency of its operation in the unique environment of orbital space. For example, its rocket engines do not need the tremendous thrust required for a shuttle, so they can be more modestly sized. The lower accelerations of its operations—a maximum of three gravities or three times the acceleration of Earth's gravity—permits engineering economies to be made in its structure. This deep space ship—oftimes called an "orbital transfer vehicle"—is the second category of spacecraft in our space transportation system.

However, the payload that both a shuttle and a deep space ship carries can be divided into two classes: (a) people, and (b) cargoes of materials and supplies. Each class of payload will require a different sort of care during transit.

People must have pressurized, temperature-controlled environments around them and cannot be subjected to any accelerations exceeding three gravities, this being considered the maximum permissible acceleration for people who have not undergone extensive training in high-gee maneuvers. (When I pull three-gees in my airplane during a maneuver, I know it, I don't like it, and I'm not trained to endure such acceleration for more than a few seconds because it becomes difficult to breathe and almost impossible to move.) People will require feeding and sanitary facilities on any trip lasting more than a few hours.

Cargoes of materials and supplies, on the other hand, may or may not require a compartment that is pressurized and temperature controlled; some cargoes may need only rudimentary temperature control with no pressurization requirements whatsoever. Some cargoes are acceleration insensitive, permitting boost accelerations that are higher and therefore more efficient in terms of how rocket propellant is used. In addition, a great deal more non-human cargo than human help is going to be required to build an SPS. Therefore, cargo freighters will probably be much larger and will transport heavier payloads.

A cursory look at a passenger liner versus a tramp steamer or a wide-bodied jet airliner versus a heavy-lift cargo plane reveals the simple truth that engineers design and build passenger vehicles differently from cargo vehicles. Although it's true that passengers often ride in cargo vehicles and that cargo is often transported in passenger vehicles, this swap of payloads usually occurs because of reasons of urgency, expediency, or economy.

We've thus divided our space transportation system into a basic requirement for four types of ships:

1. Earth-to-orbit-and-return passenger ships—Passenger shuttles.

2. Earth-to-orbit-and-return cargo shuttles—Freight shuttles.

3. Orbit-to-orbit passenger ships—Deep space passenger ships.

4. Orbit-to-orbit cargo ships—Deep space freighters.

Let's look at each of these in turn and discuss their basic characteristics because, regardless of who builds the ships, the technology used to build them, and when they're built within the next twenty years, each category will have certain basic characteristics.

The characteristics shared by *all* four classes will be (a) lowest possible operating cost, (b) highest possible reliability, and (c) maximum possible use rate. These three characteristics are shared by *any* commercial transportation system on Earth, and there's no reason why a space transportation system should be any different in these respects, or why a space transportation system cannot possess any of these three basic characteristics.

The *size* of each type of ship depends upon the nature of the SPS construction job and its engineering details. Up to a point, the bigger the ship in terms of numbers of passengers or tons of cargo, the more efficient it becomes. But in the case of the shuttles, a limit on size is reached because of the time and facilities required to handle them, load them, launch them, and recover them on Earth. This doesn't hold true for the deep space ships. Another limit on size is the amount of space transportation capability that's lost when a big ship must be repaired or maintained . . . or in case it's lost due to accident. (It would probably be most efficient to have *one* super-sized wide-bodied jet transport leaving each day from LAX to JFK, and vice-versa. But unless you've got a stand-by in case one of them needs repair, you're in trouble. And if one of them happens to have an accident, you've lost not only a very large number of passengers but also a highly expensive airplane.)

The sizing of the space transportation vehicles in the DOE Baseline Study came about as a result of a series of re-iterative trade-offs between all of the factors that were taken into consideration. This means that a "first cut" at sizing was taken, and the various effects upon system costs were determined as a result. Then changes were made in the sizing to determine effects on costs and other SPS elements.

The general ground rules followed were:

(a) The system elements were to be dedicated and optimized for the construction, operation, and maintenance of an SPS system. If other uses happened to "fall out" of these designs—as we will see that indeed they do—so much the better.

(b) The transportation system was designed for minimum total project cost—not just of the transportation system, but of the *entire* SPS system.

(c) The energy and therefore the rocket propellant costs would be minimized consistent with minimum overall system costs; energy costs money.

(d) The design of the transportation system would be made to minimize the environmental impact at the launch and landing sites and any environmental protective measures would be factored into the costs.

(e) The transportation system would require the minimum use of critical materials consistent with low cost, minimum energy, and environmental impacts.

The optimum spacecraft sizes that came out of the study were as follows:

The freight shuttle should be capable of lifting at least 424 metric tons (932,800 pounds) to LEO. This was not surprising. Space transportation planners have known for some years that the ''million pounds to orbit'' booster would be highly efficient for whatever large space projects were undertaken. N.B.: Both the Saturn 5 and the best-guess estimate of the Soviet Heavy Launch Vehicle (the Class G launch vehicle) are quarter-million pound to orbit launchers, but the Saturn 5 was designed with 1960 technology. The freight shuttle designed with 1980 technology is nowhere near as large, and the unique requirements of the space transportation system not only reduces the cost of such a launch vehicle but its size as well. For example, the Boeing version of the freight shuttle would be 76 meters (243 feet) tall and about 74 feet in diameter with a base diameter of 131 feet.

The passenger shuttle can be achieved by using the existing NASA space shuttle orbiter, putting a 75-passenger module in the cargo bay, and launching it as a two-staged vehicle with a reusable fly-back booster. The ultimate passenger shuttle is, as we'll see, a totally reusable single-stage spacecraft carrying up to 75 passengers.

The deep space passenger ships are also designed to carry 75 passengers in a variation of the 75-passenger shuttle module. Propulsion is provided by liquid hydrogen/liquid oxygen rocket engines.

But the deep space freighter is something totally new because its job is to propel SPS subassemblies put together in LEO out to GSO where the final assembly of the SPS takes place. Since such a craft is a freighter, and since it will be propelling a very large solar array, propulsion is by means of an electric rocket motor using solar electricity generated by the array itself. The thrust is not as great as for liquid propellant rocket engines, but the array doesn't have to be boosted up to GSO in a big hurry. As a matter of fact, because of its size and structure, it's more efficient to boost it very, very slowly with numerous electric rocket motors attached at various points of the structure itself. The deep space freighter becomes a very small electric rocket motor module capable of being attached to an array and capable of being remotely-controlled from LEO or GSO if necessary during its flight. There may also be a manned electric rocket module in case people are required to perform guidance, navigation, control, maintenance, or other tasks during trans-orbital flight.

And it was no surprise to the study participants who'd thought through the whole space transportation concept for years that the "easy" portion of the system was the deep space portion. Going back and forth between LEO and GEO is nowhere near as difficult in terms of technology, engineering, and energy as that first step: Earth to orbit.

There are several ways to crawl up through the Earth's thick atmosphere and out of her deep gravity well. Airplanes have been successfully (most of the time) doing it one way for more than 75 years. Their horizontal takeoff and horizontal landing (HTOHL) uses the aerodynamic lift generated by motion of the craft through the atmosphere. Until the advent of the NASA Space Shuttle, our space vehicles have been using vertical takeoff and vertical landing (VTOVL), this being the classic mode of rocket operation. The NASA Space Shuttle uses a new mode of operation: vertical takeoff and horizontal landing (VTOHL).

All three operational modes are useful for the Earth-to-orbit step of our space transportation system, and advanced designs using the three modes have left the drawing boards already.

The initial passenger shuttle will probably be based on an extension of current NASA space shuttle technology which, when operating at full-bore, will be capable of launching a space shuttle once a week utilizing VTOHL. But this operational mode requires separate facilities for takeoff and for landing. The passenger shuttle used in the DOE Baseline Study foresaw the extension of the current NASA shuttle with a reusable booster, but this still means that a large external tank is thrown away on each flight—and that's a cost item that can't be overlooked.

The ultimate for the shuttle task is *single-stage-to-orbit* (SSTO), a single vehicle that ascends to space and returns without dropping off anything and by using only rocket propellants to do the job. The SSTO approach can be done with either a winged vehicle such as the NASA space shuttle (albeit much, much larger) or with a ballistic vehicle.

A ballistic shuttle appears to be the way to go for cargo and freight using the VTOVL mode. Such a freight shuttle will be large—larger than the Saturn 5. Although an interim cargo shuttle can be cobbled-up using NASA space shuttle technology and hardware, the ultimate freighter shuttle for our space transportation system will be a ballistic VTOVL craft.

As a result of considerable study by Rockwell International and Boeing Aerospace in order to establish the DOE Baseline SPS System, three conclusions were drawn.

With both winged (VTOHL) and ballistic (VTOVL) modes, two-stage configurations required less development of technology and could be done with a great deal of existing know-how; such two-stage designs turned out to be less sensitive to differences in operations which in turn led to the possiblity of lower operational costs.

Winged vehicles (VTOHL) showed greater operational simplicity and reduced recovery and turn-around time when compared to ballistic vehicles (VTOVL), even when the ballistic shuttles were landed in special recovery ponds adjacent to the launch sites.

All types of shuttles, VTOHL and VTOVL, were more efficient if designed to use liquid oxygen and hydrocarbon fuel in a first stage and liquid oxygen and liquid hydrogen in the second stage. This is because of the greater bulk of liquid hydrogen which has low density and requires a very big tank to contain a given weight of this fuel.

SSTO came out second-best *only* on the basis of the available technology, in spite of the fact that SSTO is *the* way to go for Earth-to-orbit transportation, just as it was the only way to go for transatlantic airline transportation.

Before World War II and the advent of the four-engined Douglas DC-4 (C-54) transport plane, there was no airplane except special ships like Lindbergh's that could fly the Atlantic Ocean non-stop. Most transatlantic airplanes were flying boats, and all of them had to stop to refuel, usually at the Azores. There was a requirement for a very fast transatlantic mail plane, and Major R.H. Mayo of Imperial Airways of Great Britain came up with a solution. The biggest problem faced by a heavily-loaded airplane is taking off and climbing to its best cruising altitude. This is particularly true of a seaplane. Mayo suggested the use of a large Short Brothers *Empire* Class flying boat to lift a smaller seaplane pick-a-back until cruising altitude was reached, whereupon the smaller airplane would release itself from it's first stage and proceed non-stop across the Atlantic Ocean with 600 pounds of freight and mail. On 21 July 1938, using the *Empire* Class flying boat *Maia* as a first stage, the little *Mercury* seaplane made it from Ireland to Montreal non-stop in 20 hours and 20 minutes. This "composite" was perhaps the first "two-stage airplane."

It didn't last because the development of the DC-4/C-54 airplane made the two-staged concept impractical, costly, and uneconomical.

History doesn't repeat itself, but historical patterns often do repeat themselves, and it is quite likely that we will see this pattern repeated in space transportation. SSTO designs—both winged and ballistic, VTOHL and VTOVL—are now under intensive study and could become reality within a decade. The economics of space transportation requires the development of the SSTO shuttle.

The ultimate in SSTO shuttles will be the horizontal takeoff, horizontal landing (HTOHL) ship. This, too, is foreseeable today although the technology to achieve such a ship isn't yet in our hands. But, by the year 2000, it would be. The HTOHL shuttle would take off from an ordinary airport runway and climb into space using wings, composite air-breathing engines such as turbofans converting to ramjets at altitude, plus rocket motors for power above the atmosphere. On its return, it would land on the same runway from which it took off. The HTOHL shuttle will be the ultimate because of its lower cost, its ease of operation, and a flight profile whose accelerations are comfortable to passengers. Because the HTOHL shuttle's payload isn't as great as that of a ballistic VTOVL or VTOHL shuttle, it will probably be used only for passengers.

How many of each type of spacecraft are going to be required to build two ten-gigawatt SPS units in geosynch orbit every year?

Five of the freight shuttles, the heavy lift launch vehicles capable of placing a million tons of cargo in LEO at each launch, will be required. This means that each of the five ships is going to make seventy-five flights to orbit and return every year, or once every five days. Thus, there will be at least one freight shuttle launch *every day*. And one freight shuttle landing every day.

Two passenger shuttles will be required, each making a flight every three weeks. This is one flight every twelve days, about the same rate as the programmed NASA space shuttle launches. But the passenger shuttles will be lifting or landing seventy-five people on every flight. The number of passenger shuttle flights is determined by the number of people required in LEO and GEO for SPS construction and assembly, assuming that crews will be rotated back to Earth every sixty days to prevent any possiblity of long-term physiological deterioration due to weightlessness.

Two of the deep space passenger ships will be required to shuttle people back and forth between LEO and GEO, carrying seventy-five people per flight.

The number of deep space freight ships required depends on whether it is decided to build an SPS using silicon solar cells or gallium arsenide solar cells. If silicon cells are chosen, twenty-three deep space freighters will be required because there will be thirty flights per year from LEO to GEO with SPS subassemblies.

This fleet of ships and the frequency of operation far exceeds the capabilities of any of today's 1980 space launch sites or facilities. There is literally no way that Cape Canaveral can be expanded to handle the job because of the simple fact that they've run out of room at the Cape. A new flight operations site, a true space port, will have to be built. It will require lots of land area located in a place remote from the high population density of cities. It will require several landing strips and several launch pads. It will require easy access from the nation's transportation network of railways and highways because of the thousands of tons of materials that must be transported to the spaceport. It will require electric power, which will mean that it must be sited near large existing power plants and high-capacity transmission lines. The huge volume of propellants needed will require that propellant manufacturing facilities be on the spaceport itself. Tons of liquid oxygen will be required along with tons of liquid hydrogen, both available from electrolytic decomposition of water and liquified by known industrial processes. The rocket fuel chosen by DOE for the launch phase of flight is methane because of the ease with which it can be obtained from either natural gas or from the gasification of coal; there are abundant reserves of both natural gas and coal in the United States, far more than are required for the entire long-term SPS project.

These basic requirements for a space port can be met either with a single spaceport or multiple sites. A single spaceport would be more efficient in terms of land, logistics, and environmental impact. And there is only one part of the United States where all conditions for a single spaceport could be met: the western region that includes the states of New Mexico, Arizona, southern Utah, and southern Nevada. There are several locations in this region that would be suitable for the nation's first real spaceport.

The size of the SPS project also means that there will be a large facility in Low-Earth Orbit (LEO): the LEO Base. This is where freight is off-loaded from the freight shuttles and people are transferred from passenger shuttles to deep space passenger ships if they're going on out to GEO. LEO Base is a pass-through or staging base, but it will be large and will require the presence of at least a hundred people at all times for service, maintenance, etc.

At the far end of the line, the Geosynchronous Earth Orbital facility, GEO Base, will be the place where people assemble the SPS itself from subassemblies brought up by deep space freighters from LEO Base. As many as seven hundred people will be living at GEO Base at any given time, working three shifts around the clock, living in space, eating in space, and sleeping in space. They will require logistical services, personal services, health services, food services, waste disposal services, environmental services, entertainment and recreation services, religious services, and a host of everyday services that we take for granted here on Earth. In many ways, life in GEO Base will resemble living in the construction camps of the Trans Alaska Pipe Line or on an off-shore oil rig. There's nothing new about what needs to be done at GEO Base. What's new is the fact that, for the first time, we'll be doing it in space. But it's a matter of difference in kind, not degree. If the United States can keep three astronauts alive, healthy, happy and working for 84 days at a time in Skylab, and if the Soviets can keep two cosmonauts alive, healthy, happy, and working for six months at a time in *Salyut-6*, it's totally possible to keep seven hundred people alive, healthy, happy, and working at GEO Base, rotating the crews every sixty days to start with. As our experience grows, crews will be exchanged at longer intervals.

Thus, the transportation system for the Solar Power Satellite project is big. It will cost money. But its cost is something that must be considered in the total view of space power and all the consequences that flow from the possession of space power.

CHAPTER FOUR

Why even consider putting Solar Power satellites in the sky? Why not look for other terrestrial sources of energy instead?

There are two reasons for this.

The first reason revolves around the growing need for electrical power.

The second has to do with the consequences of getting our needed energy in space instead of on the Earth.

Let's look at these reasons one at a time.

There has been much said and much written about our "energy shortage" and about our growing need for increasing amount of energy. The philosophical reasons for this were touched upon in the first chapter of this book. But what are the hard facts? What are the numbers?

You don't have to depend upon data from the U.S. Department of Energy to get your numbers. And anybody can be an energy forecaster. The electrical energy requirements of the United States can be estimated with a very high degree of accuracy by finding out what the electrical consumption has been in the past and simply extrapolating it out into the future.

(There are some problems that arise in doing this, especially when we get out to the year 2025 and beyond. But *this* forecaster knows that. And this forecaster had discovered some interesting consequences that come about because of the growth of space power, especially in terms of what it really means to the U.S. electric energy requirements in the long haul. This is because the drive for space power will be "synergistic"—i.e.: it will develop some fascinating consequences as a result of its own accomplishments.)

Table I shows the U.S. production in gigawatt hours, capacity in gigawatts, the change in capacity over the pre-

TABLE I
UNITED STATES ELECTRIC ENERGY
PRODUCTION AND USED CAPACITY

(Production in gigawatt-hours. Capacities in gigawatts.)
Source: The World Almanac, 1946, 1962, 1970, 1976, & 1980
editions.

Year	Production	Used Capacity	New Capacity	% Increase
1925	61,451.1	7.015		
1930	91,111.5	10.401	3.386	48.27%
1935	95,287.4	10.877	0.476	4.58%
1940	141,837.0	16.191	5.314	48.85%
1945	222,486.3	25.398	9.207	56.86%
1950	329,141.3	37.573	12.175	47.94%
1955	547,038.0	62.447	24.874	66.20%
1960	753,350.3	86.000	23.554	37.72%
1965	1,055,252.0	120.462	34.462	40.07%
1970	1,531,609.0	174.841	54.379	45.14%
1975	1,917,638.0	218.908	44.067	25.20%

ceeding 5-year period, and the percentage increase in capacity over that 5-year period from 1925 to 1975 based on actual data. It can't be argued because it is recorded history.

The U.S. electrical energy usage is given in terms of gigawatt-hours per year. (A gigawatt is technical shorthand for a billion watts or a million kilowatts.) The U.S. electrical *used capacity* in gigawatts that produced this was determined by dividing the gigawatt-hours number by 8760, the number of hours in a year. This is the "used capacity" in gigawatts shown in the table.

The data sources used were the 1949, 1959, 1962, 1970, 1976, and 1980 editions of *The World Almanac*. Some additional data came from the *Encyclopaedia Britannica*. These references are available to *anyone* who has access to a public library. The older editions of *The World Almanac* were used in order to get data going back to 1925 to permit a true long-term look at electric energy consumption trends, especially as they were through the Great Depression and World War II, two periods that reflect energy consumption trends during periods of economic difficulty due to a depression as well as economic stimulation caused by general war.

Two items of interest surfaced during this research.

First of all, the current issues of *The World Almanac* printed since the U.S. Department of Energy became a reality do not contain electrical energy consumption data that go back earlier than 1971. This made some fascinating conjecture as to whether, and if so why, the federal bureaucracy might not want trend-indicating data available? Never mind: the data was available from other, earlier sources and was used.

Secondly, the trend of electrical energy consumption *continued to increase* even during the Great Depression, albeit at a slower rate. Even in the depths of the greatest world economic dislocation in this century, the U.S. electrical energy consumption increased. Basically, the rate of electrical energy consumption in the United States has been increasing at a long-term rate of 5% to 7% per year over the past fifty years.

Table II shows a projection to the year 2025 based on a trend of an average 5-year percentage increase of 25% in capacity.

The historical data over the fity-year time span between 1925 and 1975 showed this percentage rate increase to be reasonable, and this sort of reasonable extrapolation is the basis for many forecasts used by marketing people in industry and commerce as well as government forecasters and high-powered future-oriented think-tanks. One can assume any percentage increase one wants except zero or negative for several reasons. Firstly, there hasn't been any indication of a reversal of trend over the past fifty years. And secondly and most importantly, because we *can't* continue our civilization if we don't *increase* our electrical energy capacity. There is one simple reason for this: there's a new human being born in the United States every 9.5 seconds. That's 380 new people

TABLE II
FORECAST U.S. ELECTRIC ENERGY CAPACITY
(Assumed 5% annual increase in capacity)

(Capacities in gigawatts)

Year	Capacity	New Capacity	Annual New Capacity
1975	218.908		
1980	273.635	54.727	10.945
1985	342.044	68.409	13.682
1990	427.555	85.511	17.102
1995	534.443	106.888	21.378
2000	668.054	133.611	26.722
2005	835.068	167.014	33.403
2010	1,043.835	208.767	41.753
2015	1,304.793	260.958	52.192
2020	1,630.992	326.199	65.240
2025	2,038.740	407.748	81.550

per hour, 9,120 per day, or more than three million per year. They require heat, light, transportation, and other amenities that require energy. Most of this energy comes from electricity, the most convenient form of energy we've ever managed to harness.

There are two solutions to the continuing need for more and more energy: (a) zero-population growth, or (b) continual increase in electrical energy generating capacity.

The first is probably impossible to achieve over the next twenty-five year period, human beings being what they are. Wars don't seem to do the trick, in spite of the fact that warfare now kills millions of people in a decade or less . . . and in a microsecond if thermonuclear weapons are used. Famine, disease, pestilence, and natural disasters don't seem to make much of a dent in population growth, although epidemic disease once had the capability to do so for periods of up to a century. Witness the Black Death and the Plague in

Europe. If anything, these factors have shown a stubborn tendency to cause the population growth rate to *increase* rather than to decrease. Malthus, that early-day advocate of "limits to growth," has been proven wrong because he didn't understand that the human mind, working with a knowledge of the universe, could reverse what appeared to be a natural trend. Even modern population control methods based on scientific knowledge don't seem to be able to stem the tide of people doing what comes naturally. Neither widespread knowledge of the human reproductive cycle nor the infamous Pill really stemmed the tide of population growth. Demographers are ecstatic when a population growth rate trend even starts to level off, but they don't have much to say when that curve continues to go up. The population growth trend curve has exhibited temporary "glitches," inflections, and changes in slope, but it hasn't shown any indication of leveling off, much less turning around or inflecting, when considered in the long term. The upshot of this is the fact that we simply can't count on the miracle of zero population growth . . . not this century, at any rate.

In his book, "The Next 200 Years," Dr. Herman Kahn forecasts the possibility that the population trend curve will inflect at a "cusp" in the next century. Dr. Kahn claims that what we're now seeing is a rapid growth rate caused by technology that has permitted us to expand to more completely fill our ecological niche on Earth. The population trend may well turn around in the 21st Century. There may be technological reasons for this aside from thermonuclear war, or it may be caused by an increasing number of people leaving the Earth to live in the solar system over the next 120 years.

If we can't count on a decline in population to solve the problem, we must increase the energy supply.

Increasing the electrical energy generating capacity is difficult, expensive, necessary, and possible. It's the easier way out. It may not be the *best* way out, but it's the *easiest*. Human beings will opt for it in spite of massive and seemingly overwhelming problems caused by such things as high cost, technical difficulty, potential environmental impacts, social consequences, rules, regulations, laws, propaganda, threats of force, and other political and ideological coercions by those who say they have "the welfare of society at heart" but who, in their hearts, really want to control people and make them do it *their* way by exercising control over energy.

One solution was not mentioned above because it isn't a solution but suicide: shut down the nukes, close down the power plants, break up the big utilities, decentralize the power sources, and do all these things now. It's no solution because we can't do without the energy we've got now and we won't do without it or cut it back.

Where are we going to get all this new electric generating capacity?

There really isn't time to stop and study it to death—not when we'll have to build enough new capacity in the 1980–1985 time period that equals the *total* U.S. capacity in 1938. We will have to continue building new capacity using tried and proven technology while we are developing new technology.

Beset as they are with problems, the current methods of generating electricity work and don't need to be tested. So we'll have to continue building new capacity using existing technology while we develop new technology.

We'll continue to build electrical generating plants using the abundant coal reserves of the United States. (The Soviet Union has the world's largest known coal reserves, followed by the People's Republic of China as a close second in Asia. The U.S. has almost 30% of the known coal reserves in the world.) There are huge coal deposits in the western U.S., but they are the greatest distance away from the population and industrial centers where the energy is needed. There are also large coal deposits in the Appalachian Mountains and in the area of southern Illinois, southern Indiana, and western Kentucky. There is enough coal there to supply our energy needs for more than 200 years, which means that we'll continue to build coal-fired electrical generating plants in the U.S until such time as the newer energy technologies can assume most of the baseload requirements. Therefore, we'll have to continue to deal on an ever-increasing scale with the problems of the ecological consequences of strip mining and surface mining. We'll have to face up to and deal with the fact that such massive combustion of coal releases radioactive carbon-14 into the Earth's atmosphere, thus releasing far more radioactive material into the environment than has ever leaked from any nuclear electric plant.

We'll continue to build generating plants that use petroleum products and natural gas as energy sources. However, it's highly likely that they'll be built in decreasing numbers as the years go by because of the increasing problems of supply and the potential problems of resource allocation. But to handle daily peak loads, *some* oil-fired and gas-fired plants will have to be built because they can be brought on-line rapidly to handle demand and can thereafter be put on standby just as rapidly. Because of the problems of sulfur emissions from oil-fired plants, more gas-fired plants will be built in the future because, if proper combustion technology is used, the emissions from gas-fired plants amount to nothing more than carbon-dioxide and water.

Hydroelectric plants will continue to be built to supply demand, and they'll be built to last a long time because, of all the current electric energy technologies, hydroelectric has the least severe environmental impact in the long run and in the overall picture. While it's true that hydroelectric projects destroy the local ecology, the lakes created by these projects in turn create a new ecology in the locality, one where land ecologies are replaced by water ecologies. While hydroelectric projects have taken crop lands, forest lands, and wilderness lands out of the picture, they've created lakes that have succored new aquatic life as well as land wildlife. And they've created whole new human recreational areas as well. There is no question that hydroelectric projects have a severe impact upon the local environment, changing it completely from what it was. But the Earth's overall *and* local environments are not and never have been static systems. Changes wrought by natural causes are usually far greater than those created by human projects such as hydroelectric plants. If nothing more than this was learned from the 1980 eruptions of Mount St. Helens in Washington, this should have become abundantly clear, even to those who could only read about it. Therefore, we must honestly ask the question whether or not these changes wrought by humans have truly been harmful. In fact, carefully and thoughtfully carried out, hydroelectric projects can and have been extremely helpful to the environment.

A great controversy rages today about nuclear-powered electric generating plants. But the controversy is basically emotional because nobody believes anybody else's data, especially the data that originates in the opposite camp. However, one cannot argue the validity of the overall safety of nuclear generating plants because they've proven themselves to be at least as safe as other types of electrical plants. Nobody ever said that nuclear plants were *safe*, but only that they're at least as safe, if not safer, than other thermal generating plants and hydroelectric plants. However, even though the infamous Three Mile Island incident resulted from human operational error and even though all safety systems operated properly, it is quite unlikely that any new nuclear plant starts will be made during the 1980 decade, although existing nuclear plants under construction such as Arizona's Palo Verde complex will be completed and put on line during the 1980 decade. This is likely to cause a shortage of electric energy in the long haul. By 1985, nuclear plants will be producing about a tenth of a gigawatt of electric energy, less than a hundredth of a percent of the 1985 estimated U.S. capacity. But other nations aren't suffering from the same nuclear anxiety as the U.S.. France has fifteen nuclear reactors working and forty-five under construction, a factor which is likely to make France the leading energy producer in Europe. By 1985, France, Japan, and West Germany will be producing 60% of the free world's nuclear electricity.

Geothermal plants are in operation around the world, taking advantage of the natural heat of the interior of the Earth. In 1977, geothermal plants supplied 1.8 gigawatts of electricity, most of this coming from four well-established geothermal complexes: Laradello, Italy; the Geysers, California; Cerro Prieto, Mexico; and White Island, New Zealand. Current estimates place the world potential for geothermal electricity at only 60 gigawatts, equivalent to six SPS units or a three-year SPS construction project.

There are other terrestrial energy options currently being studied.

The combustion of biomass—wood, fuels derived from plants, and waste materials—simply cannot provide enough heat energy. If we were to burn *all* the available biomass on Earth in one year's time, and if it could be converted 100% to electricity, it would amount to 9500 gigawatts or roughly five times the needed 2025 capacity for the United States. But since that would involve burning everything on Earth in one year, there wouldn't be anything left to burn the following year because it takes time for biomass to accumulate.

Wind power offers an attractive terrestrial energy option because it can provide a worldwide annual electric energy capacity of a billion gigawatts. But the wind must blow—and sometimes it doesn't.

Ground-based solar energy technologies offer additional options even though they suffer from an interrupted duty cycle due to the day-night cycle on Earth.

A really favorable energy option, if it could be developed, would be the solar photoelectrolysis system in which solar energy would be used to dissociate water into hydrogen and oxygen, both of which are gases that can be liquified, stored, and transported because of what we have learned about handling these gases in the space program. Of course, hydrogen would be the only product of the photoelectrolysis system that would be stored, transported, and used because when it's burned, the oxygen will come from the Earth's atmosphere. The "Hydrogen Economy" energy option is a very feasible one for the 21st Century and will work along with wind power, nuclear fusion, passive solar, geothermal, and hydroelectric to help pick up the baseload now being carried by coal-fired, oil-fired, and gas-fired electric generating plants.

We will still have to depend upon *some* fossil fuel plants and all of the nuclear fission plants well into the 21st Century if we stick to terrestrial options.

However, if we pursue the goal of space power as quickly as possible, we *can* begin to shut down the nukes early in the 21st century because we can build enough Solar Power Satellites in space fast enough in the next twenty-five years to permit us to shift a very large portion of our electrical baseload requirements away from earthbound generating plants to the space power source.

And the earlier we get at it, the better.

Table III shows what happens if we opt to proceed with space power at the earliest opportunity.

The 1990 start on building an SPS system is realistic. We can get to work on obtaining space power *right now* if we have the will to do it. We can begin by using the NASA space

TABLE III
FORECAST U.S. SPACE POWER
1990 START

(Assume 2 10-GW SPS per year.)

(Capacities in gigawatts)

Year	No. SPS	SPS Capacity	% Total US Capacity
1990	1	10	2.34%
1995	11	110	20.56%
2000	21	210	31.43%
2005	31	310	37.12%
2010	41	410	39.28%
2015	51	510	39.08%

shuttle as quickly as it becomes available. With the shuttle, we can begin to check out some of the new technology that will be required to build and operate the SPS system, technical factors that look "iffy" today, about which little is known, or that need to be tried out to find out the best way to make them work. This means using the shuttle to investigate (a) construction of large space structures, (b) fabrication of solar cells in space, and (c) conversion of the DC electricity from solar cell arrays into high-power radio beams.

This could lead to a decision by 1987 on whether or not to proceed with the construction of a 10-gigawatt SPS "pilot plant" in GSO for on-line operation by 1990.

A 10-gigawatt Solar Power Satellite is suggested here as a goal rather than one half that size as detailed in the DOE study. It doesn't take much more in terms of mass or size to increase the output of an SPS to 10 Gw, and a 10 Gw SPS turns out to be more economical than a 5 Gw SPS. Besides, we just can't do the job that needs to be done by putting only two 5-gigawatt SPS units in orbit every year. We must put twenty gigawatts up there every year to even begin to make a dent in the new electric power requirements.

To really do a job with space power, it might appear that we'd need to increase the number of SPS units put on-line from two per year up to ten per year to handle the continually increasing energy demand forecast in Table II. But this isn't the case, as we'll see later.

Table III tells us that if we get a move on, quit wasting precious time, and start putting two 10-gigawatt SPS units in orbit every year beginning in 1991 (with the pilot plant being on line in 1990), almost 40% of our electric power could be coming from space by 2015, twenty-five years after we start building the SPS system in earnest.

What happens if we delay things? If we suffer from a lack of will? If we can't manage to get the capital requirements together? If we throw away the valuable years by studying the whole project to death and worrying over possible impacts when there's no solid data to support such worries?

Table IV shows what happens when start-up is delayed to

1995. We lose about 8%. We can never count on more than 32% of our baseload being taken up by space power if we delay five years.

Table V shows the consequences of a 2000 A.D. start. The most that space power can achieve is 25.5% of our baseload requirements.

The data of Tables III, IV, and V indicate that we are in a Red Queen's Race and that if we don't start to run as quickly as we can as soon as we can, we begin playing a losing game of catch-up. This assumes that the U.S. electric energy forecast data of Table II has some validity to it.

One could rationally question the forecast of Table II in either direction. Table II was based on a conservative rate of increase of 25% over five-year periods.

If the rate of increase is greater than this—and it could well be because it has been greater at times in the past fifty years when we were trying to catch up after the Great Depression and World War II—we may never make it and we'll *have* to

TABLE IV
FORECAST U.S. SPACE POWER
1995 START

(Assume 2 10-Gw SPS per year.)

(Capacities in gigawatts)

Year	No. SPS	SPS Capacity	% Total US Capacity
1995	2	20	3.74%
2000	12	120	17.96%
2005	22	220	26.34%
2010	32	320	30.66%
2015	42	420	32.19%
2020	52	520	31.88%

TABLE V
FORECAST U.S. SPACE POWER
2000 A.D. START

(Assume 2 10-Gw SPS per year.)

(Capacities in gigawatts)

Year	No. SPS	SPS Capacity	% Total US Capacity
2000	2	20	2.99%
2005	12	120	14.37%
2010	22	220	21.08%
2015	32	320	24.52%
2020	42	420	25.75%
2025	52	520	25.51%

opt for space power as only part of a solution rather than the biggest part of the energy answer.

If the rate of energy increase is less, we'll come out as a winner because the SPS system will be able to take over an increasing percentage of the baseload, permitting us to dismantle the nukes and bank the fires of the coal plants, saving the coal to be used as chemical feedstocks instead.

Beyond 2010, it is highly likely that we'll see a *decrease* in both the rate of increase and the total demand . . . but *only* if we exercise the space power option *soon*.

The longer we wait, the more dollars we're going to have to spend to get space power.

There is a constant, historical inflation rate of 7% per annum that has been affecting the purchasing power of the dollar for the entire 200-plus years of the United States of America. True, there have been peaks and valleys in this inflation trend curve caused by wars and panics, heavy government spending and severe economic depressions. But, over the long haul of 200 years, there has been a long-term

7% inflation rate. This means that the purchasing power of the dollar is cut in half every 14.28 years . . . or that the price of anything will appear to double every fourteen years and three months. Note that it *appears* to double in price but really doesn't. The one factor that remains relatively constant, even in the grip of severe inflation, is the true *value perceived* and *value exchanged*.

And energy isn't free. In fact, there's no cheap energy source. The only reason that some forms of energy seemed cheap for a time was because there were artificial government-imposed price ceilings placed upon them. When these artificial price ceilings eventually came off—as they had to, otherwise the suppliers would have gone bankrupt—the price of the formerly controlled energy shot up and finally stabilized just where it should be on the 7% inflationary curve.

If there's one thing that we've learned in the 1970 decade, it's the plain fact that there is no cheap energy source.

In 1980, the average cost of any energy system is $2.00 per watt—or, to put it in terms that the utility industry uses, $2000 per kilowatt installed.

If you build an electrical generating plant that's coal-fired, oil-fired, gas-fired, geothermal, hydroelectric, or even nuclear, the cost will run about $2000 per kilowatt by the time the plant's on line and providing energy and revenue.

It should come as no surprise that the preliminary estimates of the cost of a Solar Power Satellite is $2000 per kilowatt installed. This number has been independently arrived at by think-tank study groups, by the utility industry, and by the U.S. Department of Energy.

But there's a very important difference when it comes to the cost for an SPS system to provide space power:

The $2000 per kilowatt installed cost for an SPS includes a pro-rata cost of the space transportation system needed to place the SPS in geosynch orbit, said cost based on a reasonable figure for costs of repair, maintenance, and replacement of worn-out spacecraft.

By doing the SPS system instead of the other Earth-based

energy alternatives, we open the door to the Solar System on a massive scale that affects even the future of the SPS system.

All of these numbers, all of these forecasts, and all of these facts tell us some important things:

(a) To meet forecast electric energy requirements, we're going to have to continue to build electric generating plants.

(b) It costs the same to build *any* kind of an electric generating plant: $2000 per kilowatt installed.

(c) If we build the generating capacity on Earth, we will have to use non-renewable fossil fuels or nuclear energy.

(d) If we build the generating capacity on Earth, we will slowly deplete the energy sources here, and the result will probably be fuel allocations before twenty-five years (or the life of the generating plant) have passed.

(e) If we build the generating capacity here on Earth, we will have to get rid of the waste products somehow—and these waste products are combustion gases, waste heat (no system can operate without wasting something), radioactive carbon-14 from coal burning, sulfur from petroleum burning, carbon dioxide and water from natural gas burning, and nuclear waste from nuclear plants.

(f) If we build our generating capability in space in the form of an SPS system, it isn't going to cost us any more money than if we build comparable capacity generating plants on the Earth.

(g) If we build the SPS system, it will use a renewable energy source, the Sun, and the SPS units will have a design lifetime of thirty years or more.

(h) If we build the SPS system, we also buy ourselves one very large and very versatile space transportation system which permits us to achieve the ultimate: space power in all its forms.

CHAPTER FIVE

A capital investment in a Solar Power Satellite system is not the same as investing the same money to obtain the same electric generating capacity from terrestrial sources. Although the costs per kilowatt (installed) are the same, there are definite short-term and long-term worldwide benefits that accrue if the capacity is built in space as an SPS system.

The primary benefit, of course, is the use of a renewable energy source. The SPS system is solar. But it is *constant* solar, available day or night, and solar energy that is transformed into electricity that can be delivered via power beams to inexpensive ground rectennas which in turn can deliver the energy on electric transmission lines to the place where the demand exists. There are no fuel allocation problems to be faced years down the line as there probably will be with terrestrial power plants using fossil fuels. SPS power is clean with minimal impact upon the natural environment.

But the most important benefit to the SPS system comes from the synergistic nature of the program.

"Synergy" is a fancy word that basically means there are systems in which two plus two can equal five or seven or even fifteen. In other words, the nature of the system is such that it *creates* new opportunities, activities, and systems *because of itself*. Its mere existence permits other things to happen as well as the thing it was originally created to accomplish.

The growth of technology over the past 200 years is a prime example of synergy.

One of the social and environmental synergies has already been mentioned: As the SPS system grows in the early decades of the 21st century, it takes over more and more of the baseload electrical requirements of the United States. This permits utility firms to retire the older generating plants that are expensive to maintain, that are environmentally unacceptable, that may be getting hazardous because of their increasing age, and that are inefficient. It permits us to shut down the nukes, if we want to, without causing severe energy shortages. This in itself is a strong motivation for undertaking the difficult, expensive, and capital-intensive SPS project.

The SPS project also permits us to bring electrical energy to parts of the country where there's room for people, towns, industry, and future growth: the western United States. The biggest problem with the western U.S. isn't that the land is rugged and difficult to traverse or to live on. The big problem in the West is *water*. On any map, you can draw a line along the 100th degree of longitude. East of that line, there's enough natural rainfall to support the heartland of America—the cities, the industries, and the farms that feed the world. West of the line, the natural rainfall is sparse, requiring water be obtained by pumping or by diversion. Farms take on a different appearance because of the requirement to irrigate them artificially with water using free-flow irrigation from canals, drip irrigation, or circular spray irrigation. The siting of towns and cities depends upon the water supply, while in the eastern part of America towns and cities were originally established because of commercial advantage or in a network where no town was more than one day's journey from any other town. There are room and resources in the American West even today, and all that's lacking is energy.

A prime example of the synergy of energy projects in the American West is the Boulder Canyon Project created by the Swing-Johnson Bill signed by President Calvin Coolidge in 1928. This created Hoover Dam, then the largest energy and land reclamation project tackled in the United States. It was complete a mere eight years later at a cost of $165-million. It's capable of producing an electrical energy output of 1.835 gigawatts. Hoover Dam not only made possible the farming of the lower Colorado River Valley, but also the Imperial Valley of California. Its electrical output not only permitted the growth of the Los Angeles metroplex but also transformed a small railroad town in the desert into the glittering resort of Las Vegas, Nevada. Its electrical output created the nearby town of Henderson, Nevada, which produces a large percentage of the magnesium used in the aerospace industry. The Boulder Canyon Project was originally conceived as a flood control program with hydroelectric capability. The historical spin-offs that created the intense social activity in this southwestern corner of the United States are an example of the synergism of projects similar to the SPS.

There's room in the West for the SPS system ground rectennas. With the energy from these rectennas, water can be pumped or diverted and thus create oasis towns were nothing exists today. With this SPS energy, sea water desalinization becomes possible, providing even more water resources for the water-scarce regions of the western U.S. The vast areas of the American West still beckon as a frontier, but it's an energy frontier out there today.

But the most important synergism of the SPS program comes from the fact that, in buying the SPS system to provide us with safe, clean, and abundant electrical energy from a renewable source, we are also paying for the transportation system that enables us to build, man, and maintain the SPS system.

It's going to be a big one, the first true space transportation system we've possessed.

It will permit us to send large payloads and large numbers of people into LEO and GEO. It will enable us to establish and maintain very large space facilities in LEO and GSO capable of housing hundreds of people at a time.

Out of this SPS space transportation system will come explosive progress in space science, space manufacturing, and development of extraterrestrial material resouces.

Let's look at each of these one at a time, then look at the social implications that spring from the synergism that *they* in turn create.

As this is being written, space scientists are engaged in the incredible attempt to appropriate the entire non-military space mission capability and schedule of the NASA space shuttle. They do not want the NASA space shuttle's "limited'' capability to be used for any space industrialization research and especially not for any development work on such programs as the SPS. Basically, a paraphrase of what they're saying is as follows: ''We stood aside in the Mercury, Gemini, and Apollo manned space programs and let them be conducted as engineering missions because of the national prestige involved. Now we do not intend to permit the space shuttle to be pre-empted by commercial and industrial interests. We have subordinated our own interests in doing space science long enough. We want the non-military activities of the space shuttle devoted to space science as first priority with commercial and industrial engineering development work secondary to our requirements.''

This attempt to pre-empt the space shuttle for the exclusive non-military pursuit of basic scientific research in space has some justification: We *should* be doing more space science research—much more of it. Basic scientific research serves to keep the cupboard of knowledge full of information which can later be used by those people developing the engineering technologies for products and profit.

But the way to get a lot more scientific research done in space isn't to attempt to grab all the space shuttle missions.

The way to insure that there will be copious space science done in the 1990 decade is to back the use of the space shuttle for SPS development work to prove out the unknown areas of engineering and technology. This, when accomplished, can lead to lowered risk and justifiable capital investment which, in turn, leads to a commitment to the SPS program. This, in its own turn, requires the development and operation of the very large space transportation system.

The SPS space transportation system is so large and so flexible that it contains within its scope the capability to support more space scientific research than the space scientists will be able to find funds to carry out—even if the scientists are given a free ride on the coattails of the SPS space transportation system's capabilities!

With the ability to lift a million pounds to orbit every day, there will be the inevitable volume and weight ''holes'' in the payload schedule that can easily accomodate ''payloads of opportunity'' for space science. With a passenger shuttle taking seventy-five people into space and back every two weeks, there will be inevitable open slots in the passenger manifests that space scientists can take advantage of in order to go into space themselves to conduct their work on site, rather than by remote control as they're forced to do today. With the SPS project's ability to sustain more than a hundred people at LEO Base and almost a thousand people at GEO Base, space scientists will be able to *live* out there with their experimental apparatus for months at a time.

We've been talking about putting a maximum of seven people into space at a time on a weekly basis with the NASA space shuttle, and only three of these ''crew slots'' may be available for space scientists. We have a totally different game when we're shuttling ten times that number of people into space weekly and keeping a hundred times that number alive and working in space facilities.

The SPS program is going to provide space scientists with a Golconda of opportunities to do so much space science that they'll have ''wall to wall'' data. To some extent, they've already achieved this on the Viking Mars mission, where there's so much data that it will take years to reduce it to information that can be studied . . . and millions of dollars that they don't have.

When the pie is too small to allow everybody to have a suitably-sized piece, the worst thing to do is to fight over the existing pie. The answer to giving everybody more pie is to *make the pie bigger*.

With all of the things that various groups of people want to do in space, the only answer to being able to accommodate the desires of all is to get a bigger space transportation system.

The one way to get a big space transportation system is to go to work as soon as possible on a big energy project in space. Then everybody will have a shot at doing what they want to do out there.

That's the basic message of this entire book: *Conservation* of resources isn't a long-range answer to our obvious energy problems now and in the near future because it leads to rationing. This means that some people will have to decide who gets the limited slices of a limited-size pie, a pie that's already too small. By *expanding capabilities*, we make the pie bigger so that everybody gets a piece large enough to satisfying his hunger. When there's plenty to go around, nobody can ration or control it except by either consent or coercion.

It's difficult to ration soup when it's raining soup, everybody's got a bucket, there's a surplus of buckets, the roof's leaking, and everybody's hungry.

It's not only difficult, it's unnecessary. It wastes time and effort that could and should be devoted to other matters.

If we go ahead with the SPS program, there's something in it for everybody. That can't be said for any other energy option that's under consideration today, and it certainly isn't true for the energy conservation options. Because of the space transportation system spinoff of the SPS program, nobody loses and everybody wins . . . including some people who never thought that a space program would affect them at all.

The favorable social consequences far outweigh any potential environmental problems or technical difficulties that would (and have) caused some people to tend to write-off the SPS energy option.

Another good example of this in addition to the increased space science capability is the golden opportunities the SPS space transportation system offers to space manufacturing.

As of 1980, we *know* that there are products that we can make in space that cannot be made here on Earth, and products that can be made better in space. This is because of two major characteristics of orbital space around the Earth: (a) weightlessness or apparent lack of gravity, and (b) the good vacuum of orbital space.

Although the latter—good vacuum—can be obtained in terrestrial laboratories at a very high cost, the weightless characteristics of space cannot be duplicated for more than a minute without going into orbit.

We know this to be so because of preliminary research and

investigations that have been made by American astronauts in the Apollo and Skylab programs.

We know this to be so because the Soviet Union's cosmonauts have already carried out the manufacture of special materials in the long-duration flights they've made in the 1977-1980 time period aboard the Soviet space station, *Salyut-6*.

The weightlessness available in orbit permits the use of many manufacturing processes that cannot be carried out with gravity pulling on them. It also permits the manufacture of many materials that can't be produced when gravity is present.

For example, perfect crystalline materials can be produced in orbit because gravity doesn't exert a strain on the crystalline structure and cause imperfections and dislocations between the atoms and molecules that make up the crystal. So what? Why should anybody except crystallographers be interested in the perfect crystals that can be produced in space? The answer is that modern microscopic electronic circuits are made on crystalline bases. These crystalline structures must be perfect because any imperfection leads either to a high rate of rejects of completed parts or the necessity to make microelectronic circuits in a series of small units on pieces of small, perfect crystals cut from larger crystals with the imperfect portions being discarded. Separate microelectronic circuits are more costly than circuits that are more highly integrated. Components and materials that must be rejected after long and expensive fabrication's been completed adds to expense. General Electric has already determined that the manufacture of near-perfect crystalline materials in space could reduce the cost of microelectronic parts by a factor of ten or more. Space crystals would not only reduce price, but also reduce reject rates and permit larger and more complex electronic circuits to be made on larger crystal chips.

Microbiology will benefit from the weightlessness of space. The absence of gravity means that there are no differences in density between materials. Oil and vinegar salad dressing won't stay mixed on Earth because the oil is less-dense than the vinegar and therefore weighs less, therefore, it immediately goes to the top of the salad dressing bottle after you've finished shaking it. In orbit, the oil and vinegar would stay mixed because there is no gravity to separate them. Because of the total absence of density effects on materials, weightless processing means that it's possible to mix things that won't otherwise mix. It also means that warmer materials won't rise because of lowered density, and therefore convection heating won't result in separation of materials.

Many single-cell products such as blood-fraction leukocytes are used today in the pharmaceutical industry to produce drugs. There are great problems maintaining a suitable suspension of microbes, blood fractions, or single-cell materials in a nutrient solution that will also carry off the drug element being produced by the cells. The cells will settle to the bottom of the processing chamber. As a result, some of the cells will not get any nutrient because they're buried on the bottom of the pile, and these cells die. This reduces the efficiency of the process and also adds impurities created by the suffocating and dead cells. The obvious answer is to keep the cells stirred up so that they stay in suspension. But the cells usually aren't tolerant of being battered by any sort of mixing device that will keep them stirred up; if they don't die from the physical beating they take, they often just quit working or work in a manner that doesn't produce the end product the pharmaceutical engineer is looking for. But by putting this microbiological process in the weightlessness of orbit, the cells will stay in suspension and cannot settle to the bottom of the processing vat. Furthermore, they aren't being battered by a mixing machine, they can work surrounded by nutrient solution that feeds them and carries away their precious end product which may be an important pharmaceutical.

These examples are but two of the products of space manufacturing that have been carefully researched by myself and others over the past decade. The initial research led to my book, *The Third Industrial Revolution* (Ace Books, 1978) which goes into considerable detail concerning the various industrial processes that could be carried out in space. The interest in space industrialization sparked by this book resulted in a funded study by NASA in 1977–1978 to Rockwell International and Science Applications, Inc. (SAI).

As a member of the latter team, I helped identify 147 possible space products. Careful marketing research was carried out by the SAI team on ten of the most promising products whose production might be realized in the 1980 time period. Total revenues for these ten examples were forecast to be as much as $10-billion by the year 2000. This NASA study identified other areas of space utilization such as the Solar Power Satellite system as being a viable space goal in this century.

The results of the SAI and Rockwell International studies, performed independently, were part of the data I used for the follow-up book, *The Space Enterprise* (Ace Books, 1980).

The technical and economic potentials of space industrialization are discussed in detail in these two prior books which should be consulted for additional information on space manufacturing processes and products.

A major problem was identified by these studies and through contacts with individuals in managerial and planning positions in a variety of non-aerospace industrial firms.

In order for space manufacturing to become a truly viable economic part of the American industrial scene, it's necessary to reduce the cost of space transportation to $20 per kilogram placed in LEO. Otherwise, there were some terrestrial options that appeared to be more economical, and it would be difficult for any corporation to justify the combination of high risks and high transportation costs. Nearly everyone with any input to these studies agreed that low-cost, reliable and available space transportation was the important key to opening up Earth orbital space to American private enterprise for new industrial operations.

The SPS space transportation system offers the solution to this dilemma as one consequence of its development and operation as part of the SPS program.

Inexpensive space transportation will be immediately perceived as a competitive opportunity by people in domestic industry already aware of the potentials of space manufacturing. Thus, the SPS space transportation system satisfies a market need that currently exists. Once the opportunity has been grasped by only a few companies, and once profitable operations have been established by these pioneer firms, the need will grow.

This is confirmed by the fact that many of the more conservative industrialists and managers who provided inputs to the space industry studies said that they "wanted to be kept informed of what was going on," and that they "would probably get involved" if their competition did.

In the world of private enterprise, nobody wants to be left behind in the competitive race but almost everyone is reluctant to start running hard immediately after the gun goes off. It's only after a couple of the more venturesome runners look like they're going to win the whole race that the reluctant ones begin to run hard.

Once the SPS transportation system makes it possible for a few companies to show a profit on products manufactured in space, the market will expand immensely. The SPS transportation system then ceases to become merely a part of the SPS program; it becomes an integral part of the entire space enterprise.

The U.S. airlines may have started out as the response of a few hardy souls to the possibility of making money hauling the United States air mail, but it wasn't very long before the market grew. And it was a device offering low-cost air transportation which finally broke the airlines free of the mail-hauling business and put them into the passenger-hauling business: the legendary Douglas DC-3, the first airplane that could make money for its owners by flying just passengers.

History may not repeat itself, but the *patterns* of history often do, as I have said.

And the synergism continues to grow once the SPS space transportation system enables private enterprise to become established in orbit.

A well-established SPS space transportation system that allows inexpensive, reliable, and available transportation from LEO to GEO contains within itself the capability to travel further into space than geosynchronous Earth orbit.

The maintenance of a thousand people in GEO Base to build the SPS units means that many of the problems of living in space will have been tranferred over into that technological ledger column entitled, "State of the Art." This means that suitable life support systems will have been developed and proven in GEO Base, systems that can recycle carbon dioxide and organic wastes into oxygen and potable water. The only thing that can't theoretically be recycled is the nitrogen that will inevitably be lost in continuing small amounts from LEO Base and GEO Base. But cost requirements alone will demand that life support engineers working for the SPS project companies come up with the partly-closed life support system that can recycle oxygen and water; it's expensive to continue hauling life support consumables up from Earth. It becomes more economical to recycle them.

With the partially-closed life support system technology of GEO Base, it becomes possible for a modified deep space passenger ship to go *anywhere in the Inner Solar System*, including the planetoid belt between the orbits of Mars and Jupiter.

It is also possible for the electric-powered deep space freighter modules to do the same *and to bring things back* economically from the planetoid belt.

There are two very simple reasons for this. The principles go back to the science of celestial mechanics started by Johannes Kepler: (a) it isn't the distance that's important, it's the energy required to traverse that distance that counts, and (b) the time required to traverse the distances in the Solar System isn't important for non-living cargo as long as there's a load arriving at the terminal end with regularity. Insofar as people go, once even the partially-closed life support system becomes available, the time required isn't as important any more because things that were formerly consumed by the life support system operation are now recycled, meaning there's considerably less mass that's required to be carried along to keep people alive.

Travel to the Moon and the planetoid belt can begin to take place in the opening decades of the 21st Century because the capability will exist within the SPS transportation system.

But why bother to go out to the planetoid belt when all the action's taking place in LEO and GSO around the Earth?

Answer: To obtain more economical materials for building more SPS units at a lower cost.

Reason: Until the SPS space transportation system builds itself to the "takeoff" point where it can "boot strap" itself into a Solar System transportation system, it has to lift every pound of every 42,000 ton SPS unit up from the Earth's surface through a very powerful gravitational field to orbit. It takes energy to do this. Energy costs money.

It takes *less* energy to go the planetoid belt, set up mining operations there, and send SPS construction materials back to Earth orbit than it does to haul those same materials up from the Earth's surface to GEO.

It even takes less energy to get the SPS materials from the surface of the Moon, in spite of the Moon's gravity field that's one-sixth as strong as Earth's.

The cost of a Solar Power Satellite can be *reduced* by a factor of *four* when extraterrestrial materials from the Moon or the planetoid belt can be used instead of materials hauled up from Earth.

This is an important consequence because we cannot continue to strip the Earth of its raw materials to support our operations in space. Sooner or later, we will have to shift to using raw materials from elsewhere in the Solar System.

And abundant materials exist out there, waiting for us to come and get them and use them. See *The Third Industrial Revolution* and *The Space Enterprise* for details of what—and how much of it—is likely to be there.

The use of extraterrestrial materials will become mandatory for several reasons. First of all, it will reduce the cost of an SPS. It will also permit more SPS units to be built. It will permit SPS units to be built at a greater rate than two per year because the raw materials are no longer coming from Earth, but coming from extraterrestrial sources at one-fourth the cost.

The rate of construction of SPS units in GEO will probably increase from the programmed two 10-gigawatt units per year to as many as eight per year.

This increase rate of construction permits us then to do one or both of two things:

It permits us to transfer even more of the U.S. electrical baseload over to SPS power as more rectennas are built to accommodate the increased satellite capacity. This means we *really* shut down all the nukes. And that we begin dismantling some of the fossil fuel plants as well, including some that were built in the late 20th Century.

It permits the United States and the private enterprise companies who design, build, and operate the SPS units to begin selling either the output of an SPS or the entire SPS to organizations in other countries, thus making the United States an *energy exporter* in the early 21st Century.

This can have a profound effect on world affairs.

And that's probably the understatement of this book.

But there are other things that are affected by the availability of low-cost space transportation, the ready availability of extraterrestrial raw materials, and the abundance of low-cost space power.

CHAPTER SIX

It's always a difficult task for a forecaster to correctly and completely identify all the consequences of his forecasts, much less even to consider them all in detail if he could spot them. The best one can do is to attempt to target a few of the more obvious consequences, then to study them to see if and to what extent they affect the synergy of the forecast itself.

This certainly holds true in the case of space power.

We've already seen how the SPS program can create some spinoffs or consequences that affect the future of space activity and, to some extent, the future of allied activities on Earth. To summarize the most important ones: (a) the SPS program creates a large, reliable, and low-cost space transportation system operating on published schedules, (b) the SPS system creates large space facilities capable of housing up to a thousand people, (c) the large space transportation system fosters an increased level of activity in space science as well as in space manufacturing, (d) the capabilities of the SPS space transportation system permit Inner Solar System transportation of people and cargo, thus permitting the use of extraterrestrial materials for SPS construction, reducing SPS costs by a factor of up to four times.

Meanwhile, back on Earth . . .

Regardless of the future scenario that's chosen—short of the one that prognosticates all-out general war with massive thermonuclear warhead exchanges—the SPS program and its consequences begin to have growing effects on earthbound activities starting approximately five years after the program goes into high-gear, building two 10-gigawatt SPS units in space every year.

One of these consequences is the increasing assumption of the baseload energy demand by the SPS system approximately ten to fifteen years after the program starts. If SPS units can be built at a faster rate than two per year, the SPS system is able to assume a greater percentage of the baseload demand; if the program start is delayed, the SPS system is able to pick up a reduced percentage of the baseload demand because of the catch-up game characteristics of energy demand.

But, with the inevitable introduction of extraterrestrial materials into the SPS program and the resulting reduced costs of SPS construction—perhaps dropping as low as $500 per kilowatt installed, which is a *very* attractive cost figure—an increased number could be built in Earth orbit, eventually to the point where we've ringed the Earth with SPS units in GSO.

How many SPS units could be placed in GSO?

If all SPS units are placed in the equatorial geosynchronous orbit at a distance of 35,890 kilometers (22,400 miles) from Earth, if each SPS unit occupies an area of fifty square kilometers in that orbit, and if we allow for a spacing of fifteen kilometers between SPS units, it's possible to place 17,700 SPS units in GSO. That would supply a total space power capacity of 177,000 gigawatts.

That's almost eighty-seven times the total forecast U.S. energy demand for the year 2025, which is as far as we dared to take our demand forecast.

We'll never build 17,700 SPS units.

We may never have to build more than two hundred SPS units to supply the U.S. demand.

This is because a strange consequence falls out of the SPS program after approximately twenty years.

With a mature SPS technology functioning in space along with the accompanying space transportation system that permits low-cost industrial operations in space, *plus* the availability of extraterrestrial materials, we could look forward to seeing the relocation of an increasing amount of industrial activity into space. This includes the strong possibility of relocation of even the ''heavy industries'' of Herman Kahn's secondary industrial category, the refinement category.

More and more companies are going to find it attractive to locate the new industrial facilities in space for one or all of a number of reasons.

Among these reasons are the following:

Energy will cost less in space, and the cost of energy is a critical item in many industrial operations. On Earth energy comes primarily from the combusion of fossil fuels. By the early 21st century, there will be severe social pressures to conserve these non-renewable resources by using them for chemical feedstocks instead of sending them up the stack as combustion products.

Space has no biosphere to pollute. And industrial operations in space cannot possibly pollute the terrestrial environment. Even rocket operations providing transportation to the space facilities from the Earth's surface will produce only carbon dioxide and water in their exhausts . . . and there's no way that enough rocket vehicles can be launched to even equal the pollutant volume that's being vented into the atmosphere in 1980 by industry everywhere, in spite of pollution controls. And by the early 21st century, social pressures are going to create some *very* difficult and demanding anti-pollution laws. It's going to be cheaper and easier for industry to move from an expensive site where their operations may harm the ecology out to a place where there is no ecology to damage.

Raw materials will be easier and cheaper to obtain in space than on Earth. Most of the high-grade ore bodies on Earth have been worked-out or are reaching the point where it's possible to forecast that they will be exhausted within a finite period of time. Our industrial civilization is based on iron, and there is plenty of iron in space. There are also aluminum, magnesium, and other basic metals available in the Solar System because we've already sampled the Moon and Mars and because we can make a very intelligent estimate of the composition of the rocks in the planetoid belt as a result of studying the composition of the meteorites that have fallen to Earth from space. There is also a very good chance that the most critical element, nitrogen, will be available in the upper atmosphere of Jupiter. For a more detailed discussion of extraterrestrial materials, see *The Third Industrial Revolution* and *The Space Enterprise*.

The ready availability of low-cost energy and abundant raw materials along with the absence of any need to worry about pollution are three very serious and attractive factors that will cause industry to move into space, and these three factors become attractive as a consequence of the SPS program.

As industry moves into orbit in the first two to three decades of the 21st century, the relocation activity begins to have a profound impact upon terrestrial activities, specifically upon energy consumption.

In 1980, more than 60% of the energy demand of the United States is used for industrial purposes. Only about 40% is used for domestic purposes to provide heat and light for commercial and domestic activities.

If we can shift even 50% of the baseload energy demand into space by making it more attractive for industrial operations to be relocated there during the first half of the 21st century, the total baseload demand of the United States can be *reduced*.

The upward trend of energy demand shown unmistakably in Table I of the previous chapter can either be stabilized or reversed by the year 2050.

At that point, *all* of the United States' energy demand can come from the SPS system, from decentralized terrestrial passive solar systems, from geothermal sources, from hydroelectric plants, and from wind turbines. *All* of the old electrical plants that used fossil fuels can be retired and dismantled as they reach the end of their design lifetimes.

All of the nuclear reactor electric plants will have been shut down long before this as they, too, reach the end of their depreciated lifetimes and can be written off. No new nukes will be required in order to maintain the baseload capacity dictated by demand.

We will have completed a major shift in direction of our high-technology culture by converting to renewable energy resources without severe energy shortages and with the minimum amount of dislocation in our culture because we will have done it sensibly over a long enough period of time to permit people to be retired without having to be retrained, a new generation of people to be educated and trained to work with the new systems, and existing facilities to be depreciated over their design lifetimes with little financial dislocation.

We will have made the shift to space power.

And it will cost the same as trying to stay on Earth, build new facilities to eke out another fifty years' worth of energy from non-renewable resources, modify or build new industrial facilities to meet a growing trend of concern for a safe and healthy environment, and search the Earth for new sources of raw materials from an ever-decreasing storehouse of mineral wealth.

Big as the Planet Earth may be, it is still finite, and the activities of the human race are rapidly making the world a smaller and smaller place for a growing number of things. Staying on Earth and trying to "make the best of it" by conservation is no long-term solution and we do not know what the long-term consequences may be. However, we suspect that some of the short-term consequences may be fatal.

Continual technological progress and its corollary of expansion into the Solar System offers a *better* chance for the future because we *know* that progress and expansion have been historically workable. Granted that there are problems with progress and expansion, but these problems *can* be solved.

Better the Devil we know than the Devil we know not.

Space power offers a hopeful solution to the problems of today and the future.

This is not true of any other proposal for future action.

Nor does any other proposal offer the same or better degree of hope for improvement to the low-tech nations of the world, the so-called Third World, the smaller countries emerging from the grip of colonialism, the have-not peoples of the world. Space power does.

Why? Because space power means the ability to deliver energy anywhere in the world on a power beam.

And energy makes a culture go. Energy in excess of that required to sustain mere survival can be diverted into growth and improvement. Without it, people are fated to subsist forever in a climate of poverty and want. They can't grow enough high-energy food or even enough food, period, to have any excess personal energy to accomplish anything more than stay alive from day to day. There is no excess energy to turn into capital wealth in the form of facilities to provide products, jobs, services, and protection. There is nothing to put away for the contingencies of the future. There is not enough energy to permit growth and improvement.

Energy is the food of social progress.

How can a low-tech people obtain SPS power?

How can they best put it to use?

We can make a few educated guesses. But each people, each nation, each culture has different problems and different needs because of their unique history, geography, and cultural elements. There is no single solution to either of the two questions asked above. There is a different set of answers for each culture, each nation.

But we can take a crack at it in order to produce examples of how low-tech people could benefit from space power.

One of the first forecasters to take a serious look at the problem is Dr. J. Peter Vajk, author of *Doomsday Has Been Cancelled* (Peace Press, Culver City CA, 1978).

Dr. Vajk considered how an SPS could be used by India, which is a country with vast potential but lacking in energy resources to support its large population. India can be considered as a "typical" low-tech country, if such a thing exists in light of the statement qualifying differences made above. Although part of India's problem lies in the structure of its socio-economic system (as has been pointed out by Dr. Milton Friedman in his book, *Free to Choose* (Harcourt Brace Jovanovich, New York, 1980), and in his public television series of the same name), this self-same centralized economic control system provides the means to acquire and use SPS power effectively for India *if* the planners and officials think through the system to discover the sort of solutions that would be most workable. Dr. Vajk did.

Most of the world thinks of India in terms of the teeming masses of humanity crowded into the larger cities of Calcutta and Bombay. But about 80% of India's population is rural, living in some 600,000 villages averaging less than a thousand individuals each. More than half these villages have populations of less than five hundred. In spite of the fact that one of the legacies of the British Empire in India is an extensive railway system, there are vast areas of the country where little or no transportation is available to rural villages. The road system is inadequate to support extensive trade between rural and urban areas, increasing the problems of feeding the people in the cities.

India has an energy problem in common with the rest of the world, but the nature of the problem is different. There is no established national electric power grid. Most of the larger cities have electric utility systems, but this power grid doesn't extend into the countryside.

How would India use the electricity of an SPS?

It would seem at first glance that the primary beneficiaries of SPS power in India would be the inhabitants of the cities, if they could afford the electric lighting and heating fixtures. However, the primary users of SPS electricity would probably be factories and heavy industry, which is not developed to the point where any single location in India could use even ten gigawatts of SPS power. It seems unlikely that India would undertake a massive expansion program for her primary industries merely to use the output of an SPS because the capital investment would be several thousand dollars per created job, which amounts to hundreds of man-years of labor with a national average GNP of less than $200 per capita per year.

This conclusion results from looking at India's problems from the point of view of a person from a high-tech nation such as the United States. India *can* use the output of not one SPS, but *several* SPS units, and this electricity will help the country solve not only its energy problem, but will also assist in increased agricultural output, better land management, development of a rural transportation and communication system, and development of low-tech industrial capabilities whose output and know-how is marketable in other low-tech nations as an export.

The primary energy sources in rural India are firewood and cattle dung which are transported for short distances by animals, oxcarts, or bicycles and are primarily used for heating and cooking in rural homes. One ton of firewood or dung is used per person per year. It has led to increasing deforestation which in turn has led to land erosion. And the animal dung could be better used as agricultural fertilizer to increase the crop yield of the farmlands without resorting to the expensive importation of chemical fertilizers as is now done and which doesn't reach many rural areas because of the lack of suitable transportation.

To distribute the SPS electricity to the rural areas would require a massive capital investment in a power grid along with capital investment in rural electrification of homes and production of electric heating and cooking appliances.

The need is therefore for solid or liquid fuels, not electricity.

Methanol (methyl alcohol) is an excellent liquid fuel that can be burned in small, easily made, simple stoves that will provide heat for both cooking and comfort, in spite of the fact that such stoves deliver only about 9% of the chemical energy content of the fuel to cooking utensils versus about 36% for electric or natural gas stoves. Methanol can be transported in glass or plastic containers of any convenient size. Methanol can be made from air, water, and organic material using electricity.

Approximately 400 kilograms of methanol per year per person, about two liters per day, would replace the ton of firewood or dung presently consumed. Assuming a 50% efficiency in converting electrical energy into the chemical energy of methanol, one 10-gigawatt SPS would supply enough methanol for sixteen million people per year. Thus, seventy-five SPS units would be able to supply the rural energy needs of India in the early 21st century.

If 1200 methanol synthesis plants were built within fifty kilometers of rectenna sites, the average distance for transportation of methanol to rural customers would be about twenty-five kilometers, comparable to distances over which firewood is now being transported.

Although rectennas contain some high-technology semiconductor components, the labor for the assembly of a rectenna requires only semi-skilled people easily obtained in the large cities and readily trained. Assuming that the seventy-five SPS rectennas were constructed over a fifteen year program, this would provide jobs for 850,000 people. When the program was completed, this labor force then becomes an exportable item capable of assembling rectennas in other low-tech countries. Once the rectenna system is in place, it would require 75,000 semi-skilled people for operation, maintenance, and repair.

Each methanol synthesis plant would produce some 1,100 metric tons per day and require about two million eight-liter containers or their equivalent per year. These can be manufactured from glass or ceramics using very old technology. About 60,000 glassblowers and potters would be needed to manufacture the containers. Thus, a large container industry is developed with a capability to export large numbers of containers to other countries in which this same program of utilizing SPS power would work.

With methanol transported in eight-liter jugs, delivery of this fuel to rural users would require as many as ten million rural workers distributing the jugs entirely by bicycle, handcart, and oxcart. Eventually, regional pipeline networks would be built using ceramic or plastic pipes to reduce the average distance of transportation.

Thus, space power in India could be used to create new industries and new jobs to supply methanol fuel, stoves, and containers to eliminate the current use of firewood and dung.

The dung could then be used for agricultural fertilizer, reducing foreign exchange imbalances due to fertilizer imports. It would also increase the viability of the soil and produce greater crop yields, thus providing more food for India's population.

The substitution of methanol for firewood means that this fuel source which uses 20% of India's biomass production would be left in place for soil erosion control. Alternately, the land that was formerly used to grow firewood could be used for other crops, thus further increasing the food production.

This is a prime example of using the systems analysis techniques developed by high-tech nations to solve the problems of the low-tech nations. It's also an example of how high technology can be used to solve problems that are critical in the world of low-tech.

The critical item is the recognition of the problem. It requires, in the case of India, a knowledge of the massive scale of ecological damage caused by the dependence on firewood and dung for heating and cooking by the rural population of India.

However, India is not a truly poor country. It has a very long history of cultural and intellectual excellence. Even in 1980, it is a space power with its own satellite launching vehicles. Its basic problems lie in its socio-economic organization which is a legacy of its own historical development as well as its brief colonial period as part of the British Empire. It can organize and develop its capabilities to use space power as detailed in this example.

How about a truly poor country?

It's not my intention to single out one specific country to provide an example just because of any bias. But there is one African country that has immense problems whose solutions could be at least initiated by the proper use of space power.

The *Republique du Niger* (not the Federal Republic of Nigeria; look at the map of Africa) is a landlocked country in central Africa that gained its independence from France in 1960.

It has a mixed population of 4,300,000 people with sedentary Negro peoples—Djerma-Songhai, Hausa, and Beri-

beri-Manga—existing alongside nodmadic herdsmen such as the Fulani, Berber Tuaregs, and Tebu. Only about 10% of the population is urban. The population growth rate is about 2.3% per year.

The Niger River runs through the countryside, but the river isn't navigable to the sea. The climate includes the Sahara Desert in the north and the savannah in the south with rainfall averages from zero to 20 inches per year.

The Gross Domestic Product in 1971 was $400,000,000, or about $100 per capita. Imports exceed exports. There is practically no industrial base. The economy is based upon stockbreeding and agricultural crops such as millet, rice, cotton, and peanuts.

Except for uranium and tin, there has been little development of natural resouces. Prospecting and exploration have revealed economical deposits of copper, molybdenum, nickle, iron, and phosphates. Recent test drillings have revealed a deposit of more than 4,500,000 tons of coal.

Niger has no railway and only three airports. The road system has been improved in recent years, and the Niger River was finally bridged at Gaya in 1958, providing a road link to Dahomey and the coast.

The principal energy source in Niger is firewood whose continued and increasing use has accelerated the encroachment of the Sahara Desert and aggravated the effects of drought in the Sahel region.

Niger lacks the energy resources to build a transportation system to permit the extraction of its coal for additional energy, the development of its natural resources as additional export items, and the improvement of its agricultural base along the Niger River and on the broad savannahs.

If Niger could obtain the foreign capital investment to build a rectenna and buy the output of a single 10-gigawatt SPS, it would have the energy necessary to begin the development of its social institutions and its untouched natural wealth.

The Niger River is the largest river in West Africa and the third longest on the continent after the Nile and the Congo. In many ways, it's like the Rio Grande River in North America. It drains an area of 580,000 square miles. But it isn't navigable to the Bight of Benin. And it flows through the country of Niger with no favorable locations to build hydroelectric dams or impoundment reservoirs that might make more water available for agriculture. But it does provide a water table for 450 kilometers of river valley through southwestern Niger. And where there's a river valley, wells can be drilled and water can be pumped to sustain irrigated agriculture.

If there's energy available to pump the water.

A rectenna located on the broad savannah near Tahoua about 400 kilometers northeast of the capital city of Niamey on the Niger River, along with two electrical transmission lines—one leading to the Niger River Valley near Niamey and the other leading to the ore and coal deposits near the Air Massif mountain area—would permit the people of Niger to pump underground water for more intensive irrigated agriculture both in the Niger River plain and on the broad savannahs that, in some ways, are akin to the Great Plains of the United States. The Air Massif transmission line would permit the working of the ore and coal deposits and the operation of an electrified railway. Since Niger is a member of the Common Organization for the Saharan Regions and the West African Monetary Union (part of the French franc area), the railway could be extended to Lagos or Cotonou with the co-operation of Nigeria or Dahomey, or to the existing railway link terminating at Ouagadougou in Upper Volta and leading down to Abadan on the Ivory Coast. This would provide railway access to the interior of Saharan Africa for the natural resources of ore and coal that exist there, untapped because of the lack of energy, as well as for the agricultural output of reclaimed and irrigated river valley, savannah, and Saharan lands which, properly managed with modern agricultural technology, could not only feed Niger but most of West Africa as well.

Energy is the key. Without energy, the wealth of the North African region lies locked in the land and mountains forever. With energy to pump more water and grow more food, people have the extra energy to undertake low-technology people-intensive capital improvements in their environment.

True, Niger would be in competition with the space enterprise in the area of raw materials. However, abundant and economical as extraterrestrial materials may turn out to be, the ore bodies of Earth will probably continue to be richer and more concentrated and, to some extent, will continue to be competitive in many respects with some extraterrestrial sources. For while we are blithely forging ahead in space, we must keep in mind that not all peoples on Earth are adverse to the exploitation of their natural resources because these natural resources may be the only export they have until they establish, through technology they can buy with these exports, their own measure of self-sufficiency, whatever that level of regional economic autonomy may be.

But these two examples should show the tremendous variety of responses to the question of how the SPS system can help the low-tech and poor nations of the world as well as the more advanced economic units.

Regardless of the socio-economic condition or system, and regardless of the social institutions involved, *energy* is the key to survival as well as to civilization.

And space power can provide the energy anywhere on Earth . . . or in space.

CHAPTER SEVEN

Some of the consequences of space activities as a result of the development of the build-up of both space facilities and the space transportation system were discussed in Chapter Five.

It's a natural and almost trivial forecast to anticipate that the ready availability of space power would result in an increased demand for space transportation.

But it was not so obvious that the development of cheap space transportation from Earth to orbit would bring in its wake the relocation of earthbound industries and hence 60% of the United States baseload electrical requirements into space.

And few forecasters and planners have yet discovered that the availability of cheap and abundant electricity from the SPS system creates a climate for the development, phase-in and operation of totally new forms of space transportation other than the chemical rocket.

To some extent, this is presaged by the deep space freighter, a module consisting of an electric rocket engine that would be powered by the solar electric output of the SPS photovoltaic array that it propels from the LEO Base construction site up to the GEO Base assembly site.

Electric rocket engines have been around for several decades but have generally taken a back seat in the public mind. The requirement for rocket power has been for large, high-thrust rocket engines capable of performing what has been and will continue to be the most difficult and energy-consuming portion of space flight: the boost from the Earth's surface to low Earth orbit where the space vehicle must fight its way against the persistent and strong pull of Earth's gravity. The high-thrust characteristics of this type of rocket propulsion plus the absence of any well-developed technical means for transmitting energy to the rocket vehicle from any sort of a large and permanent energy conversation facility have made it possible to use only one type of rocket propulsion system: the chemical rocket.

Everything we've launched into space to date has been flown under the thrust of a chemical rocket. Usually, the oxidizer has been liquid oxygen (LOX) although the Titan-II and Titan-III launch vehicles used nitrogen tetroxide. Solid propellant rocket motors have been used in the NASA Scout, as the third stages of all the U.S. *Delta* launch vehicles, and as the boosters for the Titan-IIIC and the NASA space shuttle. The solid propellants of this type of rocket normally consist of potassium perchorate as the oxidizer and some sort of metallized synthetic rubber formulation as a fuel, both propellants being mixed together in solid form. Liquid propellant chemical rockets have used numerous fluids as fuels. The most common of these has been RP-4 which is a form of highly refined kerosene. Other liquid fuels have included ethyl alcohol, unsymmetrical dimethylhydrazine, and the most powerful of all liquid fuels, liquid hydrogen (LH).

There have been two basic problems in the use of chemical rockets of all types using both solid and liquid propellants.

First of all, there is only so much energy that can be obtained from the combustion of a fuel and an oxidizer, and this energy shows up as exhaust velocity (which should be as high as possible) and in the rocket performance factor called "specific impulse" (thrust produced per unit weight of propellant consumed per second). The propellant combination with the best energy efficiency—liquid hydrogen and liquid oxygen—is already in use, and the only way to increase its exhaust velocity and specific impulse is to burn the propellant combination in a rocket engine at the highest possible temperature and pressure. The most energy efficient hydrogen-oxygen rocket engines used to date are the main engines of the NASA space shuttle orbiter. These Space Shuttle Main Engines (SSME's) operate with a combusion pressure of 3000 pounds per square inch. This pressure is equivalent to that used for the storage of welding gases in those heavy steel tanks that accompany every gas welding outfit. The high combustion pressure—the highest that's ever been used in a large rocket engine system—creates difficult engineering problems in the design of pumps and turbines which have to deliver these exotic super-cold propellants to the rocket engine at these pressures. With what rocket engineers and propellant chemists know today, the SSME's represent the absolute ultimate in liquid propellant chemical rocket engines. At pressures and temperatures only slightly higher than those in the SSME's, dissociation of the combustion product—water—takes place, thus robbing the system of any additional energy that's gained by increasing combustion pressures and temperatures. We've just about reached the end of the road insofar as being able to increase the exhaust velocity and specific impulse of chemical rocket engines.

Secondly, every space vehicle propelled by chemical rocket engines must carry along with it all the propellants required to complete the vehicle's flight. For Earth-to-orbit space vehicles, this means that more than 90% of the vehicle's launch weight must be made up of rocket propellants. Deep space vehicles can operate with less of a percentage of their mass being required by rocket propellants. However, regardless of whether the space vehicle is a shuttle or a deep spacer, the common and primary part of a chemical rocket's design and structure is its large, bulky, and heavy propellant storage tanks.

The same two drawbacks also affect the nuclear rocket engine. Because of the nuclear test ban treaty of August 5, 1963 that prohibits nuclear tests or explosions in the Earth's atmosphere, under water, and in space, the extensive development carried out on the nuclear rocket engine by the United States Atomic Energy Commission and NASA slowly wound down and come to a halt in the early 1970's. Billions of dollars of research and development had been poured into the nuclear rocket engine project for more than twenty years and had resulted in a series of successful nuclear rocket engines beginning with the experimental Kiwi-I and culminating with a nuclear rocket engine designed for flight, the

Nerva, which would have delivered 250,000 pounds of thrust with a specific impulse 2.5 times that of the SSME's.

Basically, the method of operation of a nuclear fission rocket engine is simple. A nuclear reactor is used to heat hydrogen—carried as liquid hydrogen aboard the space vehicle. The hot hydrogen at more than 4500-degrees Fahrenheit is then expelled through a rocket nozzle to produce thrust.

The nuclear rocket engine, had its development been permitted to continue, would have made possible extensive space operations above the Earth's atmosphere. It's still in contention for possible future use in space where there is no possiblity that its exhaust could contaminate the Earth's atmosphere. However, even though a nuclear rocket engine need carry along only one propellant—liquid hydrogen as "working mass"—it still must carry along its own energy source. And secondly, its specific impulse is limited to only about four times that of chemical rocket engines.

Because of its extremely high exhaust velocity, the electric rocket engine has a very high specific impulse in terms of thrust produced per unit weight of propellant consumed per second. The electric rocket principle is the same, regardless of the category of the electric rocket engine—arc, plasma, or ion. Electricity is used to produce charged particles such as electrons or ions which are then accelerated to very high velocities by electromagnetic or electrostatic fields and ejected from the rocket engine to produce thrust. But electric rockets don't generate very much thrust and must operate in a vacuum. To date, electric rocket engines have been used on satellites and manned space craft as attitude control thrusters because high thrust is not required for this application. Electric rockets will be used both in the Deep Space Freighters of the SPS program and on the SPS units themselves in order to provide attitude control of the big photovoltaic arrays. Here again, high thrust is neither desired nor required, but high efficiency is. And, unlike chemical rocket engines, the electric rocket engines that will be used in the SPS program do not require that all their energy supplies be carried along in the form of propellants; they can get their energy directly from the Sun itself via the solar arrays of the SPS.

This makes the electric rocket very efficient for deep space use once the SPS system is in place.

Deep space flight from orbit to orbit in the Earth-Moon system doesn't require high thrust rocket engines; it just requires steady, persistent, highly efficient thrust such as that produced by the electric rocket engine. In fact, deep space flight with constant electric rocket thrust, even at a fraction of one-gee acceleration, can result in trip times that are significantly shorter in duration than the usually-considered sort of rocket flight—a short period of high thrust followed by a long period of coasting flight terminated by a final short duration flight phase of high thrust to match velocities with the destination.

Electric rockets have been confined to such prosaic uses as attitude control to date because there's been a major technical problem of providing the electric rocket with a low-mass, high-efficiency electric energy source in space.

The SPS provides such an energy source.

The SPS also means that the deep space vehicle doesn't have to carry along the electric energy source, only a small amount of reactive mass such as argon or whatever the electric rocket engine uses to produce its charged particles that are accelerated to produce thrust.

Furthermore, a *lot* of electric energy can be provided, permitting the use of much larger electric rocket engines than formerly possible.

We have visualized the solar power satellite thus far only as an energy source for Earth. But the same technology and the same design could also be used and will be used as a space power source. We've alluded to the forecast that industries would begin moving into space in the early 21st century because of the abundant and low-cost energy available in space from an SPS system. This means that some SPS units won't be directing their power beams toward rectennas on Earth but toward rectennas in space.

And instead of a single SPS projecting a single power beam, it will be projecting several from a multitude of transmitting antennas to a large number of smaller space rectennas mounted on space facilities . . . and on space vehicles propelled by electric rockets.

Naturally, it isn't absolutely necessary that a large, centralized system such as an SPS be used. Solar electric energy could be obtained by space facilities and space vehicles from large photovoltaic collectors that are integral with their design. It's just that the large SPS unit is more efficient and will provide power at a lower cost to space facilities and vehicles, at least in the Earth-Moon system during the early years of the 21st century.

Now it becomes possible for deep space vehicles to venture as far as lunar orbit carrying only one working propellant—and not very much of that—for its electric rocket motors. The system could be built today, but it can be operated only in space after the SPS system is in part a reality. The SPS unit would have a small, steerable transmitting antenna. The space vehicle would carry its own rectenna— and it can be much smaller and use a higher density power beam that is possible for Earth use—as well as a pilot beam that would tell the SPS where the ship is and where and how to direct the individual beam that's providing electric power for the ship.

It also means several SPS units—probably originally fabricated from terrestrial materials but later built from extraterrestrial materials—that are dedicated to providing electric energy exclusively to space facilities and vehicles.

This ready availability of cheap solar electric energy also makes possible the use of several other types of propulsion systems.

This includes one that doesn't use *any* propellant mass whatsoever.

The first suggestion of using a catapult device to propel a vehicle in space probably was discussed by none other than the French author, Jules Verne, in his book, *De la Terra a la*

Lune, (From the Earth to the Moon), first published in 1870. Although Verne's book wasn't the first to talk about travel in space, it *was* the first to be written using the known science and technology of the day as its background. Verne's catapult was a huge cannon, the *Columbiad*. The space vehicle that was launched by the *Columbiad* carried no propulsion systems; all the energy for the circumlunar flight was imparted by the cannon's propellant charge, a fulminate of nitrocellulose Verne called "pyroxyle." The *Columbiad* was a space catapult.

Robert A. Heinlein, in his 1947 *Saturday Evening Post* short story, "Space Jockey," and in his 1949 novella "The Man Who Sold the Moon," suggested the use of an electric-powered Earth-surface catapult running up the east face of Pikes Peak in Colorado as a means of eliminating the need for a two-stage Earth-to-orbit shuttle in favor of a catapult-launched SSTO shuttle. In his 1966 novel, "The Moon Is a Harsh Mistress," Heinlein postulates the use and consequences of a solar-electric lunar surface cargo catapult.

However, space catapults didn't begin to receive intense attention until Dr. Gerald K. O'Neill became involved in his work on space colonization at Princeton University in the early 1970's. Dr. O'Neill publicized the concept of the "mass driver," a solar-electric space catapult that could be used both on the lunar surface and in deep space. Since 1976, Dr. O'Neill and his associates at Princeton have carried out additional research work on the "mass driver" which is based upon the established technology of the linear electric motor or sequential solenoid, both of which have been widely used in industry for decades. Today, space advocates use the term "mass driver," most of them not knowing that this is an old concept.

Perhaps the biggest difference between the historic space catapults and Dr. O'Neill's mass driver is the size and frequency of the payloads launched. Classic space catapults have considered launching multi-ton space vehicles or cargo payloads much like the catapults used to launch aircraft from warships. Dr. O'Neill's mass driver would launch payloads of about 2 kilograms every few seconds in a constant stream toward the destination.

The biggest problem with space catapults and mass drivers is not the energy required to make them work, that energy will be readily available from an SPS system. It's the question of manipulating the catapult's payload when it reaches its destination, especially if said payload has no on-board propulsion system. An Earth-to-orbit catapult launching an SSTO shuttle doesn't have that problem because the SSTO shuttle has propulsive energy to match orbits with its LEO destination. A lunar surface catapult designed to lob unmanned payloads to Earth doesn't have that problem because the payload or its container can be designed to be slowed down by atmospheric entry and land in the ocean. But everywhere a space catapult or mass driver might be considered for use in the early years of its deployment, there is a problem of catching the payload.

An unmanned, unpowered payload of any size launched from orbit to orbit or from lunar surface to orbit simply returns to the launch site unless an additional change of energy is imparted to it at the proper time and place in its trajectory. It's like a cannon shell. It's like the manned projectile launched from Jules Verne's *Columbiad*.

Technically, the problem of catching the payload or of imparting an energy change to it can be solved. Dr. O'Neill has designed a catcher for his two-kilogram mass driver payloads. With abundant energy available from an SPS system, there are several approaches that can be taken toward imparting an energy change to an unmanned, unpowered payload to permit it to arrive at its space destination with zero velocity difference between it and the destination.

One of the most interesting potential solutions comes from something that was the brainchild of Dr. Arthur Kantrowitz, formerly with AVCO and now at the Thayer School of Engineering at Dartmouth College. It's also an interesting potential propulsion system for use *anywhere* in the Inner

Solar System where the energy of the Earth-orbit SPS system can be used.

Dr. Kantrowitz proposed the concept of the laser-energized rocket in the late 1970s when the potential of the high-powered lasers being developed for possible military uses was under discussion by many people.

The laser rocket would use a tightly-focused beam of energy from a high-energy laser situated as a fixed facility on a planetary body or in space. The laser beam would be directed at the rear end of a space vehicle where the energy of the beam would vaporize a solid material to provide a gaseous reaction mass to be expelled in rocket fashion from the vehicle. This is similar in concept to the SPS-energized electric rocket except for the fact that the laser rocket would be simpler and would eliminate many of the energy conversion steps of the SPS-electric rocket.

Because of the ability of a laser to generate an energy beam that can be tightly focused, thus preventing the dissipation of the beam over long distances and the increased possibility of reception of a majority of the beam's energy at extreme distances, the laser rocket offers great promise as a propulsion system for use in the initial phases of exploitation of the planetoid belt for extraterrestrial materials. The energy for the power laser in Earth orbit would come, of course, from an SPS unit. The laser could provide energy for a space vehicle all the way out to the planetoid belt and perhaps to the planet Jupiter. In fact, such a laser method of squirting energy over long distances could be used to provide the necessary energy from established facilities in Earth orbit for manned facilities and vehicles throughout the Inner Solar System during the first decades of the 21st century.

Laser power beaming may, in the final analysis, be the optimum method for beaming SPS power to the Earth's surface.

Again, we discover that we're dealing with a ''boot strap system''—it becomes possible to build systems upon systems to create synergistic multiplication of capabilities far beyond that which we could hope to achieve with one system alone.

With the energy available from the expanded SPS system in geosynchronous Earth orbit, it now becomes possible for us to provide energy for our use *anywhere* in the Inner Solar System. This will make it much easier to travel from point to point in space, and it will make it much, much easier to maintain populated facilities wherever we wish to put them.

We have just extended our concept of energy and its relationship to social organization from its original earth-bound application. We've extended it into the Solar System. Where we have energy, people can live and work. Where we have energy, we can travel. Where we have energy, we can alter the natural order to make it more useful to us as human beings.

With the propulsion devices made possible by the SPS system in Earth orbit and the consequence that we will be able to travel to and work in any part of the Inner Solar System where it's possible to use solar energy, before the 21st century is half over we will have reached the point where we no longer have to depend upon SPS units in GEO for energy beamed to the Earth.

We will be able to construct extremely large Solar Power Satellites at the terrestrial-solar libration points where they will be able to beam power to the Earth-Moon system.

A libration point is a "special solution" to the old "Three Body Problem" of celestial mechanics. Sir Isaac Newton in his classic 1687 statement of the laws of motion and gravitation, *Principia*, showed us the solution to the problem of the gravitational interaction of two bodies. But there is no known general mathematical solution to the behavior of three celestial bodies of sizes such that their individual gravitational fields affect the other bodies in the three-body system. There are, however, five "special solutions" to the three-body problem.

Figure 1 shows the Earth-Moon system drawn to scale. The location of geosynchronous orbit is shown so that we can get some perspective on distances—but *not* travel energies

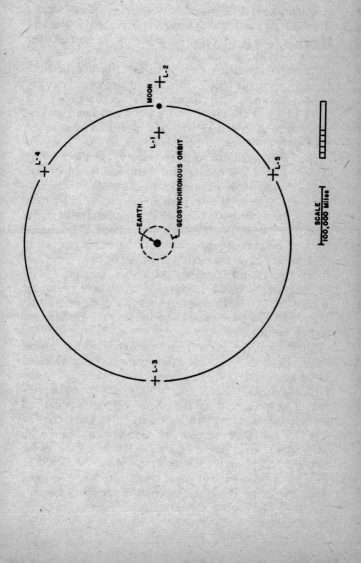

and times required. There are five points in the Earth-Moon system where another object ranging from a small satellite up to a Moon-sized celestial body could be *theoretically* located and retain its position with respect to both the Earth and the Moon. In these five locations, the gravity fields of all three bodies would be in balance.

These five locations are known as "libration points." Actually, they are regions rather than precise locations. They are also known as "Lagrangian points" in honor of Joseph Louis Lagrange (1736–1813), the French geometer and astronomer who first suggested this special solution to the three-body problem.

The First Lagrangian Point, shown as L-1 on the drawing, is located on a line between the Earth and the Moon and approximately 76,000 kilometers from the Moon. The Second Lagrangian Point, L-2, is also located on a line from the Earth to the Moon but is about 71,000 kilometers outside the orbit of the Moon. The Third Lagrangian Point, L-3, is on the Earth-Moon line but located in lunar orbit 180-degrees away from the Moon on the other side of the Earth.

The first three Lagrangian Points are "unstable"—any object placed at these Lagrangian Points will eventually wander away from them because of fact that the orbit of the Moon isn't exactly circular and because of the gravitational pull of the Sun.

But this isn't the case with the Fourth and Fifth Lagrangian Points, L-4 and L-5. The Fourth Lagrangian Point is located in the lunar orbit 60-degrees ahead of the Moon, while the Fifth Lagrangian Point is also in lunar orbit but 60-degrees behind the Moon. L-4 and L-5 are *stable* libration points and are also known as the "Trojan Points." We know that L-4 and L-5 are stable because the discovery of the Trojan planetoids (named after the heroes of Homer's *Illiad*) at the L-4 and L-5 points in Jupiter's orbit about the Sun. The Trojan planetoids have obviously been there for a long time. Thus, the Trojan Points are super-stable locations, *but they are not the only stable orbital locations* even in the Earth-Moon system.

Technically, it would be possible to put any number of objects in lunar orbit or any other orbit and have them stay in place for a long period of time—hundreds of years or more in some cases—with only minor orbital adjustments with electric thrusters. Any number of satellites can occupy a given orbit; the rings of Jupiter, Saturn, and Uranus are proof of this. (Earth has no rings; Dr. Clyde W. Tombaugh proved this as part of his extensive search for small natural satellites of the Earth in 1953–1959.)

As implied, Lagrangian libration points exist for every major body in the Solar System and for every planet-satellite orbit as well. There are equivalent Lagrangian Points in the Sun-Earth system, the most stable (because of the tremendous mass and strong gravity field of the Sun) being the Sun-Earth Trojan Points. There are mercurian Trojan Points, venerian Trojan Points, aerean Trojan Points, etc.

The Trojan Points in the Inner Solar System are going to be occupied in the first half of the 21st century. Among the many things that will be located at the various Trojan Points are Solar Power Satellites of very large size, fabricated from extraterrestrial materials, and sending their energy to various locations on radio and laser beams.

The Trojan Points in the Sun-Earth system are attractive as locations for such large SPS units because the relationship between the Sun and the SPS and between the Earth and the SPS remain reasonably constant. This means that a Trojan Point SPS doesn't need to be continually re-oriented to keep its photovoltaic panels pointed toward the sun or its energy transmitter aimed toward its consumer's rectenna.

The Trojan Point SPS system of the 21st century is only a dream today. But by 2050 or 2060, such a system could be supplying the Earth-Moon system with whatever power it needed from SPS units in the Earth-Moon Trojan Points. Additional energy would be coming from SPS units in the two Sun-Earth Trojan Point locations. The Trojan Point SPS system would also include units whose job is to provide in-flight energy to deep space vehicles via power beams, and these transportation-dedicated SPS units would have several transmitting antennas or use a single antenna with special phasing circuitry.

(Antenna design borders on black magic although it is a very solid technology based firmly on mathematical foundations. It's possible to get antennas to do a number of magic tricks depending upon their design. For example, one antenna can transmit to several receiving units, each receiver being illuminated by a separate antenna beam. And, since a good transmitting antenna is also a good receiving antenna, a single antenna can be used for both purposes by multiplexing or rapid switching.)

All that is necessary is to be willing to accept the risks, expend the capital resources, organize the effort, and get started in the 1980 decade on the development work necessary to prove out the essential technologies of the first SPS system in geosynchronous orbit. Once we have started that task in order to solve the energy crunch, the consequences are so attractive and the potentials are so enormous that the entire Inner Solar System is opened up to utilization by the human race.

Or is it?

CHAPTER EIGHT

The scenarios for the development, consequences, and utilization of space power presented thus far have concentrated on the commercial aspects. However, to a large degree the extent of space power development, its future course of development, many of the consequences, and much of the utilization and availability depends upon the answers to two important questions:

Who owns the SPS system or its individual components?

Who controls the SPS system or its individual components?

These are two separate questions because ownership and control are two different aspects of any system. They are not the same, although many people who are not intimately acquainted with finance and management techniques can see no difference between them. Regardless of the socio-economic ideologies and philosophies under which a given activity takes place, there is *always* a demarcation between ownership and control of the activity. It may be less evident in socialistic economic systems or even in a totalitarian dictatorship, but there *is* a difference.

It's possible to own something without being able to exercise management control over it.

It's also possible to control the operating policies and managerial decision-making of an organization without owning any part of it.

The larger the organization or activity, the more these statements are true and the more pronounced the demarcation becomes.

The SPS system is going to be a very large undertaking requiring a very large capital investment. What the SPS system finally does and who benefits the most depends strongly on how things are organized and upon the answers to the two questions concerning who owns the system and who controls it.

Whoever provides the capital for an enterprise is usually considered to be the owner by nearly every system of justice extant on Planet Earth. However, ownership can be divided between a number of institutions or individuals.

Figure 2 shows the possible paths of capital funding flow to any large endeavor. Not all of these paths are available in all socio-economic systems.

Regardless of who or what owns an enterprise, the basic source of all capital is the individual human being in the form of an investor of money, the user of a service whose payment for products or services contains a percentage allocation for capital improvement, or a taxpayer to a government.

Thus, the *type* of owner of an enterprise can be generally categorized according to the voluntary or involuntary nature of his willingness to provide capital investment—the extent to which he's free to make a choice and the extent to which he's coerced without a choice. This is the only factor which separates the socio-economic ideologies involved.

Under a free enterprise system, an investor makes a free choice of where he invests his capital, making a personal decision usually in favor of the investment scheme that offers or promises to offer the greatest return on his investment in the shortest period of time with the least amount of risk.

Depending upon organization of the enterprise and the socio-economic system under which it operates, the consumer of the product or services also exercises some degree of freedom of choice concerning his capital investment that's hidden in the price he pays for the product or service; he has a varying degree of freedom of choice depending upon the nature of the product or service and its importance to him. If the product or service isn't absolutely necessary to his survival and well-being, he can opt to purchase something else instead. If the product or service is essential, the extent of his freedom of choice depends totally upon the socio-economic system under which he lives. To some extent, the price he

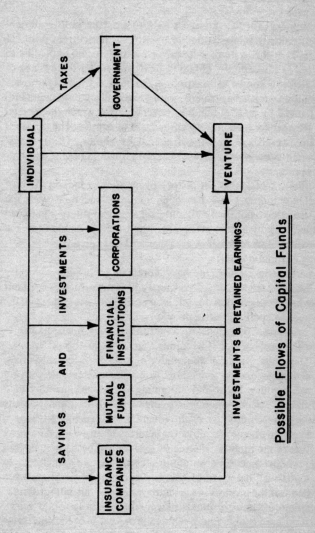

Possible Flows of Capital Funds

pays for the product or service is also dependent upon the socio-economic system.

Except for the relative power of his vote in the political area of his socio-economic system, or his current political clout in the system, a taxpayer has little or no choice as to where his capital—obtained from him under the system of coercion known as taxation—is expended by the taxing social organization, usually a politically-elected management backed by an appointed bureaucracy over which the elected element has a widely-varying extent of control. The taxpayer investor has very little freedom of choice. Under some socio-economic systems, he has no freedom of choice whatsoever.

Much of the recent history of the human race in the past five hundred years has been mainly concerned with the struggles—political, ideological, and military—between people with different outlooks and beliefs concerning the extent of freedom of choice that will be exercised or permitted to individuals.

As Eric Hoffer, the longshoreman philospher, so aptly summarized it, "In a free society, it is necessary to spell out what people cannot do, while in an authoritarian society, it is vital to spell out what people can do."

Because this question determines how space power is likely to be used, it becomes critical to this book.

Equally critical is the matter of *control* of the enterprise, and this is usually lodged in the management people who are making the day-to-day operating decisions and may also make decisions having varying degrees of impact on the long-range activities of the organization. Technically, management people are subject to controls imposed upon them by the owners, but the degree of this control by ownership can vary, from nearly absolute in the case of sole ownership, to minute in the case of the holder of a single share of a corporation's stock or a taxpayer under an authoritarian, bureaucratic government. Depending also upon the socio-economic system under which the operation of the enterprise takes place, the managers are subjected to varying degrees of governmental control depending upon the laws, rules, and regulations and upon the enthusiasm of the government people in enforcing these controls. In an international sense, organizations operate internationally according to diplomatic treaties, agreements, arrangements, accords, or protocols as agents of a national government or an international body such as the United Nations. Only the 20th century social institution of the multinational corporation can often operate without such international controls or, if controls are enforced by one or more "home nations" of the multinational corporation, operate in such a manner as to circumvent such controls.

The basic principles of management are the same regardless of the socio-economic system or the size or nature of the enterprise. The performance of any task sufficiently complicated to require the participation of more than a few people working in intimate day-to-day contact with one another involves the four basic principles of management technology:

1. Delegation of authority.
2. Delegation of responsibility.
3. Control and communication.
4. Rewards and penalties.

An activity cannot be managed effectively or for long without all four of these basic principles being observed and practiced.

History has shown time and again that the best results are obtained when the delegation of authority is matched by an equal delegation of responsibility. It is not true that absolute power corrupts absolutely; absolute immunity (lack of delegation of responsibility) corrupts absolutely, regardless of the system.

History has also provided ample data to support the contention that the best means of control and the most effective methods of assignment of rewards and penalties are achieved under a system based upon personal interest in improving one's well-being and upon an individual's ability to produce things of value to others, not upon police supervision, ideological enthusiasm, or slavery.

However, a very large project such as the SPS system, which requires a time-phased infusion of large amounts of capital and takes more than five years to achieve a fruitful and profitable position, requires more than sufficient capital (enlightened ownership) and good management people and techniques (effective control).

There are other factors that are necessary in order to achieve success, and these have become clear through analysis of numerous large projects of the past, including the Apollo manned lunar landing program of the 1960s. Because people change their minds, because new technology rapidly makes itself available in any enterprise, because new methods are learned from mistakes, and because the individuals who exercise both ownership and control change, leave the organization, and come into the overall picture with new and different ideas and methods, such "macroprojects" as the SPS program and its consequential space enterprise must have:

1. Organizational continuity, stability, and flexibility.
2. Close interaction with the environment of the enterprise.
3. Exceptional people involved in management.
4. Ability to foster and utilize innovation in all areas.
5. Avoidance of managerio-sclerosis including such syndromes as NIH (Not Invented Here), Parkinsonism, the Peter Principle, etc.

One of the big problems faced by the SPS system is the fact that a very large capital investment is going to be required over a long time period with high risk at the start diminishing to a more normal risk factor as the first SPS units go on line. This is especially critical during the first ten years of the program when most of the R&D is being carried out. Even the most optimistic scenarios for R&D and operational build-up of the SPS system cannot show a return on investment in much less than 15 years from start-up of the R&D phase of the project.

There's a general rule of thumb in domestic industry these days that says there should be no capital investment in any program that doesn't pay for itself within five to eight years, although the utility industry commonly has to wait up to ten to twelve years for a new generating plant to pay for itself.

The SPS is faced with something similar to the common dilemma of a person trying to get a first job: you can't get a job without experience, and you can't get experience without getting a job. The R&D phase will eliminate many of the technical question marks and unknowns that make the investment such a high-risk venture, but it cannot be carried out without a very large capital investment. However, once the R&D is done and the risk reduced, the SPS system should face no more difficulty in the financing area than the utility companies now face in obtaining the capital for new generating and transmission facilities.

There is an enormous difference in the financial situation between the R&D and the construction/operation phases of the SPS program. Failure to recognize this fact has led many people to assume that only government ownership of the SPS system is feasible since only the government is able to make huge capital investments in long-range high-risk ventures. This assumption is not valid if the difference between the two phases is recognized and if the SPS program is organized differently in the two phases.

However, one should not automatically assume that a single type of organizational structure can't do the entire job. And one should not assume that it's *either* a government job *or* a private enterprise job. It could be any one of a large number of organizational arrangements in between, covering a spectrum of organizational structures all the way from complete government ownership and control to completely private ownership and control.

The SPS program has posed a new problem in the intermix of ownership and control that has occurred many times in history. The stock corporation grew out of a need to share the risk among English investors of the 1600s who were interested in colonizing Virginia for profit. The multinational corporation is a 20th century invention intended to circumvent trade restrictions, monetary exchange problems, and imbalance of natural resources. There is no reason to believe that the SPS program won't also breed its own type of organization to accomplish what needs to be done. This new organization will probably be an outgrowth of existing types, taking a bit here and a bit there to form a new institution that can accomplish the establishment of space power in spite of all the pessimistic business, commercial, financial, and technical pronouncements. Too many people are now interested in the SPS program.

Since new SPS organizations will probably grow from amalgamations of existing institutions, it should be possible to investigate some of the possibilities using the techniques of technological forecasting that have been honed to a fine edge during the past quarter of a century.

It's possible to establish a matrix of organizations that might tackle the job. A matrix is a box arrangment of interactions between ownership (capital sources) and control (management principles) as in as Figure 3, which shows possible organizational forms for the full duration of the SPS program—R&D through construction and operation.

Down the left side of the chart arrayed vertically are the capital sources—government funding, corporate investment, and individual investment.

Across the top are arrayed the control agencies—government agency, government-sanctioned monopoly, and competitive corporation.

In the matrix are displayed some of the possible full-duration SPS organizations that have been considered to date.

The SPS program could be carried out by an existing government agency such as DOE or NASA. The DOE cost estimates of the SPS program run between $40-billion and $45-billion over the first fifteen years, amounting to an annual expenditure between $7-billion and $8-billion per year, a level of effort that's somewhat below the peak funding level of NASA during the Apollo program. Thus, it would seem that DOE or NASA could handle the R&D phase of the SPS program *provided* there was continuing congres-

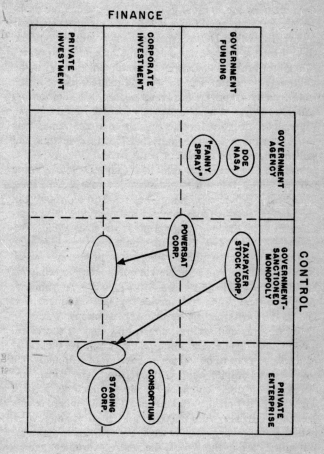

sional support for the program over the fifteen year span and
providing that the usual government-funded morasses and
traps could be avoided.

However, placing the SPS program in a new government
agency created specifically for the project would certainly
solve many of the internal political and bureaucratic problems the program would face within existing agencies (as it
already has within DOE). Management practices could be
tailored for the long-term goals of the program. However,
many of the problems of letting a government agency run the
program still remain. The diffuse and indirect nature of the
benefits to the taxpayers is a major obstacle. In addition, no
matter what government agency is involved as the prime
responsible institution for the program, there are tremendous
technical management problems that *must* be overcome and
probably have little chance of being solved.

In this regard, the reader is invited to consult Neville Shute
Norway's book, *Slide Rule* (William Morrow & Co., Inc.,
New York, 1954), especially Chapters Three through Six
describing the British experience in a similar high-risk, capital intensive, high technology program: large dirigibles. Between 1923 and 1930, the British built two dirigibles. The
R-100, the "capitalist ship," was built by private enterprise,
the Vickers Corporation, under contract to the Air Ministry.
The R-101, the "socialist ship," was built by the Ministry,
the government, using civil service engineers and managers.
The R-100 performed better than specifications, was completed on time and within budget, and made a successful
transatlantic voyage. The same cannot be said for the R-101
which turned out to be a disaster because of extremely bad
engineering, despite huge cost overruns. The end of the
dirigible era actually came on the night of October 5, 1930
when the R-101 crashed in France, killing all aboard except
six. Only Germany continued to build dirigibles thereafter,
until the *Hindenburg* disaster wrote the final end to the story.
But in the case of the R-101, the same government agency
that had built the ship also inspected it and issued the certifi-
cate of airworthiness, and there were no independent checks

on the engineering because it was *politically* impossible to have such checks made.

A similar case can be made, again with British aerospace history, in the case of the great Bristol *Brabazon* post-war airliner fiasco in which the government built an airplane that the government airline didn't want and that, by the time it was built, was obsolete because of failure of imagination on the part of the designers. In this case, the only casualties were the British taxpayers, who were gouged to the tune of 12.5 million pounds sterling, and the nationalized British aerospace industry, which lost the international airliner market to the aerospace firms of the United States.

Unfortunately the United States has its own bureaucratic disasters, such as the nuclear ocean vessel *Savannah* that turned out not to be wanted by any commercial shipping concern; the over-engineered Turbo-Train that shuddered and rocked over an existing railway between New York and Boston whose roadbed was far below the utopian standards to which the train was designed; Three Mile Island which, in spite of human error and a correct functioning of safety controls, was the fault of the Nuclear Regulatory Agency and its predecessor, the Atomic Energy Commission; and the national interstate highway system, whose engineering standards produce a bridge incapable of withstanding flood waters that don't faze an old 1930 highway span standing alongside.

If the United States opts for development of the SPS by a government agency, people must keep aware of the pitfalls of doing it this way, pitfalls that are solidly based on historical evidence. (We might also note that the government isn't doing a very good job of running a passenger railroad system called Amtrak, to say nothing of a very low technology activity known as the United States Postal Service.)

Operation of the SPS system by a government agency threatens enormous danger, as we will see later.

Since there appears to be some historical justification for concern about funding an SPS system by coercive taxation and operating it by a government agency not attuned to the feedback of the marketplace, a "taxpayer stock corporation" was proposed by George E. Fredericks and Richard D. Stutzke in 1977. The basic idea is to create a quasi-public corporation by act of Congress and to fund it by specific appropriation every year. But every taxpayer would receive some number of shares of the corporation in proportion to the fraction of his taxes that had been appropriated to the corporation every year. Such shares could then be traded openly on the stock market by taxpayers who did not wish to support the SPS program. Those who wished to support the program or to obtain a greater share in it could hold their own shares and purchase more on the open market. While the taxpayer stock corporation would be subject to significant government control during the early years of the project while risks were still high and R&D yet underway, the shareholders would elect the Board of Directors at an early time and thus exercise some control over the corporation. As the system went on-line during the operational phase, there would be no further appropriations necessary from Congress and the Directors would be answerable only to shareholders. Because of the novelty of this concept, it's hard to say how successful it would be. But it does offer a conceptual solution to the problem of capitalization during the critical high-risk R&D decade and the necessary phase-over to private ownership and control once it is in operation. It offers solutions to other problems we will later discuss, and these may create significant political opposition to the taxpayer stock corporation.

Another possiblity that has already proven itself is a federal trust fund supported by energy taxes to finance the early phase of the SPS system with development and operation contracted to private firms. During the last three decades, the federal government has provided most of the funds for domestic projects comparable in size to the SPS program. An example is the Interstate Highway System, which has a trust fund made up of revenues derived from a few-cents-per-gallon tax on motor vehicle fuels; total expenditures on the Interstate Highway System from 1957 to 1979, a 22-year period, were about $180 billion 1978 dollars. (Anyone who objects to the "outrageous cost estimates given by the space advocates for a solar power satellite" should be shown this data.) If a modest tax of two mills per kilowatt-hour were placed on electrical consumption (as a heavy user of electricity during the summertime in the air-conditioned Arizona desert, this would increase my electric bill by only $5.70 per month), such a tax would generate more than $60 billion in the 1980 decade, a figure that provides a great deal of the financing for the R&D phase of the SPS as well as for the initial construction phase. The advantage of the energy trust fund approach is that it places the burden of cost and risk on those who use the most electric energy and therefore on the very ones who demand new generating capacity. The disadvantages have already been discussed; they are the same as those which accrue to any high-technology organization funded and operated by the government. There is also the perpetual problem of keeping the politicians and bureaucrats from putting their hands in the till, using the trust fund for purposes other than that for which it was established. A prime example of this is the Airport and Airway Trust Fund, which contains billions of dollars collected from a tax of four cents per gallon on aviation fuel and four percent of every airline ticket; political shenanigans have kept this trust fund locked up so that new air traffic control facilities can't be purchased from its funds. Along with the Highway Trust Fund, the Airport and Airway Trust Fund is the target of raiding by the Department of Transportation, which would like to be able to divert those billions of trust fund dollars into other modes of transportation support.

However, another means of government financing exists and has been proved out by the Federal National Mortgage Association ("Fannie Mae"), which is a government-chartered corporation providing mortgage funds for homeowners through issuance of long-term bonds traded on the market. The government assumes some risk but speculative investors absorb the gains or losses due to changing interest rates during the lifetimes of the Fannie Mae bonds. A similar government corporation (tentatively called here the

Federal National Space Projects Association, or "Fannie
Spray") could perform the same function for the SPS program, especially during the critical R&D phase where large
capital inputs at high risk are required. The characteristics of
the "Space Bonds" could be established to resemble those
issued by Fannie Mae with a 20-year maturity and a sliding
scale of interest. Fannie Spray would be less accountable to
the taxpayers than the taxpayer stock corporation. And Space
Bonds would have to compete on the open market with other
bonds needed for capital financing; taxes don't. Since bond
financing would not appear as a line-item in the annual
Federal budget, it would be far easier to obtain continued
government support for Fannie Spray in contrast to asking for
an annual direct appropriation. And unless Fannie Spray
were organized along the lines of a private corporation (as
Fannie Mae is to a certain extent), it would be hampered by
the general managerial liabilities of government agencies.

A complex two-phased approach called the "staging company" was proposed by Christian O. Basler in 1977. A
staging company depends on investors who are willing to be
somewhat speculative and are willing to wait several years
for capital appreciation of their shares in the company caused
by accumulation of technological advances and licensing of
patent rights. The staging company is set up as a partially
closed-end non-diversified investment company similar to a
mutual fund. However, instead of distributing its dividend
earnings and capital gains to its stockholders, the staging
company spends substantially all of its income on R&D
contracts directed toward SPS technology. To stretch the
funds available from its investment portfolio incomes, the
staging company would also contract for R&D with companies whose stock it holds in its portfolio as well as with
firms willing to share the R&D costs in joint ventures. Once
the prospect for successful commercial implementation of an
SPS venture becomes assured by answers to the technology
questions answered during this R&D phase, the staging company converts into an operating company and begins to build
and operate an SPS system. The complex two-stage nature of

this form of organization is shown in the two flow diagrams, Figure 4 and Figure 5. The major advantage of the staging company concept is the ability of a private firm to proceed on the SPS system without waiting for government or political support to develop. At the same time, the magnitude of the required R&D effort could strain available sources of high-risk speculative capital. Yet this has some advantageous consequences since it would force the staging company to seek the most innovative, economical, and inexpensive design approaches, factors which have signaled the success of many private ventures when compared to their government-organized counterparts which may not come off at lost cost and with economical operating practices.

It is *highly* unlikely that we will see the emergence of a consortium of companies in the United States that would come together to provide the capital base and the technological know-how to proceed with the SPS program. Any such organization of companies would have to agree on division of tasks and of the costs involved. Because of the division of costs, they would have to agree on a division of revenues to eventually cover those costs. To the government agencies who watchdog United States industry and finance—the Securities Exchange Commission, the Federal Trade Commission, and the Department of Justice—an agreement on division of costs and revenues of the magnitude we're discussing for the SPS program amounts to a violation of the Sherman Anti-Trust Act of 1890, among a host of other federal regulations that make it totally impossible for American industry to amass large amounts of high-risk capital in 1980.

And a single corporation simply does not have all the factors required. There is only one corporation in the *entire world* that has the combination of attributes necessary to finance the SPS program. It has the necessary equity to finance the venture and has the ability and the reputation required to raise additional equity capital if needed. It can afford to take the risk and lose without having the loss destroy the company. It has a proven record of providing backing for technology that shows promise but is beyond the current state

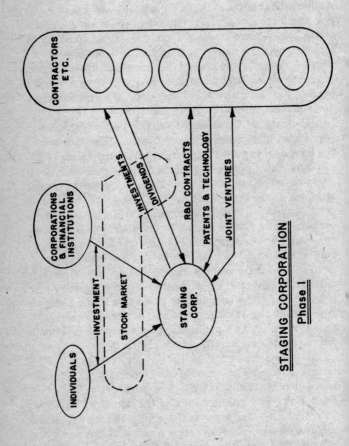

STAGING CORPORATION

Phase I

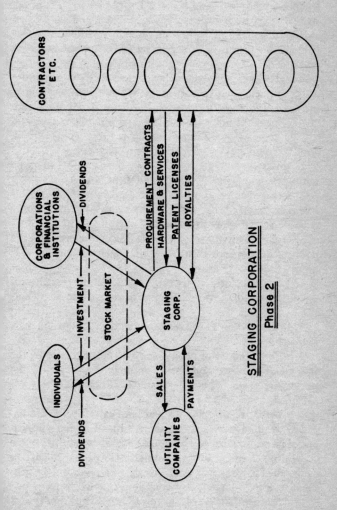

STAGING CORPORATION
Phase 2

of the art. It has the management teams, practices, and philosophies required to handle such a long-term high-technology project. And it has a Board of Directors and a staff of executive officers young enough and aggressive enough to see the SPS program through its fifteen-year development cycle to an operational phase and a return on investment. That corporation is Exxon Company.

A review indicates that there will have to be some measure of government involvement in the SPS program, especially in the early years and the entire R&D phase to the point where operational SPS units are in place and providing energy.

This means that we must be prepared to deal effectively with the problems of government involvement:

1. Possibility of getting "lost in the shuffle" in large multi-program agencies such as DOE or NASA.

2. Management problems, especially managerio-sclerosis, created by the Civil Service system and the bureaucracy in general.

3. High sensitivity to bureaucractic contingency and the political atmosphere of the time in Congress and the Administration.

4. Possibility of periods of feast and famine because of operation within the political arena of annual budgetary battles.

5. Insensitivities to the realities and demands of the marketplace.

6. Little freedom of choice or voice in the matter by the individual who is the ultimate consumer of energy and the ultimate recipient of both the costs and the benefits of the SPS system.

We will *have* to come up with an answer in the United States. The answer must be some form of organization or social institution that combines the historic capabilities of the federal government to take on high-risk, capital intensive, long-range programs to assist private enterprise and the efficient, market-oriented, cost-conscious characteristics of private enterprise. The word "historic" is used here because in the United States we have a two-hundred-year history of the government stepping in during the early high-risk period of a new venture, doing the R&D, reducing the risks, then stepping aside to let private enterprise companies take over to operate the venture and provide the government a recoupment of expenditures through an expansion of the tax base. See Chapter Eight of *The Space Enterprise* for a list of historic precursors and an analysis of the consequences that flowed from them.

We must come up with an answer because other nations with other socio-economic systems can see and evaluate the things we have discussed thus far. These other nations may not have the regulations that prohibit the concentration of the capital resources required. Some of them have historic foreign policies that are inimicable to the interests of a free people such as the citizens of the United States.

Americans *must* be the people who take the lead in SPS technology and who are the leaders among the peoples of the space-faring world—who will be in orbit too, constructing their own SPS systems. The SPS system is not just an American goal; it is of interest to others because of the energy potential and the consequences that come from carrying out an SPS program.

Only part of this is because we don't wish to face another international cartel such as OPEC where we would be forced to buy space solar energy at prices set by others and suffer the problems of a flow of cash out of the country.

Only part of this is because there is a potentially enormous international market for the output of an SPS system.

The *major* part of this is the basic consequence of space power: the political and military advantages that flow from space power.

CHAPTER NINE

Thus far, space power and its consequences have been presented against a backdrop of only *part* of the real world of human activity. We must now consider it in relationship to *all* of the real world.

In the discussion so far, space power has meant two things:

It has meant the time rate of use of energy in the classic definition of engineering and physics. Energy is the conceptual entity that causes change in the universe.

It has also been construed to mean power over the universe, the capability for one or more human beings to manipulate the forces of the universe for human well-being or to permit humans to accomplish some activity toward a goal.

Power has a third meaning: power by people over other people, the use of coercion by physical force or mental duress by people to control other people, to deny an activity or resource to other people, or to settle conflicts between people in a decisive manner.

There are two sorts of power over people (a) that given voluntarily by people under a social contract, and (b) that imposed upon people involuntarily.

Space power also means this form of power.

This is the most important and overriding category of space power.

This will determine whether or not and to what extent the first two categories of space power are developed and used as we discussed thus far.

Therefore, the military implications of the Solar Power Satellite system and its consequences *must* be included in the subject of space power and the overall considerations of the impacts of space power on the future of the human race.

This is not because of any philosophical or ideological bias in favor of that ultimate extension of diplomacy called war. Nor is it because of a belief that war is forever inevitable between human beings, regardless of where they are and *when* they are.

Military implications and the threat of warfare are current realities in the real world, unfortunate as that may be. Therefore, a discussion of the use of military force, whether it be considered to be moral or not, is necessary. If one is not prepared to fight when necessary to preserve one's freedom of choice, that freedom of choice can and will be taken away by those who only know how to take what they want and who wish to restrict freedom of choice in order to obtain the services of an individual or group without providing value in return.

Historians Will and Ariel Durant point out in their book *The Lessons of History* (Simon & Schuster, New York, 1968), "War is one of the constants of history, and has not diminished with civilization or democracy. In the last 3,421 years of recorded history only 268 have seen no war . . . Peace is an unstable equilibrium, which can be preserved only by acknowledged supremacy or equal power."

This position will be assaulted with a barrage of words from those who would unilaterally disarm and claim they "ain't gonna study war no more." Nations which are not currently at war or which have come out of a war within the last two generations show a tendency to have a larger population of vociferous anti-war agitators. As Montague said, "War hath no fury like a noncombatant."

Right or wrong, war exists and will continue to exist among members of the human race and among their social institutions as long as it's the easy way out. If it's easier to take something than to make it, people will fight to take it.

In a world of scarcity where there isn't enough to go around, war is inevitable. One answer to war is to make a world of plenty while at the same time holding the looters of the world at bay with a threat of strong retaliation against any attempt to loot. To stop war and crime, history shows that one must be armed and ready to stop both, and especially that one must not depend upon mercenaries except as a backup reserve.

But, until we achieve that world of plenty, we're going to have problems on our hands . . . especially with the SPS system. And the military implications and potential consequences of the SPS system must be discussed so that proper steps may be taken to cope with military activities of all sorts associated with the SPS system.

To some extent, the military implications of the Solar Power Satellite have already been recognized and discussed by others. However, the perception of the military implications of the SPS in these discussions has been quite incorrect. The SPS has been perceived as a weapon itself. This is not precisely accurate. As we'll see, unless an SPS is deliberately designed to be converted into a weapon, it's no more of a weapon than a coal-fired electric generating plant on Earth. An SPS may be able to support weapons systems, however.

There are two sides to the military implications of the SPS system that must be considered differently.

There is first the *perceived threat* of the SPS system—can the system or elements of the system be used to create a military threat, can they be used as weapons, and are there any means that can be used to reduce the perception of threat in the system?

The second element is the *vulnerability* of the SPS system to military activity—how can it be attacked, how is it vulnerable, and how can the perceived vulnerability be reduced to prevent attack in the first place?

Military implications of the SPS system exist regardless of which nation or multinational corporation undertakes the task and regardless of the organizational structures involved in the task. Should the United States—the government or private enterprise—unilaterally build an SPS system, the Soviet Union would certainly be concerned over potential military uses. Should the USA and the USSR undertake a joint SPS program—unlikely as that may seem at this time—a different set of military and political considerations would arise because the SPS system would change the world balance of power as perceived by the People's Republic of China as well as by Third World nations, regardless of how these nations are aligned.

The questions about military implications are important domestic issues as well. The political acceptability of the SPS system in the United States depends strongly upon the answers to these military questions. To some extent, the choice of the optimum financial-management organizational structure is affected because the SPS program should be a highly visible undertaking having minimum identification with the military.

Because the SPS program is a long-term project having at least five phases—R&D, pilot plant test and evaluation, system construction, system operation, and system up-dating—it isn't a single monolithic program. During the fifty-year period of the program as presently visualized, a large number of different types of organizations will have to be involved in a wide variety of roles, each organization interacting differently with other groups on the industrial, domestic, and international scenes. The arrangements between these organizations will also be varied and have different social, political, and military ramifications. Therefore, it's difficult—if not impossible—at this point to identify or discuss the enormous number of permutations and combinations. The reader should be alerted to this factor right from the start. The discussion should serve as an important foundation for considering any of the possibilities should they arise. In this regard, what we're doing is no different from the activity of any advanced planning job: trying to identify some of the problems so that, in the future, it may be easier to consider the options available in the real world.

The major military implications are associated with the construction, operation, and the system updating phases with some of the problems and solutions existing during the pilot plant test and evaluation phase where a single SPS unit is in orbit.

During all phases there are military implications inherent

in the existence of the space transportation system involved, but to a great extent these differ in degree rather than in kind with those involved with the space transportation system in the future phases.

So the R&D and pilot plant test and evaluation phases will not be specifically discussed because the later problems of the construction and operational phases apply to the earlier phases. In addition, the last phase—system updating—will not be considered because it lies far in the future and involves unguessable future technology that will arise out of the SPS system and its consequences.

Since the military implications of the SPS system arise from the hardware of the system and its operation, this is where we've got to concentrate our attention. The international or national organizations involved with the legal, financial, and political aspects of system operation are really outside the sphere of military implications, at least those military implications that are unique to the SPS system. The focus will be on the operational organizations—government agencies, quasi-public government-chartered corporations granted monopoly status by fiat, or private enterprise corporations—whose people have continuous hands-on access to space facilities and the space transportation system. We'll also concentrate on institutions that might be established to reduce or eliminate the perceived threats and vulnerabilities of the SPS system by technological or other means. It's these organizations involved in the day-to-day, on-site, hands-on operations that are most vulnerable to being co-opted by military interests, to being subverted for military uses, or to being threatened by military action. It's also these organizations and their people who will have to defend the SPS system against military threats.

In order to get a better grasp of both the perceived threats and vulnerabilities that are involved in the military implications of the SPS system, we should discuss them against a background of possible reality, against a scenario of the future as it might occur. The relative merits of each scenario and its probability of turning into reality aren't issues, but the military implications that may stem from each are important matters affecting the subject. If you want an interesting exercise, come up with your own scenarios and then run through them with the SPS military implications in mind. Such an exercise will not only give you a better idea of SPS military implications but will also acquaint you with the ways in which forecasters and planners work.

Thus far, we've considered only the first scenario. There are others.

Scenario 1: The United States undertakes the SPS system alone with some workable combination of government and private enterprise organizations to carry out finance and management. This is feasible since the whole SPS program could be done with an expenditure of less than 0.5% of the Gross National Product during the next twenty years, after which time the program would be self-supporting. Once the SPS system can supply most of the new baseload requirements of the U.S. energy demand, the U.S. organizations begin to build SPS units for other countries with no international SPS regulatory organization being created (although the International Telecommunications Union assigns frequencies and geosynchronous orbital positions, and the United Nations continues to require national registration and reporting of space vehicles and activities).

Scenario 2: The USA and the USSR undertake an SPS program as a joint venture in a renewed era of *detente*. Two different SPS units are designed—one optimized for equatorial GSO to supply the USA, and other optimized for a Molniya-type 12-hour high-inclination orbit to supply the USSR. Export controls on high-technology are relaxed to permit the joint development of an SSTO passenger shuttle, a large freight shuttle, and a joint LEO staging base from an equatorial launch site in Africa. The People's Republic of China doesn't participate and denounces the whole arrangement. Other countries are permitted to participate only as customers for SPS units or their power output.

Scenario 3: The USA gathers a group of friendly nations (Canada, some of the Western European nations, and perhaps Japan) into an SPS alliance composed of international consortia of companies. One of these operates the international launch bases in the USA, French Guiana, and the South Pacific area. Another builds, owns, and operates the space transportation system vehicles. Another consortium builds and operates LEO Base and GEO Base. Yet another builds the SPS units, while another builds rectennas, and another operates the SPS units. SPS units and rectennas are first completed for members of the SPS alliance. Later SPS units and rectennas are built to export power to other nations. It's strictly business similar to INTELSAT, and the USSR doesn't like it.

Scenario 4: The Organization of Petroleum Exporting Countries (OPEC) decides that the SPS system is a viable concept and a natural extension of their world energy cartel. They form the Organization of Space Energy Countries (OSEC) which is given access to the enormous amounts of capital OPEC members have received from their petroleum exporting activities. Contracts are made with companies from the USA, Western Europe, and Japan to perform the work, build the hardware, and operate the SPS system for OSEC. OSEC acquires major stockholder positions in most of these companies, and companies in which OSEC can't get majority control receive only minor contracts if they can supply or perform unique products or services.

Scenario 5: Multilateral negotiations involving the USA, Western Europe, Japan, a number of other industrialized countries, and a few energy-starved Third World nations with large untapped raw material resources create INSOL-SAT, an INTELSAT-like organization which channels funding for the SPS system into various corporations around the world. The first SPS units are built with multiple power beams to provide token amounts of energy to participating countries at the earliest opportunity. A dozen launch sites around the world are used, and space workers are recruited from everywhere including some non-participating countries. The USSR may be invited to join. Sub-scenarios depend upon the response of the USSR to this invitation.

There are more possible scenarios, but these five will serve
to show that there can be very different military implications
involved in each scenario.

For example, the concern of the USSR military analysts
and planners about the possible strategic uses of the SPS by
the USA would be largely defused in Scenarios 2, 3, and 5.
Similar concerns by the People's Republic of China (PRC)
exist in Scenarios 1, 2, and 3. In fact, Scenarios 1, 2, 3, and
some sub-scenarios of Scenario 5 might also raise charges of
superpower hegemony among Third World and non-
participating countries. The same charges could be directed
against OPEC and its OSEC in Scenario 4.

No scenario is without its problems of military implications, however.

The heart of the problem lies in the nature and make-up of
the operational organizations. How can any country, especially a superpower or a group of nations organized into a
multinational joint military activity, be assured that their
security interests aren't threatened when the SPS operational
organizations are based in another country, especially within
the national jurisdiction of a superpower? These concerns
arise in *all* scenarios, even the ones in which a large number
of diversified national interests are involved. Contrary to the
belief that such varied participation by different national
groups would necessarily lead to great difficulty in deploying
weapons systems in the SPS space facilities, sub-scenarios in
which national entities of countries belonging to multinational security groups such as NATO, SEATO, the Arab
Union, the Pan American Union, or the Warsaw Pact were a
part of an SPS alliance, INSOLSAT, or OSEC would still
create the mistrust syndrome.

In short, no matter what is done in the way of SPS organization, there is no way that mistrust can be eliminated among
those countries who might perceive that their national security interests were endangered by the potential perceived
threats inherent in an SPS system. Whether these perceived
SPS system military threats are real or imagined, their continued existence creates uneasiness which in turn breeds the

potential of military action against the SPS system to counter them.

The only answer is to attempt to eliminate the element of mistrust, which is *very* difficult to achieve, given the antici- pated international scene over the next fifty years.

But perhaps at least a partial answer can be obtained by carefully analyzing the perceived threats and the vul- nerabilities of the SPS system.

Threats and vulnerabilities may be imaginary because of misperceptions.

An example of a perceived SPS threat that is unreal is the common fear—mostly being perpetrated by the "small-is- beautiful" anti-technology, anti-utility-corporation, decen- tralized-energy, "consumer" groups with prominent leftist ideological beliefs—that the SPS power beam represents a weapon. The voiced fear is that the power beam can wander away from the rectenna and leave in its wake a grisly path of "cooked" people and wildlife, "scorched" cities, and genetically mutated organisms.

In the first place, the energy density in the *focused* power beam is well below standard US limits for exposure to mi- crowave radiation and orders of magnitude below the energy density of microwave ovens used daily in millions of homes.

Technically, it's very difficult to focus the power beam in any event. Were the SPS unit to lose reception of the pilot beam sent up from the rectenna, the power beam would automatically defocus into a diffused beam with much lower energy density. This amounts to a safety measure that's designed into the system, a "fail-safe" measure.

It's fashionable among the non-technical intelligentsia these days to embrace the paradox of demanding safety systems on such common devices as automobiles while at the same time loudly proclaiming total distrust of any safety system used on any technical hardware.

In *any* energy conversion system designed and used by human beings, there are both safety rules to be followed in using the system and safety measure incorporated into the system to prevent it from running away. As a person who has been employed professionally as a safety specialist in both government and industrial activities, I can honestly say that safety rules and safety systems *work*. However, it is totally impossible to design a foolproof system if the system's run by fools. *There is no safety system that will guarantee 100% safety.* However, the realization of this simple fact of life has not kept the human race from harnessing and using ever more powerful energy systems throughout history. People are still burned with fire. Steam boilers explode in spite of the fact that they represent old technology and use safety valves. Electricity continues to kill people and destroy property even with continued progress in insulation and safety equipment.

The SPS system will have safety systems installed. They will work as designed when required. They will make the SPS even safer than the nuclear reactors of electric generating plants which are the safest energy systems ever designed and built. Yes, Three Mile Island proved that nuclear energy isn't safe. But it also proved that it's safer than any other form of energy conversion and that the safety systems worked *in spite* of the mistakes made by the human beings in charge.

The only solution to countering the misperception that the SPS power beam will "fry" things is a properly conducted public education program.

Even then, there will be some people who won't believe it. But that's their problem. Some people continue to believe that the world is flat, too.

An example of perceived vulnerability is the generally accepted view that an SPS, because of its enormous size and stable orbit, is wide open to an attack by anti-satellite missiles launched from the Earth's surface. It turns out that this is only a "perceived" vulnerability on the part of the SPS because of the fact that the SPS sits "on top of the hill" insofar as an attack from the Earth's surface is concerned.

This is best explained at this point by introducing a concept that will be referred to hereafter as the "gravity well."

Looking at Figure 6, think of the Earth as being at the bottom of a deep well created by its gravity field. This funnel shaped "hole in space" extends beyond the orbit of the

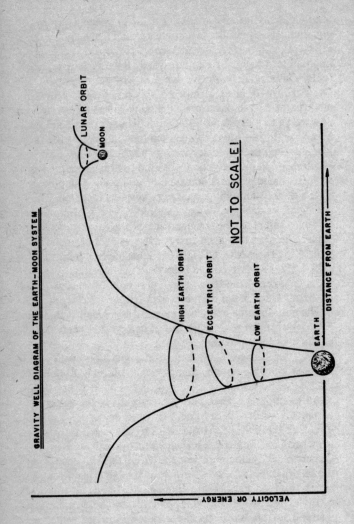

GRAVITY WELL DIAGRAM OF THE EARTH-MOON SYSTEM

LUNAR ORBIT

MOON

HIGH EARTH ORBIT

ECCENTRIC ORBIT

LOW EARTH ORBIT

EARTH

NOT TO SCALE!

DISTANCE FROM EARTH

VELOCITY OR ENERGY

Moon, which has its own gravity well that shows up as a dimple in the surface of the Earth's ever more shallow gravity well. At about two hundred million kilometers from the Earth, the gravity well of the Sun becomes predominant over that of the Earth.

The further away from Earth one goes, the more shallow the Earth's gravity well becomes.

If you stand at the bottom of the Earth's gravity well and throw a rock straight up the sides of the funnel at a approximately twelve kilometers per second, it will climb all the way up the sides of the gravity well and out into the gravity well of the Sun. Twelve kilometers per second is the "escape velocity" of Earth. If you throw the rock in the right direction, it falls into the gravity well of the Moon, which will cause it to pick up a velocity of about 1.6 kilometers per second as it falls down that smaller funnel.

If you want to put a satellite around the Earth, you must give it enough velocity to climb up the Earth's gravity well as far as you want it, then give it additional sideways velocity so that it whirls around the surface of the Earth's gravity well funnel fast enough to keep it from falling back down the well. If the direction of your sideways thrust on the rock is a little off, the rock goes into an elliptical orbit instead.

When the gravity well concept is applied to the military implications of space, it becomes evident that it is the prime strategic concept in space military operations. It means that one will have a significant military advantage in terms of energy and maneuvering capability if one is higher on the gravity well than his adversary. It requires far less energy to maneuver if one is higher up the gravity well.

The military importance of the gravity well doctrine has its roots in the proven terrestrial military doctrine of high ground. During the age of sailing ships in the Earth's ocean navies, it was called the "wind gauge" which involved getting upwind of the enemy.

A simple analogy will demonstrate soundness of the gravity well doctrine.

Put one person at the bottom of a well and another person at the top of the well. Give them both rocks to throw at one another. Which person is going to have more time to see the opponent's rocks coming at him and thence have more time to get out of the way? Who's going to have more time to do something about an oncoming rock? Whose rocks are going to have more energy when they reach their targets? Who's got the chance of being hurt the worst?

The person at the top of the well possesses an obvious, significant, and classical military advantage.

Thus, an SPS in geosynchronous orbit 22,400 miles above the Earth is well up on the Earth's gravity well. It is not extremely vulnerable to rocks thrown at it from the bottom of the Earth's gravity well if the SPS possesses *any* way to intercept those oncoming missles or to zap them out of space with even a low-powered short-range defensive beam weapon powered by the SPS itself.

SPS vulnerability hinges on something else. A single SPS is very expensive as well as being able to provide a significant amount of a nation's energy requirement. SPS owners and users are going to be very sensitive about the vulnerability of an SPS to military action.

Far more realistic threats to an SPS hinge on the right of free passage of space vehicles launched by or under the registry of states who are parties to the 1967 "Treaty on Principles Governing the Activities of States in the Exploration and Use of Outer Space, Including the Moon and Other Celestial Bodies." Article I of this Treaty, to which the USA is a signatory, states in part:

"Outer space, including the Moon and other celestial bodies, shall be free for exploration and use by all States without discrimination of any kind, on a basis of equality and in accordance with international law, and there shall be free access to all areas of celestial bodies."

This treaty could be invoked to allow a hostile or potentially hostile nation to deploy "NEARSATS" which are killer satellites or space mines flown in close proximity to an SPS or even "in formation" between the girders of the photovoltaic array, ready to disable critical components of the SPS in the event of open hostilities between the nation owning the SPS and the nation deploying the NEARSAT.

Obviously, there are going to have to be announced rules of engagement as there are today between ships and aircraft in international waters and airspace.

The SPS will be vulnerable not because it is necessarily convertible to a weapon, but because it can supply electric energy to power space weapons systems. Historically, power supplies have become a military target in the 20th century. The Mohne and Oder dams supplying electric power to the Ruhr industrial complex of Germany were a prime target for bombers of the British Royal Air Force. The electric generating plants of Hanoi and Haiphong were prime air strike targets for the United States during the Vietnam War.

An SPS can also serve as a "platform" for smaller military facilities that could be hidden in its structure. These military SPS platform facilities could be used for reconnaissance, surveillance, communications, command, or control. The microwave transmitting antenna of an SPS could be used as a deep space phased surveillance radar or, with laser communications equipment, permit the SPS to act as a relay to and from "hidden" military satellites located nearby. If this is the case, or if it is perceived to be the case, the SPS becomes a significant target for attack in time of hostilities.

Thus, the vulnerability of the SPS itself as a target must be analyzed on the basis of two extreme cases: (a) the SPS with enhanced military capabilities, either real or perceived, and (b) the SPS with minimal military support capabilities. Since an SPS can serve to provide power to other space weapons systems and to critical systems and industries on the Earth below, it can never be considered to have no military support capabilities whatsoever, and it therefore becomes a military target, albeit with perhaps reduced military priority.

As we look at these cases, we're going to see that the SPS is the prime element in the military aspects of space power.

In fact, the SPS *creates* real space power.

CHAPTER TEN

The military threat potential created by the SPS system and its sub-systems is a reality that must be taken into account in planning if the perceived threat of any SPS system put up by the USA or any combination of organizations headquartered in the Western World is to be minimized. By doing this, as we've seen, the risk that the expensive SPS system will become a primary military target can be reduced.

There's already a military threat from space, but it's not a primary threat.

As of 1981, there are military operations going on in earth orbital space that involve unmanned command, control, communications, and intelligence ("C-cubed-I") activities using various sorts of unmanned satellites. There have also been manned C-cubed-I activities being conducted from time to time by the Soviet Union with its cosmonauts in the *Salyut* space stations.

Thus, the military organizations of both the USA and the USSR (and perhaps the PRC) are already taking advantage of the high ground of earth orbit.

But, because of the United Nations' 1967 "Treaty on the Principles Governing the Activities of States in the Exploration and Use of Outer Space, including the Moon and Other Celestial Bodies," weapons of mass destruction are prohibited from being placed on the Moon and other celestial bodies in space by treaty signatories.

(Nobody really knows what would happen if a signatory nation abrogated this Treaty of Principles and began deploying some sort of space weapon with a thermonuclear warhead. It's just an agreement on principles. The most recent failure of the UN and its members to do anything in the Iranian hostage affair in spite of actions from the World Court confirms the principle of international law that says any treaty is effective only if nations tacitly abide by it, because there's *no* mechanism to enforce any provision of any UN treaty. No UN member nation has yet to agree to surrender any of its national sovereignty to the UN. The failure of the major world powers at Dumbarton Oaks in 1944 and of the founders of the United Nations in San Francisco in 1945 to insist upon a United Nations military peace-keeping organization, coupled with the insistence of the United States delegates then that the UN Security Council be permitted to be stopped dead in its tracks through use of the veto, resulted in a seriously flawed United Nations organization from the start. In retrospect, it's only fair to point out that world conditions of the time probably precluded the possibility of having a UN military organization. However, if there was ever a time in history when a democratic republic based upon individual freedom such as the USA had the opportunity to exercise world leadership, it was in August 1945 when the USA could have said, in effect, "We've got the drop on you. Throw down your guns." The USA had the atomic bomb, and everybody including the USA was afraid of it. That atomic monopoly didn't last five years, and after the USSR broke the USA's atomic monopoly the opportunity for a powerful international peace-keeping body was perhaps gone for a long time to come.)

Therefore, in spite of UN treaties and a host of international agreements, a nation could covertly deploy one or more space weapons systems in conjunction with the SPS system by employing adapters that would enhance the military capabilities of the system. These military adapters fall into three major categories:

1. *Adapters for force delivery.*
2. *Adapters for remote sensing.*
3. *Adapters for military support.*

Each of these three categories must be discussed to get the total picture because it may not be obvious that the SPS system offers opportunities to deploy military adapters.

For example, the SPS system offers entirely new possibilities for force delivery in the space environment.

First, an SPS unit can supply ten gigawatts of electrical power.

Second, an SPS unit (along with LEO Base and GEO Base) is a permanently manned space facility.

Third, an SPS unit is a geosynchronous orbital platform with complete housekeeping functions.

Adapters for force delivery fall into three sub-categories:

1. An SPS unit can be used as a base for projectile weapons which could be used to attack other satellites and even Earth targets. Such weapons include rocket-propelled missiles as well as simple projectiles such as rocks. Simple projectiles could evolve as a primary space weapon system because they could be launched with SPS-powered catapults or mass drivers. A mass driver launching hundreds of kilogram-mass projectiles per minute amounts to a Space Gatling Gun.

Any projectile weapon capable of atmospheric entry could be targeted against Earth surface sites.

For some applications it isn't necessary for projectiles to carry any sort of a warhead at all because their masses and velocities—their kinetic energies—make them destructive in and of themselves. The impact of kilogram masses at several hundred meters per second can't help but produce damage to space facilities, especially to critical components such as solar arrays, antennas, etc. Larger masses traveling at lower velocities become hazardous to larger facilities and their components.

Projectile weapons without warheads and utilizing only their kinetic energies for destructive power against specific military targets on the ground or in space could be deployed as part of an SPS unit without violating *any* provision of any UN treaty.

The UN Space Treaty prohibits only weapons of mass destruction. Projectile weapons with no nuclear warheads whatsoever can have destructive capabilities that can be pin-pointed. Even an Earth bombardment projectile weapon system deployed on an SPS need not be a weapon of mass destruction; it could be designed and launched in such a way that it would possess sharply limited military destructiveness against precise targets.

Such selective weapon systems might be tolerated. However, city-busting weapons, nuclear or not, would increase the vulnerability of the SPS system, making the system a prime target in the opening moments of any war because the SPS system could not be permitted to launch its large projectiles. We would have transferred today's doctrine of Mutually Assured Destruction (MAD) into space . . . and it might not work there as well as it apparently has on Earth. (As of this writing, MAD has prevented all-out thermonuclear war between superpowers. How long the balance of terror can be maintained is a guessing game.)

2. The second sub-category of force delivery adapters involves devices or vehicles called "manipulators." Manipulators manipulate other space craft. As part of the SPS itself, or mounted on SPS deep space ships, or even mounted on their own specially-designed space vehicles, a manipulator could be used to do one of several things. It could seize a satellite having military potential or use, thus perpetrating a new activity called "satnapping." A satnapper would simply pull a satellite out of space, put it aboard, and hold it. Or a manipulator could be used to reach out and destroy or damage part of a satellite that was too large to satnap, thereby engaging in the activity of satellite mutilation ("satmute"). Since the USSR has already demonstrated the capability to reliably rendezvous and dock with another satellite using a remotely-controlled, unmanned satellite, satmute could be carried out by remotely-controlled space vehicles if there was a suspicion that the target satellite might be booby-trapped or carry some sort of self-defense system.

3. The third sub-category of SPS military force delivery adapters involves the gee-whiz, Buck Rogers weapons that are only hinted at by both the USA and the USSR: the directed energy or beam weaponss such as high energy lasers and particle beam weapons.

There's been a lot written about these beam weapons in the

popular press as well as in the scientific and trade press. They're real and they work. There is a very good possibility that beam weapons could be deployed in space in the 1980 decade. However, they require large amounts of electrical power to function and would thus need to be housed in large satellites. But in the 1990 decade, they could be deployed as part of an SPS unit. In fact, they may be deliberately placed on an SPS unit for defensive purposes.

Not all directed energy or beam weapons are useful in space, and some are useful only for restricted targeting.

Both types of high energy lasers (HEL)—continuous wave (CW) and pulsed—would be useful for space-to-earth targeting, but only from low earth orbits (LEO). This is because the Earth's atmosphere acts to reduce their intensities, often by as much as a factor of 15 for some types of HEL(CW) devices. This atmospheric interaction reduces the effective range of HEL's. Therefore, for Earth bombardment, HEL's would have to be positioned in LEO and receive their power by relay from the SPS system in geosynchronous Earth orbit.

It's in the space-to-space targeting area that HEL's become attractive as weapons. They can be used for SPS defense because they are very effective at short ranges and in the vacuum of orbit. For example, by 1990 an HEL(CW) could have the capability to produce ten megawatts of energy in a one microradian (0.00005729 degrees) beam width. Such an HEL(CW) could produce a beam with delivered power density of three kilowatts per square centimeter at a distance of a thousand kilometers (620 miles). That's enough to vaporize steel in a very short period of time. Thus, HEL's will be militarily useful for space-to-space anti-satellite attacks, for SPS self-defense against projectile weapon attack, for enforcing blockades, and as a very effective anti-ballistic missile (ABM) defense to be used against ICBM's when they rise above the Earth's atmosphere on their way from Earth launch to Earth target.

Particle beam weapons (PBW's) are somewhat more than lasers because PBW's produce charged or uncharged subnuclear particles, whereas lasers produce beams of photon

energy. PBW's conceived and possibly built to date include
neutral hydrogen, proton (H+), electron, neutron, and
gamma ray units.

PBW's cannot be used for Earth bombardment from space.
The Earth's atmosphere interacts so strongly with all of these
particle beam types that their effectiveness against ground
targets is zilch.

Only one form of PBW appears at this time to be useful for
space-to-space targeting: the neutral hydrogen PBW. Proton
or hydrogen PBW's suffer from the fact that beams don't
propagate well in vacuum unless the beams are fully neutralized, and the charged nature of the proton PBW beams
makes them extremely difficult to focus and aim because of
the Earth's magnetic field. Neutron and gamma ray PBW's
have beam divergences that are too great for weapon use
. . . at least with technology that can be forecast for the next
quarter of a century.

There are other ways to use the energy output of an SPS
unit for military purposes in the sub-category of directed
energy weaponry.

Primary among these methods is the use of SPS-powered
r-f transmitters for electronic warfare and electronic countermeasures.

It's quite unlikely that the SPS power beam itself could be
used even against other satellites because of the low power
density nature of the beam sub-system. With the types of SPS
transmitting antennas presently planned or available, it's
extremely difficult, if not impossible, to focus the power
beam sufficiently to achieve any effect against another space
vehicle or facility unless the vehicle or satellite were to fly
into the beam of the SPS only a few kilometers away. In that
case, the spacecraft thus irradiated might become temporar-
ily warm, but it is unlikely that a power beam operating up in
the region of 2450 megaHertz could cause any damage to
properly shielded internal components or circuitry.

The *only* possible way that an SPS power beam could be
used against a ground target such as a city would be as a
psychological weapon, assuming a non-informed or

partially-educated populace. This military use is extremely infeasible. The SPS power beam has *no* possibility of being used as an Earth-targeting weapon of destruction. Upon careful analysis without the irrational and emotional element that's so prevalent among uninformed people, the SPS power beam simply does not have the energy density to heat up organic material or produce an incendiary effect.

Another category of SPS military adapters lies in the area of remote sensing.

The SPS unit is projected as a very large space facility. It can therefore be used as a space platform for a variety of sensing devices because of its stability and ready source of electrical power.

For example, the very large power beam transmitting antenna can also be used as either an active or a passive radar antenna. (Antennas can be used in the multiplex mode—they can be used to transmit on one or more frequencies while at the same time receiving r-f signals on other frequencies.) The SPS transmitting antenna will be one to five kilometers in diameter, which is a very large radar antenna indeed. As a passive radar receiving antenna, it could be used for surveillance of areas "illuminated" by other satellites that transmit the radar signals. The converse is true, the SPS unit providing the power for radar signal transmission through the SPS antenna to illuminate a target for other passive radar units to look at.

It would also be possible to install a wide variety of passive sensors and detectors on the SPS unit. These would obtain optical or infra-red imagery or could detect and monitor radio, microwave, or radar signals. SPS-mounted sensors could be used in their classical roles for reconnaissance, surveillance, and intelligence data gathering, could be used to track objects moving through space or on the Earth's surface below, and could provide early detection and warning of ballistic missile launches, anti-satellite (ASAT) interceptor launchings, or space vehicle flights.

Lasers could also be mounted on and powered by the SPS unit to provide "lidar" (Laser Illuminated Detection And

Ranging), the laser analog to radar, in active, passive, or multiplex modes.

The uses of the big SPS antenna and of the SPS itself as a very large, stable orbital platform are numerous.

The third category in which the SPS system itself could enhance military operations is in the classical support role.

For example, the SPS units in orbit could carry radio beacon transponders that respond to specific radio interrogation signals from the ground or from space craft, permitting them to provide precise navigational data.

The individual SPS unit could carry equipment to act as a communications relay between very small, low-powered transmitters on the Earth because the SPS could mount a very large, very powerful, and highly directional r-f communications system. The ability of such equipment on an SPS unit to relay communications from, to, or between space craft permits covert and secure military communications with "silent" or covert military satellites that are perhaps undetectable because of "stealth" measures. A very tightly focused laser beam could be used for such communication.

And, of course, the power beam of one or more SPS units could be redirected to provide power for other military space facilities mounting such devices as high-energy lasers (HEL) or particle beam weapons (PBW).

Because the SPS units as well as the LEO and GEO bases are military support facilities that are well isolated, they offer established facilities in which to safely conduct experiments and production of chemical and biological warfare (CBW) weapons. It's probable that such a CBW lab would be a separate module of an SPS unit to prevent access by nonparticipants and to minimize the possibility of inadvertent vectoring of agents into the SPS and other orbital facilities. Such CBW facilities could be operated under the guise of recombinant DNA research facilities or pharmaceutical production modules.

Because of the fact that an SPS along with LEO Base and GEO Base have all the necessary life support facilities to maintain a large number of people, they could serve as bases for trained military cadres which *do* have a space role in preventing seizure of space facilities by personnel of a hostile nation, for example.

And a final SPS military support role lies in the SPS system space facilities' ability to serve as alternate manned command posts similar to today's airborne command posts which serve to provide back-up in case of destruction of the main command center on the ground.

Even if these military adapters were the only military implications of the SPS system, they alone would provide more than an order of magnitude enhanced military capability in space over present systems.

And even if the SPS system is "demilitarized" by prohibiting the national military forces from placing any of these adapters in the system and by allowing open inspection of the system by international observers from, say, the United Nations, the SPS system would still possess military utility.

The SPS system demands a large and efficient space transportation capability which has military utility.

The operation of the space transportation segment could be diverted in whole or in part to the construction and operation of manned and unmanned military satellites and facilities. With such a very large number of flights required every day for the thirty-year span of the construction and operation program, the integration of military launches, flights, and other operations into this very extensive operation would not significantly increase the number of flights. In the absence of a sophisticated space surveillance, tracking, and identification system in the hands of a potential adversary, it would be possible to conduct extensive military space activity with a slim chance of detection.

In addition, the SPS transportation space craft are readily adaptable to carrying military payloads. It's analogous to the present program where the USAF Military Airlift Command contracts for military airlift with the airlines who use their commercial airliners and airfreighters. There is also the USA Civil Reserve Air Fleet program that allows the Department of Defense to commandeer and use domestic airliners for

military airlift in times of national emergency. A passenger
or cargo vehicle of any sort doesn't care whether it carries
civilian or military payloads, and it can't tell the difference
anyway. Nor can an outside observer.

And with space craft identical or outwardly similar to SPS
space craft, military crews can make inspections of their own
satellites as well as those of other nations, carrying out repair
and refurbishment of their own craft and possibly sapping
satellites of potential enemies by placing remotely controlled
explosives to disable or destroy such satellites should hostilities occur. Such inspection and sapping operations should
be considered to be highly dangerous because of the possibilities for self-defense systems or booby traps on the satellites. This possibility alone may make manned satellite inspection and sapping far too risky to be considered as a
feasible operation.

The SPS units, space facilities, and transportation system
provide means for the military organization to stockpile and
store materials and supplies against the possibility of future
use.

However, of equal or greater military importance to the
possible active or covert military use of SPS hardware or
adapters, either in the diplomatic strategy prior to a possible
war or in case of limited warfare, are the "institutional"
military threats of the SPS system.

An institutional military threat is one based upon a real or
perceived capability to deliver some type of physical force.

Today's balance of terror of the MAD doctrine is based
upon such an institutional threat. The same holds true for the
truce agreement and cease-fire line in Korea. The inability of
the United States to recover its diplomatic personnel from
Iran within a matter of days or weeks after the embassy in
Teheran was seized in 1979 was due in great part to the lack
of an institutional threat.

The lack of an institutional military threat has caused wars
in the past and is probably the rationale that justifies the
Roosevelt Doctrine. "Speak softly and carry a big stick."

An institutional military activity was used in the Cuban

Missile Crisis of 1961: blockade. A nation cannot threaten a blockade unless it possesses or is thought to possess the capability to activate it and enforce it. For example, a government could not threaten the blockade of a space station unless it possessed a demonstrable or at least a credible antisatellite capability such as ASAT missiles or beam weapons that would prohibit or make it extremely risky for enemy space craft to run the blockade.

Institutional activities of a smilar nature to blockade include denying access to space facilities, denying access, or use of space craft by hijacking. In contrast to a blockade, denial requires less force.

Orbital facilities of the SPS system provide convenient platforms for radio transmitters that could be used for direct broadcast to enemy populations to disseminate propaganda.

SPS facilities could be used as a basis for a "show of strength" or a "showing of the flag" in space for diplomatic purposes. There could be a deliberate show of military force and presence in space to back up diplomatic negotiations or to exhibit the presence of a second strike capability or the enhanced survivability of the nation's command and control organization.

Last but not least, the SPS system could be used as a tool for economic warfare.

Electric output of the SPS system could be reduced or denied not only to enforce demands of other sorts, but to produce reductions in industrial output or ability to harvest and process agricultural output, thereby permitting a manipulation of international commodity markets.

In this regard, the Earth-based rectenna possesses some military utility. It's the last link in the chain of SPS system elements. Because all the electric power interfacing equipment between the rectenna and the ground electric power grid is located at the rectenna site and because the rectenna thereby becomes one of the centers or nodes of the electric power distribution system, it offers a source of power for military support elements on Earth.

Despite the earlier statement that pointed out the multiplex nature of any antenna—a good receiving antenna is a good transmitting antenna, and an antenna can often be used simultaneously at several frequencies—the SPS rectenna is designed for use and maximum efficiency at about 2450 megaHertz. Its design precludes the possibility of using it effectively as a radar antenna or even to some extent as an electronic intelligence gathering antenna. It is also highly unlikely that the rectenna could be used in electronic warfare as a transmitter of jamming or other EW signals.

The main military utility of the rectenna is then seen to be that of providing electric power for military-oriented industries and for ground-based military facilities. The rectenna may also play a major role in supporting the SPS space transportation system launching sites by providing the power necessary to produce propellants. The rectenna may also be used to provide electric power for ground-based beam weapons such as we'll discuss during our consideration of SPS military vulnerability, but in this case the SPS system would possibly be providing energy for ground-based beam weapons that would be used to provide a credible SPS defense capability on the ground. In this regard, the SPS rectenna occupies a military position analogous to that of any large electric power generating plant.

Some of this may seem far-fetched and blue-sky dreaming in 1981. But these considerations have come about as a result of serious study of the military implications of the SPS system carried out for the Department of Energy. Regardless of how far-out they may seem, they turn out upon close inspection and study to be realistic. They must be kept in mind and dealt with in terms of the real world as it exists when the SPS system is built and operating.

Above all, however, just because these military threat capabilities exist is no reason *not* to undertake the construction and operation of an SPS system. There are military implications in technology of all kinds. A slurry plane for dumping 20,000 pounds of fire retardant chemical on a forest fire is also a very fine attack bomber capable of dropping 20,000 pounds of bombs on a bridge.

How real are these various threats during various phases of the SPS construction and operation periods? Since the credibility of any perceived threat depends upon the level of technology available, can we differentiate between "real" and "perceived" threats in these various time periods by making an educated guess at the various technologies available in each phase?

In order to do this, time periods must be defined.

Near term means out to the year 1990.

Mid-term means during the 1990 decade.

Far-term is anything in the 21st century.

If known basic physical laws and scaling relationships show reasonable indications that a given technical capability could never be constructed, it will be designated *infeasible* (with some hesitation and trepidation, knowing that the impossibilities of today are often the realities of tomorrow).

A threat is potentially real or could be perceived as real in a given time period if there's a reasonable forecast that it could be deployed then. To some extent, this will also depend upon the availability of SPS elements to support it. For example, since an effective HEL might require several gigawatts of power for operation, its deployment in space is unlikely until there is either a very efficient power supply available to accompany the HEL satellite or an SPS unit available to provide such levels of power. Thus, threats which require SPS elements are mid-term threats.

Because the R&D phase of the SPS system is presumed to take place in the 1980 decade, some of the potential threats could become real in the later part of the decade if experimental or pilot plant facilities were to be used. But, in general, most of the threats from the military utilization of an SPS system can't become near-term realities.

But this does not mean that it won't be possible to deploy significant military systems in space in the near-term period. It just means that they probably won't use any of the SPS system.

The various potential threats of military utilization of an SPS system and its various component sub-systems is summarized in Table VI for space-to-Earth threats and in Table VII for space-to-space threats.

Table VII also has a bearing on our later discussions of the military vulnerability of the SPS system.

It should also be obvious that the availability of technology doesn't make any particular threat feasible or real, although it can make the threat perceptually real.

And many times in warfare or even in diplomatic relations between nations, history tells us that a perceived threat or capability is often as effective as if it were real. On a personal basis, it's sometimes called ''bullying'' if it's used by an antagonist or ''bluffing'' if you or your friends and allies use it, especially in a poker game.

The SPS system *does* have apparent military utility, but not as many people have claimed: as an incendiary space-to-Earth attack weapon. The SPS system permits many new military operations and space weapons systems to become feasible in the space environment, but the SPS is *not* one of those weapon systems.

TABLE VI
SPACE-TO-EARTH THREATS

Weapon: Continuous wave high energy laser.

  Target: Terrestrial structures and vehicles.

  Period: Mid-term.

  Comments: HEL(CW) could be deployed in space by the late 1980's. Deployment in GEO impractical due to long ranges. LEO HEL(CW) could deliver 100 times solar flux in beam 1 microradian wide, but atmospheric effects could reduce intensity by factor of 5-15.

Weapon: Pulsed high energy laser.

  Target: Terrestrial structures and vehicles.

Period: Near-term to Mid-term, possibly infeasible.

Comment: Level of capability increases with time. Use in GEO probably infeasible for Earth attacks because of ranges. In late 1990s, values are 20 megawatts output, beam width 1.5 microradians.

Weapon: Particle beam weapon.
Target: Terrestrial structures and vehicles.
Period: Infeasible
Comment: Unlikely to be used for space-to-Earth because of effects of interaction with atmosphere.

Weapon: Entry vehicle.
Target: Terrestrial structures.
Period: Near-term.
Comment: Earth bombardment, second strike capability. Warhead not needed if large and fast enough. Capabilities increase with time.

Weapon: SPS power beam.
Target: Terrestrial structures.
Period: Infeasible.
Comment: Insufficient energy density for incendiary use.

Weapon: SPS power beam.
Target: People.
Period: Far-term to infeasible.
Comment: Possible but implausible psych war use.

Weapon: SPS power beam.
       Target: Electrical equipment.
       Period: Far-term.
       Comment: Use in jamming communications.

Weapon: SPS power beam.
       Target: Weather modification.
       Period: Infeasible.
       Comment: Requires too much power.

Weapon: SPS power beam.
       Target: Customers.
       Period: Far-term.
       Comment: Denial of power is possible.

Weapon: Radio frequency transmitter.
       Target: Radio frequency equipment.
       Period: Mid-term.
       Comment: Electronic warfare use on any fre-
                  quency.

Weapon: Radio frequency transmitter.
       Target: People.
       Period: Mid-term.
       Comment: Direct broadcast of propaganda.

Weapon: Radio frequency transmitter.
       Target: Weather modification.
       Period: Infeasible.
       Comment: Requires too much power.

Weapon: Radio frequency sensors.
    Target: Radio frequency emissions.
    Period: Mid-term.
    Comment: Electronic and signal intelligence
            gathering.

Weapon: Optical/infra-red sensors.
    Target: Structures and vehicles.
    Period: Near-term.
    Comment: Reconnaissance and surveillance.

Weapon: Radars.
    Target: Structures and vehicles.
    Period: Near-term.
    Comment: Reconnaissance and surveillance.

Weapon: Radio frequency and laser communications.
    Target: People
    Period: Near-term.
    Comment: Military communications and control.

TABLE VII
SPACE-TO-SPACE THREATS

Weapon: Continuous wave high energy laser.
    Target: Space craft and missiles.
    Period: Near-term to mid-term.
    Comment: Level of capability increases with time.
            Could be deployed in space by late
            1980s. Capabilities 10 megawatts and
            1 microradian beam width, 3000
            watts/square cm. at 1000 kilometers
            suitable for ASAT, ABM, self defense,
            blockade.

Weapon: Pulsed high energy laser.
Target: Space craft and missiles.
Period: Near-term to mid-term.
Comment: Level of capability increases with time. Electrically powered types suitable for GEO deployment because of solar electric power availability. Late 1990s: 20 megawatts output, 1.5 microradian beam width, 250 watts/square cm. at 100 km. suitable for self defense, attack nearby satellites, blockade. LEO deployment for ABM with power relay from SPS.

Weapon: Particle beam weapon (neutral hydrogen).
Target: Space craft and missiles.
Period: Possible mid-term, far-term.
Comment: 50-100 megawatts input required to deposit 100 calories per gram at 1000 km. SPS power relay to LEO required for ABM use.

Weapon: Particle beam weapon (H+ or electron).
Target: Space craft and missiles.
Period: Infeasible.
Comment: High intensity of less than fully neutralized beams don't propagate well in vacuum. Geomagnetic anomalies make focus and aim difficult.

Weapon: Particle beam weapon (neutron or gamma ray).
Target: Space craft and missiles.
Period: Infeasible.
Comment: Beam divergence too great.

Weapon: Orbital interceptors.
    Target: Space craft.
    Period: Near-term.
    Comment: In development. Space torpedoes or mines. Nuclear or conventional warheads.

Weapon: Nuclear detonations.
    Target: Space craft.
    Period: Near-term.
    Comment: Weapons exist if deployed. May destroy attacker's systems by electromagnetic pulse.

Weapon: SPS space transportation vehicles.
    Target: Space craft and non-specific.
    Period: Near-term.
    Comment: ASAT carrier. Support, shelter, logistics.

Weapon: SPS power beam.
    Target: Space craft and missiles.
    Period: Far-term.
    Comment: Insufficient power for physical damage against even moderately shielded targets at close range. Electronic warfare use possible.

Weapon: Radio frequency transmitter.
    Target: Space craft.
    Period: Far-term.
    Comment: Electronic warfare only.

Weapon: Radio frequency sensors.
    Target: Space craft and radio frequency emissions.

Period: Near-term.
Comment: Electronic intelligence, capability depends on receiver sensitivity at given frequency and signal processing ability.

Weapon: Optical and infra-red sensors.
Target: Space craft.
Period: Near-term.
Comment: Reconnaissance and surveillance.

Weapon: Radar
Target: Space craft.
Period: Near-term.
Comment: Reconnaissance and surveillance, tracking.

Weapon: Radio frequency and laser communication.
Target: Space craft.
Period: Near-term.
Comment: Military communications and control.

Weapon: LEO and GEO Bases.
Target: Non-specific.
Period: Mid-term.
Comment: Usage as shelter, logistic support.

Weapon: Space facilities for CBW.
Target: People.
Period: Mid-term but may be infeasible.
Comment: Chemical and biological warfare (CBW) facilities in separate modules to permit isolation and secrecy. May

not offer advantages over Earth-based facilities.

Weapon: Deep Space Freighter.
　　　　Target: Space craft.
　　　　Period: Mid-term but may be infeasible.
　　　　Comment: Inspection, but long-range sensors on space facilities may accomplish all goals at lower cost and risk.

Weapon: Deep Space Freighter.
　　　　Target: Space craft.
　　　　Period: Mid-term, but may be infeasible.
　　　　Comment: Used for satnap and satmute, but booby traps and satellite self defense could make use too risky.

TABLE VIII
EARTH-TO-SPACE THREATS

Weapon: Continuous-wave high energy laser.
　　　　Target: Space craft.
　　　　Period: Near-term & Mid-term.
　　　　Comment: Level of capability increases with time. For the late 1980s. A plausible HEL(CW) is a chemical laser, 10 megawatt output, 4 meter mirror, beam width 1.5 microrads.

Weapon: Pulsed high energy laser.
　　　　Target: Space craft.
　　　　Period: Near-term and Mid-term.

Comment: Level of capability increases with time.
For the late 1980s, a plausible HEL(P)
is a closed cycle carbon dioxide elec-
trodynamic laser with 10 megawatts
output, 4 meter mirror, beam width 3.5
microrads, rep rate a function of target
characteristics and range.

Weapon: Particle beam weapon.
　　　Target: Space craft.
　　　Period: Infeasible.
　　　Comment: Neutral or pulsed charged beam considered infeasible because Earth's atmosphere interactions prevent ground-
to-space or space-to-ground use.

Weapon: Orbital interceptor (ASAT)
　　　Target: Space craft.
　　　Period: Near-term.
　　　Comment: Under development in USA. Conven-
tional or nuclear warhead.

Weapon: SPS pilot beam.
　　　Target: SPS
　　　Period: Far-term or infeasible.
　　　Comment: Used as covert communications relay to
other military space facilities, probably
infeasible because cheaper and more effective means exist.

Weapon: Radio frequency transmitter.
　　　Target: SPS
　　　Period: Far-term or infeasible.
　　　Comment: Used to jam the pilot beam, but feasibil-

ity depends upon design of pilot beam
steering equipment.

Weapon: SPS space transportation system.
        Target: Non-specific.
        Period: Near-term.
        Comment: Used for transportation of men and
                 equipment including ASAT weapons.

Weapon: Launch sites.
        Target: Non-specific.
        Period: Infeasible.
        Comment: Not a threat because facilities can be
                 used for military and commercial pur-
                 poses.

CHAPTER ELEVEN

Since an SPS system has both military threat capability and utility to a military organization, it will become a military target if hostilities break out. It will also become a target for "un-war" or paramilitary activities such as sabotage, guerrilla operations, and terrorist activities.

The extent to which an SPS system is *vulnerable* to these military and paramilitary operations and activities is of great importance not only to the military organization that must defend the SPS system against such activities, but also to the planners, financiers, managers, insurance underwriters, and operational people who must reckon military or paramilitary actions into their overall assessment of system risk.

At first glance, the military vulnerability of the SPS system seems simple, but it isn't because of the unique international issues also involved.

Assessing the military and other risks of analogous electric power systems on Earth has, in the past, been simple when compared to risk assessment of the SPS system. By its extraterrestrial nature, this system brings into consideration problems concerned with the fact that the SPS unit in orbit doesn't exist on anyone's national territory—English common law precedent regarding overflight rights notwithstanding. Unlike Earthbound electric generating systems, the SPS system possesses some unique and complex international and military implications which greatly complicate any evaluation of the risks and vulnerability issues involved.

The potential of partial or total power loss at the rectenna's power grid interface is an SPS system vulnerability issue, for example. The extent to which this risk is increased by the military vulnerability of the system and its elements is of both military and commercial importance because of the great value of the SPS system as a major asset.

While the rectenna element is potentially vulnerable to most of the classic military and paramilitary operations that can be conducted on the Earth's surface, the space elements of the system are not. In fact, elements of the space-based portions of the system must be considered separately.

The only way to get a handle on complex issues such as this is to break down the system or the problem into increasingly smaller elements until it becomes possible to handle each of them individually. Then, once the assessment has been made for each of these small elements, a process of synthesis puts it all back together again. During the process of synthesis, assessments that are similar for various elements of the system are recognized. They often result in not only a simplification of what appeared initially to be complex but perhaps also a new assessment that had previously not been recognized.

This is an old problem-solving technique that's been used in the management of large systems for decades, although it often hasn't been recognized for what it is and usually hasn't been systematized.

As before, we can classify the SPS system into generic segments:

> *Space Facilities.*
> *Earth facilities.*
> *Transportation.*
> *Management* (command, control, communications, data).

Each segment has its own degree and kind of sensitivity to military threat and each has its own sort of vulnerability. Sometimes, the vulnerabilities overlap segments of the system.

Obviously, both space facilities and Earth facilities as well as the transportation system are sensitive to attacks.

And these first three categories are sensitive to attacks on the management segment, even though the threat to the management segment is significantly different from the potential threats to the others.

The types and kinds of vulnerabilities and their corresponding military and paramilitary actions can be summarized as follows:

1. Technological
    a. Sabotage.
    b. Mutiny.
    c. Attack.
    d. Terrorism.
    e. Espionage.
2. *Institutional*
    a. Strikes.
    b. Expropriation.
    c. Financial.
    d. Propaganda.

The acronym combining all the methods of physical vulnerability of the SPS system is SMAT, standing for Sabotage, Mutiny, Attack, and Terrorism.

The extent of the reality of each of these threats to the elements fo the SPS system is not as straightforward as it might appear at first glance. Some parts of the system may be vulnerable to SMAT whereas other elements may be vulnerable only to parts of it.

Take sabotage for example.

The ability to seriously affect the entire SPS system by interrupting a small but key element in the system's chain of operation means that sabotage is a serious concern for the owners and operators of the SPS system.

In all segments of the SPS system, there are a lot of complex devices involving very high technology, close tolerances, microscopic components, and tight specifications. In some portions of the construction, assembly, or operation of system elements, for example, extreme cleanliness is mandatory, requiring the use of "clean room" technology to eliminate even microscopic dirt particles as small as one micron or less. Thus, sabotage can be accomplished on the microscopic level where it can't be detected except by special equipment. Sabotage can also be carried out on the macroscopic level because of the extreme size of some of the system elements and their remote location from human examination or sensors that may not be designed for or looking at the critical item that would indicate sabotage.

Although it takes some knowledge of the technology involved in the system, segment, or device that's the target of sabotage in the case of the SPS system, sabotage can be extremely effective.

Because of the complexity of the SPS system and the number of people working in the system, it's extremely difficult to completely eliminate the work of a saboteur.

For example, extremely small quantities of gases, liquids, or solids released in the proper places can stop or destroy critical elements of space systems.

There are more overt methods such as plastic explosives, of course, that have large destructive potential against such system elements as closed and pressurized modules with life support requirements and people in them.

Even successful sabotage, however, is seldom crippling to a large and complex system where there are usually redundancies built into the system to handle emergencies. Sabotage has historically accomplished little more than slowing down an operation; rarely has it stopped it altogether. And there are workable safeguards against sabotage even for the SPS system.

Mutiny is something else again. A rebellion against established authority by some or all of the trained crew of a vessel or facility amounts to mutiny and may be successful in taking control away from command or management. Mutiny differs significantly from other types of attack because it's carried out by trained people who are familiar with the system element and especially with built-in safeguards that may be unique. Furthermore, the mutineers may have been serving in the system element long enough to study the safeguards and covertly override them. Thus, sabotage can be an element of mutiny.

There are system elements whose occupation and control by a mutinous crew could result in a disruption of system operation. Such critical nodes in the system might include the SPS unit itself and especially LEO Base whose pass-through operation is critical for both personnel and cargo in the system.

Mutiny means that an application of military force must be made to dislodge the muntineers unless psychological operations can convince the mutineers to relinquish their control.

There are safeguards that can be put into operation within the SPS system and its supporting elements that would serve to reduce the risk of mutiny. However, unless these safeguards are in place during the initial phases of system build-up, mutiny will remain a potential paramilitary risk in the SPS system.

Not all of the SPS system is vulnerable to mutiny, only those portions that are in relative isolation and that have personnel operating them who can be subverted. Mutiny would seem to be particularly effective only against critical nodes in the system such as LEO Base.

Overt attack on various elements of the SPS system is the most commonly conceived military threat; the SPS system appears to be exceptionally vulnerable. To some extent this is true. However, the vulnerability of individual segments of the SPS system is variable, depending not only on the system element attacked but on the method of attack used.

There are a lot of ways to attack the SPS system, and some of them are classical military operations: The modes of attack can be broken down into two major categories: direct physical attack on the personnel and facilities of the system, and stand-off attack where damage or destruction is inflicted by a remotely launched, directed, or operated piece of military hardware.

In this first category, a direct physical attack can be aimed at mutilating, disabling, or destroying a component in the system by simply tearing it up, so to speak, using hand or power tools as weapons of destruction in addition to explosives.

Direct physical attack can also be aimed toward the goal of leaving the system elements intact for later use but destroying the control elements, thus making the system impossible to operate or use.

These forms of direct physical attack can be carried out using directly attached conventional explosives, by careful use of chemical and biological warfare agents to disable sensitive equipment or personnel, and by the ancient method of using armed troops to board and take over the system element.

It's easier to use direct physical force against the rectenna, especially if troops, armored vehicles, or attack aircraft are used. In spite of sophisticated early warning devices such as radar, it's surprising how ineffective such systems have been in such conflicts as the Six-Day War in the Mid-East, the Vietnam War, and the Iraqi-Iranian War. Even with the plethora of aircraft detection and tracking systems used by the Department of Defense and the Federal Aviation Administration in the United States, it is feasible to broach the airspace of the USA with ease. Thousands of airborne drug runners do it every year out of Mexico, Central America, and the Caribbean. People even manage to fly through what is perhaps the most intensive radar environment in the world: the Iron Curtain border that divides Western and Eastern Europe. Thus the rectenna is eminently vulnerable to direct attack by armed contingents large enough to accomplish considerable destruction.

It may not be as easy to mount a direct physical attack on the space elements of the SPS system. In spite of the extensive space traffic expected during the build-up and operation of the SPS system, it's still quite a bit less that the air traffic in the USA. The coming and going of space vehicles will be carefully scheduled. Even two launches per day of shuttle freighters and two per day of shuttle passenger ships, amounts to considerably less air traffic than comes into any airport.

It might be assumed that direct physical attacks would come from the Earth, but they could also come from space if a military force is permitted to build up strength in such areas as the lunar Trojan Points, L-4 and L-5. In this case direct physical attack could come with both manned and unmanned weapons from space itself. The basics of celestial mechanics will allow an approach to an SPS facility only from known directions unless a very large amount of energy is used by the attacking vehicles in order to achieve surprise by an approach from an unsuspected quarter.

The last element of SMAT, terrorism, can manifest itself in many forms including direct attack. But in terrorism the motivations and human force elements involved are different from the other overt military actions discussed above. The goals of terrorists are typically more limited, and their actions may range from a single take-over to a general campaign of hit-and-run destruction and death. Generally, terrorism involves more than a single person, and human life is usually threatened. Suicidal or ''kamikaze'' missions are not unknown. Unless extreme safeguards are put into use, terrorism is a danger to the SPS system, especially to its rectenna but also to its space elements.

Even though SMAT involves the use of violence of one form or another in exploiting the military vulnerabilities of the SPS system, there are other types of warlike or pseudo-warlike activities that are recognized today as being form of warfare.

Espionage is a form of informational warfare and is carried on covertly today all over world. Historically, it has proven to be an important element in both diplomatic affairs and warfare of varying degrees of involvement and scope. It's been assumed that the SPS system would be a purely civilian undertaking, whether by government or private enterprise or by a combination of these. Regardless, prudence dictates that certain types of information containing critical details of the SPS system be closely guarded, particularly if knowledge of these system details would make it easier for SMAT to be effective. History if full of this, and a lot of ''space opera'' science-fiction is based upon it. Warfare does not have to exist as an overt reality for a considerable amount of espionage activity to take place. Ian Fleming's novels of the fictional James Bond, Secret Agent 007, are well-done fictional examples of this sort of thing and have even been extended by others to cover the space area as in the case of *Moonraker*.

Another institutional vulnerability of the SPS system is one that's shared by nearly every other human activity on Earth: strikes. In a large project such as the SPS program, workers have tremendous leverage and can shut down or partially close any or all system elements by activities that are well known today. The extent to which strikes represent a military vulnerability of the SPS system depends on how critical the SPS system and its electrical output is to the military establishment.

Expropriation is listed as a military vulnerability of the SPS system because the threat of a takeover of an SPS element such as a rectenna may appear at first glance to be a system vulnerability, particularly if the rectenna is sited in another country and military activities under joint defense treaties thereby depend upon the electrical output of the SPS system. However, judging by the sorry state of affairs in the area of space law and jurisprudence, locations in geosynchronous orbit are still being claimed by some nations because they are *over* that nation's territorial boundaries. This harks back to English common law which says that a person or a nation has jurisdiction not only over the piece of property owned on the Planet Earth, but also over a wedge of volume that goes down to the center of the Earth and outward in an expanding volume to infinity. While the subterranean rights of landowners and nations has to some extent been clarified by various laws or legal precedents, and while the right of passage of aircraft over personally owned land has been determined, the control of national airspace is still a very viable principle. Whether or not this control of airspace principle extends out to infinity has yet to be completely resolved, although right of passage of space vehicles has been tacitly granted since Sputnik-I opened the Space Age on October 4, 1957. At that time, no nation on Earth could do anything to prevent Sputnik-I from traversing their classical airspace 227 kilometers overhead. Even if there had been international laws regarding transit of space vehicles over a nation, nobody could have done anything about it. Therefore, nobody did. In the years since that time, there has been tacit agreement over right of passage of space craft. But there is no international agreement nailing down whether or not there's a ceiling on national airspace. Nations astride the Earth's equator have, with some legal justification, claimed that geosynchronous orbital segments located over their territory belong to them, and that location of satellites there by others requires their permission. Lacking that permission, the theory goes, the satellites belong to those nations and can be expropriated.

However, to date no equatorial nation has had either the diplomatic or military clout to back up its demands. This has not kept them from making noise in the UN and elsewhere.

Until space law becomes firm on this point, as more and more nations achieve space capability, and especially as more nations acquire a manned space capability, probably through joint efforts with those nations possessing the capability, a real vulnerability to expropriation of SPS units in GSO exists.

One of the SPS institutional vulnerabilities is listed as "Financial," and for a very good reason. Most people do not think of money as a weapon and of financial vulnerabilities as a credible military element. But it is. Post-revolutionary Iran under the Ayatollah Khomeni did not believe it was vulnerable to this institutional threat until the Iraqi-Iranian War, when they had no way to pay for military equipment and supplies for a military establishment based upon US military systems. An SPS system, especially one of a multinational nature where the investment capital is obtained in whole or in part from international sources such as Japan, Western Europe, or any of the OPEC countries, is subjected to an institutional vulnerability best exemplified by the facetious statement of the Golden Rule: "He who has the gold makes the rules."

An incredible amount of coercive pressure can be applied by financiers. And offtimes this pressure is indistinguishable from non-violent institutional threats made or backed up by military agencies.

An institutional vulnerability, as we've seen, is one having its roots in laws. The extent of this financial institutional vulnerability is best exemplified by the statement of the powerful European banker from Frankfurt, Germany, Anselm Rothschild: "Give me the power to issue a nation's money, then I do not care who makes the laws."

The *entire* SPS system is openly vulnerable to this, especially during the construction phase but even during the operational phase because the system will be required to return value on investment to its stockholders or to the nation who supplied the funding. It will require additional capital to expand. Capital will be required to bring Third World nations into the system. And there is a continual flow of cash generated by the SPS system, a flow that can be interrupted and diverted by any number of means known to and used by banks the world over. The SPS system is vulnerable *because* of its revenue-producing capability.

Shut off the cash flow and the capability of the management of the SPS system to collect money or to charge viable rates, and the control and use of the system is altered.

The final institutional vulnerability of the SPS system is listed as Propaganda. Many readers will not believe this to be a vulnerability, but it is a vulnerability of the SPS system *even as you are reading this*. In 1981, *any* system based on high technology—and some based on well-established technologies, as well—is highly vulnerable to propaganda designed to convince people to oppose the creation or the operation of the system. We see the propaganda vulnerability of nuclear generation of electrical power. We see the propaganda vulnerability of flood control projects, dams, supersonic transport aircraft, fluorocarbon aerosol propellants, personal automobiles, insecticides, food preservatives, highway construction, birth (population) control, and a long list of technology-based systems. It has proven *extremely* difficult to fight a system propaganda vulnerability because in order to do so one must communicate and educate. To a large extent, the means to communicate and educate have been and are controlled by those who oppose technology in favor of "humanism." However, humanism without technology is pretty grim to consider, even granting the fact that occasionally technology has *not* been used in a humanistic way (although the great percentage of it has). This is not the fault of technology but of the people who apply it and use it.

Because of the recognition of this fact, there may be few reviews of some books because the most effective propaganda weapon against counterattack is to ignore it in the communications and educational media. If people don't know about the counterattack, they won't know that there's anything going on at all. They won't know there's another side to the argument and will tend to accept propaganda as fact, regardless whether it's nonsense or not, because who can tell the difference if no difference is perceived?

Be that as it may, the SPS system is under attack by propaganda even in its formative, study stages. There is no reason to believe, given the current situation in both communications and education, that it won't continue to be under attack even when most of our baseload electrical power comes to us from space. Strongly applied, it can stop the development, construction, and operation of the SPS system. What else is that but an institutional form of military threat based on a system vulnerability?

Not all elements of the SPS system are equally vulnerable to these military and paramilitary threats. Although all SPS vulnerabilities may have some basis, not all of them are credible. The most common mistake is to underestimate the degree of effort required to carry out an attack on any of the vulnerabilities. Another mistake involves an ignorance of basic physics and celestial mechanics.

For example, an SPS unit may be perceived as being very easy to attack with an ASAT that would knock it out of the sky and send its pieces raining down on Earth. While it's true that an SPS could be attacked and possibly destroyed by an ASAT, the pieces would simply stay in GEO. An enormous amount of energy would be required to alter the orbit of the SPS or its pieces and cause them to enter the Earth's atmosphere and survive the atmospheric entry in large enough pieces to reach the ground. The fear associated with the "Skylab syndrome" may exist among the uninformed, but it is not based upon the reality of the universe. Yes, one *could* "shoot down" an SPS and get it to enter the Earth's atmosphere, but the energy requirements are so large that it forces one to consider other, cheaper ways to carry out Earth bombardment from space or even from Earth—for instance, ICBM's which are already built, in place, paid for, and ready to do the same job cheaper.

The same misconceptions hold true regarding the use of Earth-based beam weapons to "shoot" objects in orbit. Although it's difficult to second-guess the technology of a quarter of a century hence, it's perfectly possible to calculate the amount of energy required to damage an SPS unit, and it is possible to predict how much attenuation of the beam's energy will be caused by its passage through the Earth's atmosphere. There are also simple passive defenses that could be placed on the SPS unit. On the other hand, space-based beam weapons for space-to-space attack offer a totally different set of conditions.

Table IX shows the various SPS vulnerabilities to weapon attack.

And Table X is a listing of the various *misconceptions* of SPS vulnerability.

This is not a whitewash of the military implications of the SPS system. Neither is this book. There *are* military implications to the SPS system, some of them quite serious which demand our attention during this period of decision. The analysis of the military threats and vulnerabilities of the SPS system that we've just slogged our way through has shown that some of the easily-perceived ones evaporate under closer rational scrutiny, while others appear that hardly seemed possible at first.

Such analyses permit us to design safeguards into the system to prevent the worst from happening.

TABLE IX
SPS VULNERABILITIES TO WEAPON ATTACK

System Element	Subsystem Element	Vulnerabilities
Transportation	All	SMAT
LEO Base	All	SMAT
GEO Base	All	SMAT
SPS unit	All	SMAT
	Array	Shadowing
	Transmitter	Blocking beam
Rectenna	All	SMAT
	Pilot beam	Chaff & EW
Command & control centers	All	SMAT & EW
Communication system	R-f & laser links	SMAT, EW, Blocking.

TABLE X
CLAIMS VERSUS REALITY
SPS SYSTEM VULNERABILITIES

Claim: "All SPS elements except the rectenna can be destroyed by an Earth-based laser."

Reality: The Earth's atmosphere disperses and attenuates HEL beams, and space craft can be "hardened" or protected against HEL beams. SPS facilities in GEO are "out of range" of any HEL laser currently conceivable.

Claim: "A single small projectile properly placed can disable any space system."

Reality: By means of proper design, shielding, and component redundancy, most space systems can be made reasonably impervious to small projectiles although space transportation vehicles and facilities in low Earth orbit (LEO) will remain vulnerable. Space facilities will have to be shielded against micrometeorite damage in any event, and this sort of shielding is also effective against small projectile weapons.

Claim: "Objects in space are easy to hit and destroy with simple non-nuclear tactical rockets.

Reality: Non-nuclear intercept and kill in space is extremely difficult and requires very sophisticated homing devices. Very sophisticated and advanced rocket missiles are needed and nuclear warheads are required in order to justify the expense and the operational difficulties of the military deployment of such systems.

Claim: "Space-based lasers are small objects easy to conceal and use with no advance warning."

Reality: HEL weapons require very large power supplies, making such space craft very large and easily detected and tracked. The existence, orbits, and ownership of such space craft would be well known shortly after launching.

Claim: "A huge SPS satellite will fall out of geosynchronous orbit if it's hit and damaged or if its propulsion system is disabled."

Reality: Once placed in GEO, an SPS will stay there with no propulsion except attitude control thrusters to maintain alignment of the photovoltaic array with the Sun. If hit, the SPS will remain in GEO and any velocity changes that could possibly be effected by any ASAT might cause it to hit other objects in GEO over a period of time. But, since there is negligible Earth's atmosphere at the altitude of GEO, an SPS will not travel in an orbit that decays because of atmospheric drag as Skylab did. Decay from GEO would require millions of years in the worst case.

Claim: "Any hit on an SPS solar array will result in the SPS being ripped apart."

Reality: The SPS solar array and structure are designed to be damage tolerant in common with other large structures. For example, even the impact of a B-25 bomber didn't destroy the Empire State Building.

Claim: "Blast damage in space is similar to that on Earth. So shock waves from a small explosion can have devastating effects on large enclosed structures in space, meaning that living facilities in space are highly vulnerable to attack with small conventional warheads."

Reality: With no atmosphere surrounding space facilities, there is no medium for propagating the compression-expansion wave that magnifies the explosion's compression wave as it does on Earth. The explosive must be detonated close enough to a structure that the explosion's own blast wave creates the damage before it dissipates in the vacuum of space.

Claim: "If an SPS is hit and disabled, its power beam would be free to wander over the surface of the Earth, cooking people and animals and burning forests and cities."

Reality: If an SPS loses reception of the pilot beam directed to it from its rectenna, the power beam is designed to fail-safe by defocusing. However, even in the event that the power beam didn't defocus. its energy density even in the center of the beam is below USA standards for human exposure to radio frequency energy and orders of magnitude below that required for incendiary purposes. Because of transmitting antenna design, the power beam *cannot* be focused more sharply than the design allows. A microwave oven it's not.

CHAPTER TWELVE

History has lessons to teach those who will read, listen to, and heed the record of the past. Among these lessons are those concerned with threat and response as well as vulnerability and defense.

There is always some manner of safeguard that can be put into operation to counter a threat or to protect a vulnerability.

Sometimes the initial safeguard is both very expensive as well as technologically difficult, but the important fact is that the safeguard can be worked out and can be placed into operation.

And sometimes the safeguard creates a whole new direction for civilization to take.

The term *safeguard* is used in preference to others such as *defenses, countermeasures,* or *protection.* This is because the term *safeguard* has a much broader scope and can encompass everything that needs to be done to provide antitheses to military threats and vulnerabilities. A safeguard includes measure for protection of a system element from attack as well as the means to deter a potential enemy from mounting the attack in the first place. It also includes the means to effectively and credibly prevent a potential threat from becoming reality.

There are many examples in the history of technology, diplomacy, and warfare. It's unfortunate that most history courses taught in school are centered around the political and diplomatic aspects—a weary list of kings and wars with no real attempt to gain any understanding of *why* these people acted the way they did and why the wars started and ended as they did. And there is practically no discussion of the role technology has played in the course of history.

To take a single example, the invention of the stirrup, an attachment on each side of a saddle to hold a horseback rider's foot. The device may have been invented in India about 200 B.C., but it found its way north into China where it was known by 523 A.D. The stirrup had spread as far west as Turkestan by 800 A.D. where it found its way into Europe. The Franks had it about that time, and it changed the fate of nations as a result.

Before the use of the stirrup, mounted troops were restricted to archers often riding pillion behind the horseman, often riding as the horseman himself. Sometimes a foot soldier rode pillion and could dismount to fight on foot. In this event, the horse and the horseman provided a high degree of mobility to the foot soldier, being the ancient counterpart of the Soviet Red Army's tank rider infantry soldier. But fighting, for the most part, was still done on foot by a soldier standing on the ground and slugging it out with an opponent. The cavalry used by the Romans was a force of maneuver accompanied by long-range (for that period) artillery in the form of arrows launched from a short bow. All major fighting was done by soldiers on foot with pikes, spears, and short swords; the foot soldiers were sometimes armored to the extent that the armor didn't prevent rapid movement in close hand-to-hand ground fighting.

The Franks discovered the true capabilities of the stirrup: it permits the ancient spear to be used as a lance by a mounted soldier because the force of impact of the spear can be transferred from the rider through the stirrup to the horse without unseating the rider. The Franks (ancestors of today's German and French peoples) made profound changes in their weapons systems as a result. Battle axes and javelins disappeared from their armories and the short swords of infantry combat became long swords far too heavy to be easily used in combat by a foot soldier. No longer did a foot soldier have to ride pillion behind a mounted archer; the foot soldier was given mobility *and* striking force because of the stirrup. The cavalry force of maneuver became the mobile main force of attack.

In 1066 A.D., the Normans under Duke William invaded England and were met by the Saxons under Harold at Hastings. The Saxon army was based on conservative military tradition—about 5000 trained fighting men that included infantry soldiers each carrying a short sword and a throwing axe or merely a spear, plus unarmored bowmen on foot and the usual levy of farmers and peasants equipped with a motley variety of weapons. Duke William had 1000 archers, 4000 conventional foot soldiers, and 3000 cavalry troops. These cavalry troops were to win the battle. Each Norman cavalryman was mounted in a saddle with stirrups. He carried a shield to protect his off side and both an iron-tipped lance and a long sword which enabled him to strike a man on the ground from his perch atop his horse. He was further armored with an iron helmet and chain mail, the latter also an invention which had come to Europe from the East.

On Friday, October 13, 1066, the Battle of Hastings took place. (Perhaps this is the origin of the superstition about Friday the Thirteenth.) The heavy Norman cavalry acting as shock troops turned the tide and won the day.

The stirrup changed the course of history. If the stirrup hadn't been used at the Battle of Hastings, this book would be written in a different language.

The stirrup made possible the mounted, armored knight. The contact of the Europeans with the Arabs during the Crusades had also introduced the concept of both chivalry and romantic love to Europe. Our entire Western tradition of romantic love thus derives from the invention of the stirrup and its military implications.

The military threat of the armored, mounted knight lasted until the Battle of Agincourt on October 25, 1415 when the English introduced the weapon and the tactics that spelled the end of this threat: the long bow capable of throwing a very stout arrow at high velocity, thus having the capability to penetrate both horse and body armor. Massed archers with long bows could wipe out a charge of mounted knights . . . and did.

The development of a reliable machine gun for use in the trench warfare of 1914–1918 spelled the final end to mounted cavalry. Had the Germans effectively used their heavy, squad, and light machine guns in the Soviet Union—and the Germans had the best machine guns in the world at that time—they could have stopped the Red Army's cavalry attacks that were successful only because the Soviets had the cavalry in reserve and because the Germans were out of ammunition and in retreat because of logistics failures.

These are brief examples of the continual seesaw of threat-vulnerability, offense-defense, weapon-counter-weapon that runs through history. The cycle used to take centuries. Now it takes only years. The reason is that technology is involved in all cases, and the rate of technological progress is now much greater than it has been in the past. "Ultimate weapons" don't remain ultimate very long these days. They rapidly breed countermeasures.

The same holds true of the military implications of the SPS system.

It can also be said that strong military imbalances breed new social institutions designed to control new military capabilities or to render the use of the new capabilities more difficult to initiate. In other words an institutional defense or countermeasure is developed.

One of the most effective and recent social institutions developed in this regard is the insurance industry.

This may appear to be a mis-statement because most domestic American insurance policies exclude such risks as acts of war. Although this is true for many forms of American insurance, its not generally true. Because the insurance industry finds itself in very difficult straits in times of war, overt military activity isn't in the best interests of this industry. Therefore, upon closer examination, the concept of insurance turns out to be a military control device and a counter-vulnerability activity.

To better understand this, we need to take a brief excursion into how and why insurance developed because the insurance industry can have a profound effect upon the military implications of the SPS system and, in general, upon military activities in space.

Many people believe that insurance as we know it began at

the coffee house known as Lloyd's in London around the year 1688. There insurance underwriters sat around drinking coffee and underwriting risk insurance on shipping.

Actually, the concept of insurance can be traced back to the marine insurance of the Italians in the 15th Century.

Insurance is a social device wherein a large number of individuals reduce or eliminate the economic risks of loss common to all members of the group; to do this, each member contributes an equitable portion of the overall risk based on the level of his risk and the economic consequences of the loss to him. The objective of insurance is to substitute certainty for uncertainty, and its effect is to spread among many individuals the cost that would normally fall upon a single individual from an accidental occurrence leading to a disastrous event.

Risks are considered to be (a) pure risks that are unilaterial and negative, involving only the chance of loss, and (b) speculative risks that are bilateral and include the alternatives of loss or gain. Not all risks are insurable—for some risks, it isn't possible to get anyone to underwrite the potential loss. And only pure risks are insurable.

Many people also believe that buying insurance involves wagering with the insurance company, the wager being that the buyer is betting he'll lose while the insurance firm is betting he won't. This isn't true. Payment of the insurance fee or "premium" is made by the insuree to the insurer *before* the risky, insured activity actually begins. Payment by the insurance underwriter is made only if the loss stipulated in the contract actually occurs. Payment for a loss becomes an indemnity, not a gain as it would be if it were a bet.

That insurance is an institutional safeguard against certain types of military threats and vulnerabilities isn't immediately obvious until one considers that the most remarkable expansion in the insurance industry took place during the war between France and England that began in 1793. The insurance people associated with Lloyd's of London advanced enormously in wealth and importance, even though some underwriters found their resources strained by losses. From

1793 through 1815, Lloyd's exerted considerable influence on the Admiralty and upon the direction of naval operations to protect the commercial shipping insured by Lloyd's associates. The whole concept of the naval convoy came about as a result of insurance. And at that time, the state made no provisions for war victims. Lloyd's associates established a patriotic fund for that purpose in 1803. That fund is still in operation today.

With these historic facts in mind, let's look at how both technological and institutional safeguards could be established against military threats and vulnerabilities of the SPS system.

Is it possible to safeguard against the potentiality of the SPS being used for military purposes?

Probably, if the military threats and vulnerabilities are carefully studied and analyzed in advance so that pragmatic safeguards can be designed into the system and implemented as needed to reduce the risk of military utilization. The worst possible thing is to ignore the military capabilities and hope that nobody will ever think to use them; that's a very dangerous Ostrich Syndrome and has not prevented military use of technology and systems in the past. That's why a major portion of this book is devoted to the military implications of the SPS system. It's all well and good to trumpet the potential gains and benefits to come from a technological leap forward such as the SPS, but unless all the military implications are considered ahead of time we run the great historic risk of the SPS turning into a militarily controlled system to the potential detriment of all. This is not an anti-military statement because one of the military uses of an SPS system is to create multilateral nuclear disarmament if proper safeguards are incorporated into the total system to start with.

First of all, are there technological safeguards against both the real and the perceived military threats of an SPS system that were detailed in an earlier chapter?

Table XI details some of the technological safeguards that have been considered to date for use against the military threat potentials of the SPS system.

TABLE XI
SPS TECHNOLOGICAL SAFEGUARDS

Safeguard	*Used against*
Anti-ballistic missiles (ABM) (ABM)	Re-entry vehicles ASAT
Anti-satellite vehicle (ASAT) (ASAT)	Earth-to-LEO vehicles ASAT attackers Orbital vehicles
Booby traps	Satnap, satmute
Counter-ASAT	ASAT
Decoys, chaff	ASAT
Dual keys	Power shutoff
Electronic countermeasures	Electronic warfare
Encryption	Espionage & intelligence
Hardening & protective coatings	Directed energy weapons
Long Range Space Surveillance	Installation of military adapters.
Maneuver	ASAT
Monitor crews	Augmented manning
Physical attack	Military use of launch site
Pilot beam override	"Piped Piper" box
Reduced observables	Surveillance, reconnaissance, ASAT
Reflectors & shields	Directed energy weapons
Self defense	ASAT, satnap
Self-destruct	Satnap
Surface-to-air missile	Hypersonic bomber conversion of shuttle vehicle

To some extent, there's an overlap between the safeguards against SPS military threat and SPS military vulnerability, especially in the category of force delivery. Those should be obvious as the discussion proceeds.

Anti-ballistic missiles (ABM) could be used against entry vehicles launched from the space segment of the SPS system, and ASAT's could also be used, particularly against the SPS space transportation system.

The ASAT capability of the SPS system could be negated by counter-ASAT weapons and by such countermeasures as radar-jamming chaff or decoys.

In the case of the SPS military threats of satnap and satmute, booby traps become an effective safeguard whose suspected presence also amounts to a certain degree of deterrency.

The whole game of electronic warfare is a relatively new one that's played with sophisticated electronic countermeasures equipment and techniques such as increased transmitter power to overcome jamming, changing the operating frequency of the transmitter to go around jamming, and other anti-jamming techniques such as spread spectrum modulation and frequency hopping. Some of this is also effective against signature intelligence and electronic intelligence.

History has shown that the best measure for safeguarding communications against intelligence activities is encryption. Coding is not effective because computers can now be used to break codes very quickly. Encryption is another matter. A code is a system in which symbol substitution takes place, and many people have had experiences with this as children with "secret code rings" and other devices. Encryption is best examplified by the use of the phrase, "Climb Mount Niitaka," that signaled the Japanese fleet under Rear Admiral Chuichi Nagumo that diplomatic negotiations with the United States had failed, that war was inevitable, and to proceed with the plan to attack Pearl Harbor. Or the use of the phrase, "The Italian navigator has landed in the new world," whose transmission by physicist Dr. Enrico Fermi was the signal that he'd achieved criticality in the first nuclear reactor at Stagg Field of the University of Chicago. It's a password or prearranged phase, term, or series of symbols. It's secure during transmission *unless* somebody other than the transmitter or receiver knows about what it means *in advance*.

The use of "hardening" and protective coatings are both historic safeguards against projectiles. Warships, aircraft, and fortifications have used armor in the past to protect themselves. Space craft and space facilities can use the same to safeguard themselves against projectile threats from SPS elements. Protective coatings are effective against directed energy weapons. "Hardening" also includes the protection of equipment against specific threats such as electromagnetic jamming or the effects of explosives. In some cases, this sort of "armor" could be deployed by vehicles and facilities when necessary to blunt the threat.

In the event that the SPS transportation system shuttles are converted into hypersonic bombers, there are a number of physical safeguards against these including SAM's, ABM's, ASAT's, and directed energy weapons.

There are physical safeguards against all the potential military threats of the SPS system, although some are not as effective as others. All of the physical safeguards shown in Table XI are technologically feasible. One of the problems hinges on the fact that some of the *safeguards* have an escalatory nature—i.e.: they could be viewed themselves as potential military threats.

There is another problem inherent with all the technological safeguards against military threat of the SPS system. All of the safeguards require the threatened nation to develop and install the safeguard systems as part of their own military forces. Some of these safeguards can be developed and deployed only by technologically advanced nations, the so-called "high tech" nations of the world. How about the Third World or "low tech" nations? Few if any of them would have the capability to deploy such safeguards and few could afford to purchase them from high tech nations. This may require that low tech nations form space defense treaty organizations that could be viewed as "low tech NATO's." Such mutual defense organizations have been formed by several regional nation groups; an example is the Arab League. Analysis indicates that the need for such low tech mutual defense organizations would be increased in the future. The reaction of the superpowers and the high tech nations to these low tech mutual space defense leagues might be to attempt to prevent their formation. However, in the past, superpowers have not felt challenged by the creation of regional defense leagues. In the case of space defense leagues, the nature of the technological safeguards permits the use of some of them as offensive weapons.

The development of technological safeguard systems could lead to an escalating arms race scenario. If any nation opts to expend vast amounts of national resources on the development and deployment of technological safeguard systems, this could be viewed by other nations as a threat itself, leading to a competitive development of both offensive and defensive technologies to counter the real or imagined advantages possessed by the potential opponent. Such a race could have many implications in the military, political, economic and social areas. In the area of ASAT, such a race already appears to be under way between the USA and the USSR.

It's therefore a certainty that technological safeguards, effective as they may be in the hands of high tech nations, will not be viewed on a worldwide basis as a satisfactory total solution to the military threat problem of the SPS system because the safeguard systems may well have a tendency to breed their own problems on an international level.

Technological safeguards against the military vulnerabilities of the SPS system have much in common with those against the military threats.

Some safeguards are universal across the entire SPS system and can be used anywhere. These include the use of security forces, access restrictions, careful screening of personnel, enforced exclusion zones, counterforce, and first strike capability.

Nearly all vulnerabilities of the SPS system can be reduced by use of proper technological safeguards, and levels of vulnerability of elements of the system can be achieved that are similar to those that exist for Earth-based power generating systems. But there are a few vulnerabilities that are totally impossible to eliminate and will have to be considered as impossible to defend against.

Again, the best way to approach any defense of the military vulnerabilities is to break the SPS system down into its sub-systems and consider the vulnerability safeguards separately where possible.

The vulnerability of the SPS transportation system can be reduced by a number of technological means. All safeguards against SMAT (Sabotage, Mutiny, Attack, and Terrorism) are effective. The Earth launch facility could be vulnerable to attacks launched from submarines if located on a sea coast; safeguards against such attacks require extensive anti-submarine activity. A more viable solution to the problem, given the energy and ground transportation requirements to support the launch site, would be an inland location with advanced ABM protection. Protection of the space vehicle segment of the transportation system against SMAT could be achieved by use of preventive electronic surveillance ("bugs") using some of the techniques that are currently used to screen airline passengers for weapons.

The biggest problem in reducing vulnerability of the space transportation system lies in deploying defenses against ASAT weapons and nuclear explosions. ASAT defense requires both a rapid maneuvering capability on the part of the space craft—which may not be successful in the face of sophisticated ASAT terminal homing guidance systems—and the most effective defense, active systems such as decoys, jamming, and electronic countermeasures equipment either aboard the space craft or installed in one of the larger space facilities.

On the other hand, nuclear attack is a serious threat. Nuclear attack on the space segment of the system could disable space craft electronic devices due to the electromagnetic pulse generated by nuclear explosions and to surface charge phenomena from X-ray and gamma ray fluxes. Nuclear attacks could possibly subject passengers and crews to lethal radiation levels. Nuclear "hardening" represents the technological safeguard against nuclear explosions in space; such "hardening" of critical electronic elements will be required to some extent by the solar flare radiation environment.

Sneak attacks by directed energy weapons are highly unlikely because, as we've seen, such weapon systems require very large power supplies and, to some extent, are ineffective in the Earth-to-space attack mode. Space-based directed energy weapons are difficult to hide. Since their location is known, they could be easily targeted in advance by counter-weapons associated with the SPS system as a system defense force. In addition, there is also the possibility of "hardening" space vehicles against directed energy weapon attacks by use of coatings and reflectors.

Although there are workable technological safeguards for the space transportation system, LEO Base is almost indefensible. Being in a low-Earth orbit, it's reachable by modestly sized rocket vehicles carrying a number of effective warheads. It will be vulnerable to ASAT. Since it can easily be attacked with nuclear explosives, hardening and radiation protection can be used to decrease its vulnerability but may not be practical because of the extent of such protection needed. And LEO Base cannot be protected against the launch of a sounding rocket that would dispense a cloud of small projectiles. Common nails would work fine. Closing velocity between LEO Base and a cloud of nails would be approximately 8.5 kilometers per second. A hundred kilograms of common iron nails 5 centimeters long spaced ten feet apart would fill a volume of 70 x 70 x 35 meters—171,500 cubic meters. This would wreak havoc with LEO Base and destroy all but the most heavily armored portions. It would carry away antennas, destroy photovoltaic arrays, and disable heat radiators. Launching such a payload into position to shred LEO Base would be within the grasp of practically every nation on Earth. Any terrorist group with money and the ability to handle 1960 technology could do it. And there is no way to defend LEO Base because it's so deep in the Earth's gravity well.

GEO Base is another proposition altogether. It's further up on the gravity well, and any Earth-launched ASAT will require more time to reach GSO. Technological safeguards effective for GEO Base are almost identical to the ones required for the SPS units themselves, except for the fact that, to some extent, GEO Base can be hardened against nuclear attack.

SPS units can't. Power satellites are extremely vulnerable to nuclear attack because of the electromagnetic pulse (EMP) produced by nuclear explosions. Given the size and power handling capabilities of an SPS, it would be extremely expensive to harden it against the EMP. The best safeguard for both GEO Base and the SPS units is an active satellite defense system capable of getting to an Earth-launched ASAT very early in flight and disabling its warhead by preventing detonation. Preliminary estimates, however, indicate that such a satellite defense system would have to act quickly and reliably because a 20-megaton thermonuclear warhead detonated at an altitude of 200 kilometers would produce nuclear effects such as the EMP that could disable the *entire* SPS power satellite constellation up in GEO!

Clearly, we will have to develop institutional safeguards instead.

The rectenna can be safeguarded by fortification—fencing and security guards. It can also be defended by ABM and SAM batteries against missile and air attack. However, as we well know from military history, such weapons defenses are not 100% effective or successful.

Basically, one can state that if "the balloon goes up," the SPS satellite and rectenna segments are just as vulnerable as everything else when it comes to nuclear weapons but can be defended to some extent against conventional weapons systems.

When it comes to technological safeguards for the SPS command, control, and communications ("C-cubed") systems, we enter the magic world of electronic warfare. Basically, EW amounts to outguessing and out-gadgeteering your adversary. A great deal of what one does to safeguard one's system against EW depends on what the adversary tries to do, identifying what he's doing, figuring out how to counter the EW activity, and activating electronic countermeasures. Then one must observe what the adversary does to counter the countermeasures. The SPS C-cubed system can be "hardened" and safeguarded just as today's military command centers are. An example is NORAD's Cheyenne Mountain center in Colorado. However, as the level of hardening and safeguarding a C-cubed system grows in its defensive capability, so its cost skyrockets as well. It may not be economically feasible to institute technological safeguards for the SPS system's C-cubed segment.

Technological safeguards, as we've seen, involve either preventing or denying an adversary from developing or deploying a system to exploit your vulnerability or by mounting some manner of defense system, either active or passive, to counter the effects of the threat.

When it comes to technological safeguards, *nothing* is 100% effective or reliable. *Nothing* that we can do with technology guarantees that the expensive SPS system will not be vulnerable to disablement or destruction.

Some technological safeguards will result in significant reduction in vulnerability but will not totally eliminate the vulnerable aspect without incurring exorbitant costs. Some safeguards are unworkable simply because of the economics involved even at the lowest and most rudimentary level of safeguarding.

Several facts have now become self-evident upon close analysis:

The SPS system itself is an extremely poor weapons system because (a) its energy output cannot be *directly* used as a weapon, (b) it's far too vulnerable to be used as an economical weapons system, (c) it can't be adequately safeguarded against military action by technological means, and (d) for every perceived use of the SPS as a weapons system, there are simpler and cheaper ways to do the same thing without being so militarily obvious and economically risky.

The *only* way to safeguard the highly vulnerable SPS system is to let people know that it can't be used as an effective weapon. This requires institutional safeguards.

Since the SPS system vulnerability cannot be effectively reduced by technological safeguards, we therefore must consider the institutional safeguards.

CHAPTER THIRTEEN

It may be said that the greater the energy source, the greater the amount of energy that must be expended to control it through institutions organized for that purpose. This could be considered a corollary of Coon's energy hypothesis that was discussed early in the book.

The words "institution" and "institutional" have been used thus far without a succinct definition of what we mean. Many people will misunderstand what an "institution" is. In simplest terms, an institution is a group of people. It's organized for some definite purpose. It develops and follows its own rules. It has a structure—i.e.: its members have adopted an organization with means for making rules, means for enforcing rules among its membership, well-defined levels of authority, means for delegating both responsibility for carrying out certain tasks and the authority to demand compliance by other members of the group in accomplishing these tasks, means for control to insure accountability, means for communication up and down the organizational structure, and means for assigning rewards and punishment for carrying out, failing to carry out, or blocking the accomplishment of tasks.

In its simplest form, an institution consists of a leader and a few followers. In its most complicated form, it is a worldwide federation of nations or business enterprises.

All of us belong to several institutions—family, business firm, trade union, commercial association, professional association, service club, church, social club, community, state, and nation.

An institution is people. It isn't its inspirations, its rules, its customs, or the way the people in the institution accomplish the goals they've organized to achieve. It has nothing whatsoever to do with race, culture, environment, heredity, or any of the other modern buzz words of sociology because we've defined "institution" and will use that term not as the sociologists do, but as an anthropologist does. And an anthropologist is one who approaches human history and activities from the viewpoint of human biology and institutions.

However, an institutional system is indeed something that is part of an institution. An institutional system can be the rules, laws, regulations, treaties, agreements, contracts, or customs of the institution. An institution acts through such institutional systems.

Now we should have straight in our minds what is meant by an institutional safeguard.

It's a safeguard that's activated and operated by an institution made up of people.

Simplistic? So is a dictionary. Anything that clarifies meaning must be simplistic or it doesn't perform its intended function. Only insecure people who are unsure of their knowledge will hide behind jargon, complicated explanations, and the claim they possess information that can be understood only by members of their arcane group. Beware of such experts. They have helped tarnish the pages of history with a great deal of human suffering, stagnation, dishonesty, torture, and blood. They're the slave masters over the human intellect as their associates, the men on horseback, are the tyrants over human effort. Together, these two types have made a team whose exploits are sadistic.

As energy has become available, it has not only caused existing institutions to grow but has permitted the creation of new institutions.

As a result of our analysis of the technological safeguards to the vulnerability of the SPS system, our conclusion was that none of them was suitably effective.

Therefore, it appears that we're going to need those institutions of increasing size and complexity. One of the goals of some of these institutions will be to provide safeguards for both the military threats and the military vulnerabilies of the SPS system as we've analyzed them.

The institutional safeguards would appear to offer the only salvation.

This is no surprise.

Again, history has shown that technological safeguards offer no firm, reliable, long-term solutions to military threats and vulnerabilities because technology isn't a static thing. It changes, and it's changing now with great rapidity. Since the amount of human knowledge is doubling now every seven years, technology which is the result of the application of that knowledge is also progressing at an analogous rate. It is doubtful if it can be stopped or slowed down. It's even more doubtful that we would want to stop it or slow it down because we don't know what course it would take if it were restricted or forbidden.

Any engineer worthy of the title will tell you that it's not nice to fool Mother Nature; it's *impossible*. The best you can do is to work with her. If you can't get from here to there in a technically straightforward way, you've got to be devious and find a way to get around the barriers. There are usually ways to get around them. Therefore, the path of technological progress is never the straightforward one; it's as crooked as the Brownian Movement of a single particle in a colloid. It's driven always by perceived social desire—not need—by a person or persons who sees in the fulfillment of that social desire a way to improve his own lot. With this sort of a driver behind technological progress, it can't be easily stopped. Forbidding the development of a technology is, in fact, almost a sure-fire way to insure that development. Prohibit a nation from developing and possessing long-range artillery, and that nation develops the ballistic missile. Prohibit the development of weapons of mass destruction in space, and some nation will develop weapons of even greater power that are capable of selective targeting. Prohibit war as you know it, and somebody will develop war as you never conceived it could be.

What we have said about technological safeguards here could be obsolete in a decade or less. The same can be said about the military threats and vulnerabilities of the SPS system. But we must deal with the problems as they appear to exist now. Unless some UFO lands and gives us some fantastic technology from on high—and that hasn't happened lately around here—we're stuck with what we've got or can reasonably forecast that we'll have.

We *can* foresee the SPS system and, on the basis of reasonable technological forecasts, we can also forecast the likely technological safeguards that would be available for us to use against the threats and vulnerabilities of the system. Thus far, the technological safeguards don't seem to be efficient.

Because the problems inherent in the SPS system as a solution to world energy demands appear to be formidable and, in some cases, not only insoluble but fatal, there is a tendency for many people to try to ignore the problems and dismiss the SPS system in hopes that the problems will go away if the development of other less centralized terrestrial energy sources were pursued instead. The consequences of doing this are of such importance that they deserve to be discussed separately . . . and we will do just that once we have confronted the problem of how to handle the SPS system military implications by means of institutional safeguards, the only approach left.

The human race has had some experience in the area of institutional safeguards, and some of them have worked reasonably well for a period of time after they were activated.

Since military threats and vulnerabilities are international rather than domestic issues, they have to be dealt with against the background of international law. Therefore, we can consider the realistic options that are currently available to us within which the facets of international law can be brought into play. To do this requires that we first consider the organizational structure of the SPS system itself and then investigate the sorts of international institutions, existing and potential, that could be used to reduce the military threats and vulnerabilities.

The basic form of organization of the SPS system is a determining factor in the international perception of the military implications of the system itself. If the SPS system is a totally government owned and operated system, it would be extremely difficult for it *not* to be perceived as a system that could be quickly and easily utilized for military purposes to add to the military capabilities of a country and back up its diplomatic capabilities.

Given the importance of the SPS system, it's likely that the United States will choose to develop the system initially for its own domestic use. This would probably be the fastest and most efficient manner in which to do it from the USA viewpoint. Unless there is a very strong trend toward nationalization of major industries and utilities in the next twenty year period—a trend which does not appear to be developing—the SPS system developed, constructed and operated by the USA will probably be funded during the R&D phase with some sort of government involvement by direct grants, subsidies, contracts, tax incentives, or even a government-chartered corporation. As the SPS system begins to enter the construction and operation phases where technical risk has been reduced by proving the technology, the government will probably act in its historic manner by backing away to let private enterprise take over more and more of the system financing. The federal government has already done this with the canal system, the railroads, and the airlines. Where it has stepped back into government control and operation of the passenger rail transportation industry, it has failed miserably to date and would probably like to unload Amtrak to private interests if the market for passenger rail transportation was there . . . which it isn't, not at ticket prices and costs that would permit a private firm to break even, much less show a profit for its stockholders. And the government recently backed away with alacrity usually unknown in bureaucracy when it came to a suggestion to nationalize the airlines.

A major argument pointing toward financing and management of the SPS system by private enterprise can be made in light of the furor that resulted when the proposed Moon Treaty was passed for signature by the UN General Assembly and came before the US Senate for consideration and ratification. An extremely strong effort was mounted by private individuals and entrepreneurs in the USA—not by large corporations with heavily funded lobbying organizations—to block ratification. As of this writing, this grass roots space advocacy group has succeeded. The UN Moon Treaty as worded was both obscure and lacking in foresight. It would have prevented *any* exploitation of space—except for the grandfather exemption for communications satellites—by private enterprise or even governments because it declared that the resources of space were "the common property of all mankind." Regardless of the semantic nonsense of that phrase, one wonders what fictional inhabitants of Beta Lycris IV would think of such an anthropocentric term!

Internationalization appears to be a non-viable option for financing and especially for management unless the multinational corporations or OSEC scenarios become realities. The history of projects run under the auspices of the United Nations is a long and dreary list of excess delays, funding difficulties, and management problems. In addition, internationalization involves a number of current USA policy concerns such as technology transfer and energy independence. These factors would tend to place internationalization in disfavor in spite of an apparent capability for reducing the military implications. Granted that the perceived military implications may be reduced by internationalization, the control of the SPS system jointly by several governments or by an existing international body such as the UN poses real problems in *non-military* areas, problems that could be so severe as to render an SPS system ineffective as even a stand-by energy source.

This leaves us with two possibilities—domestic ownership and management by organizations in a single nation such as the USA, and ownership and management by a multinational corporation operating as much as feasible outside the overall jurisdiction of national governments and totally outside of international organizations such as the UN.

Both approaches do little to ameliorate the perceived military implications.

In the case of the domestic private enterprise approach, there is the real concern of nationalism and the real possibility of nationalization during periods of international tension or diplomatic crises escalating toward war.

The fear of military implications in the case of ownership and control by a multinational corporation is just the opposite: national governments would fear the military implications because they would have no control over the use of the system and no way to prevent control from being seized by a potential agressor.

There is in existence an international institutional safeguard that works. To date, its history of working over extended periods of time has been well established and makes the few instances in which it has not worked all the more important in our discussion.

This safeguard is international law.

This so-called "law of nations" is a body of rules and principles which nations consider as binding upon them. It came about in the late 16th century because some institution was required to bring order to the relationships between the emerging independent sovereign nations of Europe.

International law differs from national, internal law in several respects. First of all, international law is probably more consistently applied and obeyed than many systems of national law, contrary to the belief of many people. The apparent lack of capability to compel nations to observe and obey the tenets of international law is nowhere near as serious as people believe. International law is generally obeyed because there's little temptation to violate it, because it's easy to live with, and because habitual violations would invite reprisals in a tit-for-tat response. By and large, however, international law is obeyed because it's in the best interests of a nation to obey it. It's rarely broken except in war time, and even then the portions of international law dealing with relationships and conduct during time of hostilities is usually obeyed. The perceived consequences of ignoring international law are usually deemed too serious, and this was borne out in the aftermath of World War II.

International law is less effective than national law because it doesn't reach into some of the most important aspects of national law that deal with external relations—nationality, armament, immigration, fiscal policies, trade policies, etc. Even the right to wage war is still left to each state to exercise at its complete discretion in spite of numerous international sanctions against this right.

There is also a relative lack of international institutions in the area of international law. A real system of national law depends upon a strong legislature to adopt laws, an executive to enforce them, and a judiciary to interpret them and adjudicate conflicts under the law. The international machinery for doing this is still far short of that required for a mature, developed legal system.

Nevertheless, international law embraces agreements and disagreements between nations, peace and war, treaties and declarations.

There are thousands of international agreements called conventions that are now in force and that form much of the basis for international law. They amount today to more than agreements relating to peace, alliances, and the like. Multipartite treaties are relatively new on the international scene, dating only from the 19th century.

There are numerous problems with treaties. One of the most serious is their contractual nature. Contracts are agreements between parties that have been reduced to writing and mutually agreed upon. There are always provisions in any contract for unilaterial cancellation, recourse measures to be followed in case of abrogation, and provisions for enforcement of agreed conduct of the parties to the contract. As has been pointed out, there are no international institutions capable of enforcing treaties or *any* aspect of international law. This flaws the overall system.

Treaties may be mutually beneficial to all parties when signed. They rarely remain that way because people change their minds and institutions change their people.

In discussing the treaty as an international safeguard, we must keep in mind the ephemeral nature of most treaties.

There are few treaties of any consequence that have remained intact, inviolate, and unchanged for more than twenty-five years.

One of the few exceptions to this is the agreement reached between US President James Knox Polk and British Ambassador to the United States, Richard Parkenham, on 15 June 1846, establishing the boundary between the United States and Canada at the 49th parallel. This is the longest unfortified international boundary in the world, and the one that has been unfortified for the longest period of time. It is also the only international boundary established in the 19th century that has not seen a war fought back and forth across it by the nations involved. As the exception to the rule, it shows that international agreements *can* work for a long time exactly as their creators proposed.

However, the obituary list of treaties is long, and if we are thinking of the international agreement as an institutional safeguard for the SPS system, we *must* keep these in mind. Here are a few of the most recent and important ones, historically speaking:

The Treaty of Tordesillas in 1494 divided the Western Hemisphere between Spain and Portugal, while the Treaty of Zaragoza in 1529 divided the Far East between the same two powers. The authority standing behind these two treaties was the international equivalent of the United Nations at that time: the papacy. Neither Spain nor Portugal followed either agreement, and the other European nations who were busily carving out their colonial empires ignored the treaties entirely. The only surviving consequence of the Treaty of Tordesillas is that the language of Brazil today is Portuguese while that of the rest of South America is Spanish.

The Congress of Vienna in 1815 established the international order and national boundaries of Europe following the Napoleonic blood bath and consequent stirring of the pot there. By 1871, nothing was left of the agreements because the Franco-Prussian War was in full swing, setting the stage for the European holocausts that were to follow.

The Congress of Berlin divided the Balkans in 1878. It

didn't stop the fighting there. The Balkan Wars of 1912–1913 put the final *coup de grace* to that long-forgotten agreement.

The Covenant Provisions of the Treaty of Versailles in 1919 established the League of Nations. No additional comment is necessary.

The Washington Naval Treaty of 1922, including the four-power Pacific Peace Treaty signed at the same time, set limits on naval forces in the Pacific Ocean. Less than twenty years after it was pompously signed amid much publicity, the signatories were involved in a general war with each other.

The Kellogg-Briand Pact of 1928 outlawed the use of war as an instrument of national policy. *Sixty* nations signed it, including the United States. Some of them were at war when they signed it. All of them were at war with one another a mere eleven years later.

The very intelligent people who drafted the Constitution of the United States of America were careful to insist that a legislative body, the United States Senate which at that time amounted to a convention of "foreign ministers" from each state, must ratify every international treaty signed by the executive branch of the government. They forgot about the ephemeral nature of international agreements because they made no provision in writing about abrogating the national agreement to a treaty. Now the precedent has been set. It requires Senate ratification to make the United States a party to a treaty, but any international agreement can be abrogated by a simple Executive Order of the President without the advice and consent of the Senate.

Therefore, in the case of the United States of America which is one of the world superpowers, it's difficult to get the nation involved in an international agreement but very easy to get out of it.

This doesn't mean that treaties are useless or that they shouldn't be considered. On the contrary, treaties are international agreements, and our world could not function without them. But they must be looked upon as one would view any agreement: a contract between two or more parties which, when made, is of mutual benefit to all participants under the circumstances of the time and the circumstances in the future *as they can be foreseen at that moment*.

This last item is why lawyers will always have work to do. Lawyers are specialists in the resolution of human conflict.

Treaties *do* work and *have* worked in the past. They usually resolve some sort of conflict between the parties or they divide up responsibilities, accountabilities, property, etc. The biggest problem with a treaty is the same problem that exists with any agreement: When circumstances change, as they inevitably will, treaties, agreements, and other forms of contracts must be renegotiated rather than considered as something cast in concrete and immutable forevermore. Unless the benefits of the contract inure to all parties involved, there is an imbalance . . . and one of the parties will break the contract.

There are a very large number of international treaties that bear upon the SPS system. The most important ones are those adopted by the United Nations and passed out for signature by the UN member nations.

The most important of these for our consideration is the 1967 Treaty of Principles which has now been ratified by over 100 countries and stands thus far as the basic statement of the rights and responsibilities for space-going peoples. Its seventeen articles make the following points:

1. The exploitation and use of outer space should be for the benefit of all mankind and all nations.

2. Outer space and other celestial bodies cannot be claimed as territory or occupied as territory by any nation.

3. Nuclear weapons and weapons of mass destruction must not be stationed in outer space or on other celestial bodies.

4. People voyaging in space are envoys of mankind, are due all assistance in emergencies, and must be returned to their country if they accidentally land in another nation.

5. Nations bear international responsibility for activities in space whether these activities are carried out by their governments or by nongovernmental agencies. Activities of nongovernment entities in outer space require authorization

and continuing supervision of their national government.

6. Nations are responsible for damage done by their space craft or component parts thereof. If the launch site is in a different nation or if the launching is carried out by another nation, that nation is jointly liable.

7. Ownership of space vehicles is not affected by space travel and subsequent return to Earth, but nations exercise the same jurisdiction and control over space craft and personnel as on Earth.

8. Nations must confer before doing anything in space that might harm the Earth or interfere with the activities of another nation in space.

9. All space facilities, space vehicles, and space equipment in space are open to inspection on grounds of reciprocity and reasonable notice.

The 1967 Treaty of Principles might seem at first glance to offer an umbrella to cover the potential of military implications of the SPS system. But the Treaty wording has a looseness and ambiguous nature that leads to a wide variety of interpretations.

The USA has signed three other treaties since the 1967 Treaty of Principles. These three develop concepts from the Treaty of Principles into specific international law. The rescue and return of space personnel and equipment was formalized in a 1968 agreement. The 1972 International Liability Convention established the concept of "absolute liability," requiring the launching nation to pay for damage caused by its space craft on the Earth's surface. If the damage is done in space or to another space craft, the launching state is liable only if the damage is due to its fault or the fault of persons for whom it is responsible. The 1976 Registration Convention provides a mechanism for nations to register a space object. If an SPS unit is on the USA registry, then the laws of the USA apply to it and the courts of the United States have jurisdiction over it and over all events that transpire within it. A registered space object is also subject to all applicable national laws, including tax and patent laws.

None of the international treaties now in effect provide any sort of safeguard against SPS military threats or protection of SPS military vulnerabilities. The United Nations Moon Treaty might totally eliminate both the military threat and the military vulnerability of the SPS system by making it impossible to construct and operate the SPS system in the first place . . . which means that the world will be shortchanged in the amount of several hundred gigawatts of energy or more that it will desperately need in the coming decades.

So treaties and other forms of international agreements such as a *memoire*, a *proposal*, a *note verbal*, or a *proces-verbal* will need to be negotiated as a form of institutional safeguard.

The question then arises: which should be done first, the SPS system or the treaties? This is a legitimate question because if one were to attempt to draft a suitable treaty to reduce the SPS military threats and vulnerabilities presently conceived and foreseen, the treaty might be and probably would be meaningless within a decade. The reason is that the treaty must be based on the reality of the technology used, not upon even a good forecast of that technology. The construction and operation of the SPS system cannot be put off until more experience in the operation of large space systems is gained because the SPS will probably be the only system of its kind. We're dealing with a unique system in terms of the size of the undertaking, the potential of the military implications that can be estimated in advance, and the extremely limited analogs from which we can draw experience. The answer to the question of which comes first, the system or the safeguards, might seem at first to be a Catch-22 situation. However, it can be kept from becoming a chicken-or-egg matter *if* there is an awareness of the military implications and a willingness to negotiate the safeguards as a series of improving and expanding international agreements as the program progresses. No single international agreement could be drawn at this time that would satisfactorily reduce the military implications.

Another question inevitably arises: Why bother? There are military systems deployed in space as of 1981. There seems to be very little public concern about the threats posed by such systems. Even military managers and planners appear to be worrying very little about the situation today. Military space systems deployed today are primarily supportive in nature—C-cubed-I. The ones that can probably be deployed in the next decade seem to pose no real threats. We've learned to live with MAD and with ICBM's staring down the backs of everybody's necks, and Soviet cosmonauts haven't zapped Akron or Yakima with bolts of lightning like gods on high as everybody feared they might in 1961. Conversion of today's commercial space systems to military use is unlikely since such an effort would not only take time—which might not be available in the next general war—and since such conversions offer no significant improvements over existing military systems that would make the cost and effort worthwhile. Other nations will not seize these systems because they can't. Why worry?

This question fails to consider the enormous difference in scale between current military space systems and the SPS.

And it fails to recognize the march of technology. Twenty years ago, the two most technologically advanced nations in the world had to stretch their technology to the limit to merely place an unmanned satellite in orbit. The USSR managed to do it first with big satellites because they had developed the first ICBM, the Korolev R-7 *Semyorka*. Less than a quarter of a century later, five more nations had developed their own launch vehicles and orbited their own satellites with these vehicles; four more nations, using launch vehicles purchased from space nations or based upon such vehicles, had orbited their own satellites. By the year 2000, less than twenty years from now and closer in time to us than *Sputnik-I*, it will be well within the technical capabilities of Western Europe, Japan, and the People's Republic of China to launch manned space craft into orbit.

We based our discussion on the scenario wherein the United States unilaterally constructs and deploys the SPS system. This scenario leads to the very strong possibility that international multi-partite negotiations will not result from

US initiatives. They will come instead in response to foreign
initiatives taken within the United Nations and within such
international bodies as the International Telecommunications
Union. Indeed, the ITU's World Administrative Radio Con-
ference in 1979 recognized the potential feasibility of the SPS
system and recommended a study of all aspects of the effects
of SPS power beam transmissions on radio communications
services as well as the ecological and biological implications
(which now we understand to be minimal).

Fortunately, we've been down a similar road before and
can undertake a search for institutional safeguards through
international law by studying the case history of communications satellites. Here, the United States formed a corporation,
the Communications Satellite Corporation (COMSAT) and
authorized it to act on behalf of the USA in implementing
international agreements concerning space communications,
the INTELSAT connection. Communications has been
strictly controlled under international law for decades, and
there is a web of international treaties and other agreements
by which the United States is bound. And although there are
military implications inherent in radio communications, the
USA has managed to work within the international community to properly control international telecommunications
while at the same time permitting private enterprise to make
maximum use of the technology.

International agreements within the existing scope of international law provide one approach to adopting institutional safeguards. There are others.

CHAPTER FOURTEEN

No agreement has any real teeth unless there are provisions to insure that the parties concerned do what they said they would in the agreement. Therefore, no international agreement is ever an absolute assurance against military threats and vulnerabilities.

The only reason why it's possible to rationally consider something like the Strategic Arms Limitations Treaties (SALT) is that both parties to the agreement have means for independently monitoring the military activities of the other through surveillance satellites. The technology of surveillance satellites has gone far beyond the capability to achieve very high optical resolution—good enough, some reports say, that it's possible to kibitz on a card game from 200 kilometers up in LEO. Today, surveillance satellites carry detectors so sensitive and sophisticated that it's possible to determine whether there's an ICBM housed in a given covered silo launcher or whether the silo houses a dummy; the dummy must be as large and complex as the real ICBM.

Today, it's possible to use computer analysis of the radar return from a space vehicle being tracked by Earth-based radars and to determine from the characteristics of that return signal the size and the shape of the satellite.

The technology of remote sensing has therefore come a long ways.

While it's entirely possible that the technology of remote sensing may develop into a suitable safeguard against military threats of the SPS system, it still amounts to a question of the reliability of the hardware and the believability of the data. Sensors can be designed only to sense those signals which are expected. There are no assurances against the deployment of new technology by the adversary.

In short, we've seen that there are no sure-fire technologi-

cal safeguards and no institutional safeguards based on international law that will reduce or eliminate the military threats
and vulnerabilities of the SPS system.

Therefore, in order to protect the huge investment of time,
money, and effort, whoever deploys the SPS system will
insist on deploying a military capability to defend it because
it cannot help but have a perceived military threat and therefore possess a military vulnerability. It must be capable of
being defended if attacked.

But this tends to exacerbate the problem. How can those
parties who fear the perceived military threat of the SPS
system be assured that the defensive capabilities aren't really
offensive?

What's needed is some manner of on-site inspection by
properly equipped and trained people who will verify that the
military defense systems deployed on in the SPS system are
truly defensive in nature.

It was stated earlier that new technologies and new energy
resources usually create or permit the creation of new social
institutions, especially those institutions which can exercise
some control over the military uses of the energy. The SPS
system will not only require the development of some new
social institutions to finance and manage the enterprise, but
also the development of a totally new institution to assure that
space power is not used to the military advantage of those
who operate the system.

It's obvious that what's needed is some sort of non-
partisan, non-aligned, international inspection organization.
We'll call it the International Space Inspection Group (ISIG).

Before such a new institution can be dismissed out of hand
as being impractical, we must look at what ISIG is designed
to do, how it could be organized and financed, and how it
could operate. Although there is no precedent in international
law or relations for such a supra-national organization,
perhaps the potential benefits of the SPS system are so great
and the military implications so severe that the problems can
be worked out.

The principal function of ISIG would be to provide interna-

tionally acceptable assurance to all nations that the SPS
system is not being used as a threatening military weapon,
that it's not being converted into such a weapon, that its
defensive weapons systems are indeed for self-protection,
and that none of its elements is being used to support offensive military systems in space. Naturally, the electric power
delivered to the rectenna can't be monitored and would not be
expected to be used solely for non-military purposes any
more than the power output of an Earth-based generating
plant.

Basically, ISIG amounts to a manned insurance policy in
the form of a novel social institution.

In order to effectively perform its intended functions, ISIG
must at all times be both *effective* and *trustworthy* in the eyes
of the international community. To be effective, ISIG must
be able to operate as intended even in the face of political,
economic, or physical coercion. To be trustworthy, its activities must be carried out in the open and above suspicion
and its reports must be available openly to everyone.

ISIG must therefore be free of dominance or undue influence by any vested interest nations, groups of nations, international organizations, and even the owners and managers of
the SPS system itself.

Several problems exist in organizing and managing ISIG
in order to achieve this goal.

The first of these is the problem of independence.

Regardless of the organizations that finance and manage
the SPS system, the ISIG must be acceptable to these organizations. Although the SPS system personnel may in some
instances tend to treat ISIG personnel as necessary evils,
there must be an arrangement between SPS management and
ISIG that will permit free access of ISIG personnel to any part
of the SPS system at any time with due regard, of course, to
the safety of both personnel and equipment of both organizations. Open inspection rights are part of the 1967 Treaty of
Principles which is, however, a consensus by a multinational
committee and is not yet an integral part of international law.

ISIG must also be acceptable and believable to the political and military leaders of the nations of the world and to the general public in those nations where public perception and reaction forms a part of the governing process. Since ISIG cannot show the slightest hint of conflict of interest, it cannot be organized and staffed by the owners/managers of the SPS system.

Nor can it be organized and staffed by any government or organization that can exert any form of political, economic, or ideological leverage on ISIG. This means that it could not and should not be organized and administered as part of the United Nations, where it would be subjected to possible superpower veto action in the UN Security Council or to the crippling effects of power struggles between political blocs that are so endemic to UN activities.

However, although independent of UN control, ISIG *must* be in constant liaison and communication with the UN Secretariat.

To maintain its effectiveness, ISIG must be able to report potentially threatening activities on a worldwide basis. ISIG must therefore possess its own communications systems which must be, to all intents and purposes, non-jammable and non-interrupted. Interruptions or electronic warfare against the ISIG communications systems must be viewed as an aggressive act, and ISIG must have the capabilities to detect the source of such interference and the means to report it to the world. ISIG communications system will be used for its own internal secure communications as well as for communications with world leaders, world news media, and even the general public through existing communications networks. Communications is an important and essential element in ISIG effectiveness, and the independence of these communications must be established in such a way that any interference constitutes grounds for suspicion of whatever organization perpetrates the interference.

Because the functions of the ISIG must be solely those of observing and reporting, it is probably advisable that ISIG personnel and space vehicles not only be *unarmed* but incapable of carrying or operating any sort of weapon, even in self-defense. This is only one of the highly debatable issues surrounding ISIG, but it should be pointed out that unarmed police organizations do exist and are very effective. Domestic police officers in the United Kingdom are unarmed, but their effectiveness is certainly comparable to that of the armed policemen of other nations. (This issue is complicated by major differences in social attitudes, history, and cultural factors as well.) The only weapon of ISIG is instant, believable, and effective worldwide communication.

Because ISIG must be apolitical, independent, and pannational in order to eliminate conflict of interest and maintain trust, its organization must be designed for immunity to bribes, both monetary and ideological. It must therefore be a tightly organized and highly motivated organization with high *espirit de corps*, dedication, discipline, pride, and a set of unique, developing traditions that set it apart from other social institutions. These characteristics are typical of paramilitary organizations, and ISIG should therefore be considered in such a light. Similar organizations are already operating, although they may not have paramilitary characteristics. The International Red Cross is one of these. There are also analogs on the commerical level with such industrial security and police forces as Brink's, Pinkerton's, Wells Fargo, and Purolator. However, ISIG has to be a new type of *international inspection agency* and cannot be precisely equated with any existing organization.

ISIG must be developed on a higher social level than any existing organization. This is why it must be considered as a new institution springing from the needs of the new technology of space power.

The final element in ISIG effectiveness and trust is its basic component, its personnel. ISIG personnel must be selected using the best psychological screening technology such as the current human reliability programs proven and used by the USAF Strategic Air Command for bomber crews and ICBM silo launching officers. Training must be strict and demanding. Discipline must be tight. There must be respect for ISIG on the part of its people, respect that is earned and that stems from pride in being one of the highest social institutions yet developed. It must be considered by its people as a life's work. In spite of modern anti-war, anti-authority, and anti-discipline philosophies that appear to dominate the thinking of people in the Western or Free World nations today, dedicated organizations similar to ISIG do exist. Modern psychological theories to the country, it's eminently feasible to form and maintain such an organization today.

How can such an organization as ISIG be formed? There are a number of "umbrella" organizations that might provide the initial roots for ISIG, but each of them presents problems involving the effectiveness and trustworthiness of ISIG under their umbrella.

The UN has already been mentioned. It's probably the first organization that comes to mind as a root for ISIG. However, ISIG as a paramilitary organization is closely analogous to the pan-national UN Security Force originally proposed in 1945. A UN-based ISIG would certainly be saddled with constraints that would impair its effectiveness. Because of its importance in the military sphere, it would certainly be subject to reorganization, restaffing, restructuring, veto of operations, and other restraints by UN member nations or distinct UN power blocs. Such restraints would not only impair ISIG effectiveness but also its trustworthiness, especially if it were perceived to be the tool of any UN power group.

Operation of ISIG under *any* national umbrella is unacceptable. Virtually any existing political group can be ruled out as a potential umbrella organization because of certain perception of military threat by other political bodies. There's one possible exception to this: the sponsorship of ISIG by a nation with a long and established history of neutrality such as Switzerland or Sweden. However, almost every nation on the world has covert ties with some international power group, banking interest, multinational corporation, financial base, monetary system, vested interest, or ideological bloc.

Obviously, operation of ISIG under the umbrella of a multinational, apolitical corporation is unacceptable to a large part of the international scene.

As could be suspected from the start, ISIG is going to have to be a truly independent institution. If operation as part of any existing world organization of any type is unacceptable for one reason or another, how does ISIG get started?

To get a different perspective on ISIG, we must consider the simple question: *Who stands to lose the most should the SPS become a military target because of real or perceived SPS military threat?*

Answer: The people and organizations who have accepted the risk of insuring the system against loss.

Not the least of the basic characteristics of the SPS system is the huge capital investment and the high capital risk not only in building the system initially but in continued operation of the system if it is perceived as a military threat by others and thereby becomes a military target because it is vulnerable.

Regardless of *how* the SPS system is built and operated, the sheer magnitude of the loss will require that the financing organization seek to distribute the risk of loss. No single organization in the world could weather the financial crisis that would result from losing the SPS system it financed or helped to finance. It makes no difference whether the SPS system is financed by private enterprise, a combination of private enterprise and government, a government, or an international consortium of governments and private enterprise. The risk of loss of the SPS system is too great to consider. Therefore, the various elements of the SPS system will be heavily insured against loss just as large terrestrial power stations are today.

Granted, the sort of insurance obtained and the institutions through which it is obtained to share the risk of loss will probably be different. There is no single insurance company or association, including Lloyd's of London associates, capable of underwriting the potential loss.

Whoever underwrites the insurance of the SPS system against loss will require the institutional safeguard inherent in the ISIG concept.

And of all the potential umbrella organizations, the most internationally uncommitted, apolitical, and pan-national is the insurance group.

It might seem that this argument does not hold true for the socialist nations of the world such as the USSR and the PRC in which the political group owns everything and insures itself. Basically, however, the socialist nations must be looked upon as super-paternalistic national proprietorship companies possessing super "goon squads" that are their military forces ready to back up their company policy decisions with physical force if necessary. However, the question regarding the willingness of the USSR and the PRC to permit access to their space facilities by ISIG is unanswerable at this time. Much depends upon the degree to which either nation becomes involved in its own SPS system, the extent of its SPS system, and the degree of co-operation that happens to exist between it and the remainder of the world at the time. It's often difficult to forecast future developments in the socio-economic and political area of international affairs because leadership changes in all countries and international policies are often quite opportunistic. To some degree, both the USSR and the PRC have been co-operative, at least on tacit basis, to satellite surveillance and sensing. If their leaders perceive an advantage to be gained by co-operation, they have co-operated in the past. Thus, the ISIG must be organized and set up with the participation of these questionable nations and, in fact, with the full co-operation and participation of *any* nation that so wishes.

Since ISIG amounts to a manned insurance policy, who pays the premium? Shall the costs be borne by the users and customers, by the SPS system owners, by national governments whose concern over the military threat is reduced by the operations of ISIG, or by the United Nations? Here again, the organization that pays the bills usually has strings attached to the money. "He who has the gold rules." Just as the basic organization of ISIG must be as independent as possible, so the financial support of ISIG must be similarly arranged.

If risk-sharing institutions are the roots for ISIG, they'll consider the operation of ISIG as part of their operational costs and will therefore see to it that ISIG is suitably funded to remain as effective as possible. If, on the other hand, ISIG is not part of the assurance group and is set up and operates as an independent international institution like the International Red Cross, the insuring organizations may *require* that the SPS system owners contract with ISIG to provide inspection and reporting services for the insurors and, because of the importance of the perceived military aspects, to the world as well. Eventually, regardless of operational procedures, the costs of ISIG will be passed along to the users and customers of SPS services in concert with current practices in similar industries.

In spite of the difficulties in establishing ISIG and maintaining both its effectiveness and trustworthiness, and in spite of the fact that there are enormous inherent difficulties in establishing such a new international institution, these problems are probably far less serious and much easier to solve than those associated with any other program for internationalizing the SPS system. Even nations that are ideologically opposed to the USA, to the SPS system, or even to a great degree of international co-operation, have a very strong interest in seeing to it that the SPS system does not become a real military threat to themselves. Something like the ISIG will become a reality because there is no other way.

How should ISIG operate and how many people will it require?

Ideally, the ISIG inspection program should consist of two elements. One of these is a resident inspection team on each power satellite, in both LEO Base and GEO Base, and at the launch site. The other is several spot inspection teams which are free-roaming units not based at any specific location.

An ISIG resident inspection team would consist of four to six ISIG personnel (or more, depending upon a more detailed analysis of the inspection power required based on a large number of factors) at each power satellite. More people would be required on the resident inspection teams at LEO Base and GEO Base. More than a thousand would be required at the launch sites to monitor personnel and cargo payloads. However, the critical inspection team is the one located at each power satellite. Here, a minimum of four ISIG inspectors can do the job. This is enough for one inspector on each eight-hour shift plus a supervisor who can step in in case of the absence of another team member.

The ISIG team would live with the operations crew aboard the SPS and would have its own dedicated and secure communications channel to ISIG headquarters. They would not operate on any scheduled inspection routine but would inspect and observe on a highly random basis. SPS operating personnel wouldn't know from one shift to the next what the ISIG team would be looking for, where they would look, or how they would look.

Much of the ISIG team's equipment would be highly automated to provide an alarm in case of any change. For example, should some military hardware be attached out in the girders of the photovoltaic array, the mass and moments of inertia of the SPS would change. This would make the attitude control system perform differently and require different burns on the attitude control thrusters, creating a computer-detectable change in the overall system.

Basically, the ISIG team would look for *changes* that would indicate that the SPS was being modified. This presupposes that the SPS unit is on line; during the construction phase, ISIG would have to closely monitor the design of each SPS component and sub-system to insure its non-military function or potential.

The ISIG teams would be changed, rotated, and mixed at short and irregular intervals. They wouldn't remain in the same SPS unit, and inspectors wouldn't remain with the same team for any long period of time. This is to prevent inspectors from forging friendships, arrangements with SPS personnel that might result in conflict of interest or abrogation of the function of ISIG. It also prevents any team from growing too comfortable with its members and therefore becoming complacent. Frequent changes also enable individual inspectors to get to know the entire SPS system and to be able to spot any change made in any part of it.

Leaves and R&R would be frequent and would be taken in dedicated ISIG recreational facilities on Earth among other ISIG personnel. The objective of this is to maintain close contact at all times with the highly dedicated members of ISIG and a minimum of regular contact with other non-ISIG people. This would act to prevent the same sort of conflict of interest situations as long periods of service in an individual facility would produce.

No inspection team can be perfect, however. And there is always the question, *Quis custodiet ipsos custodes?* (Who shall watch those self-same watchmen?) This problem is addressed by the spot inspection teams.

An ISIG spot inspection team would function to check up on both the SPS system personnel and facilities as well as the resident inspection teams. The spot inspectors would make unannounced and irregular visits to facilities. There would be no advance announcement of their schedule nor of their inspection procedure. No one, not even the resident inspection team in a facility, would know what to expect, when to expect it, or what the spot inspectors would be looking for, or how long the spot inspectors would be there. The only thing known about the spot inspection teams is that they'll show up, probably when least expected.

The spot inspection team concept presupposes that ISIG would have its own space transportation system as well as its own communications network. Without its own transportation system ISIG would become subject to the whims of those who control the SPS space transportation system. There can be no instance in which a spot inspection team can be denied transportation because of scheduling, payload restrictions, unavailability of space craft, etc. This sort of thing could happen even if ISIG had absolute priority over SPS passengers in the regular space transportation system.

The ISIG space transportation system is also essential to provide logistical support for the resident inspection teams, especially with regard to life support consumables. Each inspection team must have its own stand-by life support system that can sustain it in emergency because team reliance upon SPS life support systems could place a team in a difficult if not untenable situation in a crisis or emergency.

The ISIG communications system is the key, critical element in the inspection philosophy. This communications system must not only be secure but also contain fail-safe elements. For example, coded or encrypted reports must be made at irregular but scheduled times by each resident inspection team. Failure of a team to report as scheduled and in the cipher or with the pass words expected would be cause for immediate suspicion, communication of the fact from ISIG headquarters to SPS headquarters, a report to world leaders, and a prompt inspection visit by a large spot inspection team.

Some ISIG communications would be made ''in the clear'' while others would be made on secure, scrambled channels. SPS operation personnel and especially world military personnel must not know what ISIG is doing at all times. A secure channel to ISIG headquarters is necessary to handle potentially dangerous situations in which ISIG command would be able to work quietly with SPS management to clarify or rectify a perceived problem without bringing it to the full attention of others.

ISIG will amount to a drop in the bucket in terms of personnel and facilities required in comparison to the SPS system. Assuming a full-blown SPS system in operation with thirty SPS units on line, some 15,000 SPS personnel will be required, including more than 1,400 in space at any given time. Only 718 ISIG people would be in space at any given time out of a total of 1,200 ISIG personnel.

An international Space Inspection Group organized somewhat along the lines we've discussed would do a great deal to solve the problem of military use of space power. The big question that now remains is: Can something like the

ISIG be organized and operated? And another question arises from this: What are some of the logical consequences of introducing an ISIG organization into the space power equation?

CHAPTER FIFTEEN

It's obvious to anyone who knows anything at all about international relations, current events, and the intense feelings of nationalism rampant today that there are a lot of problems associated with putting an organization such as the International Space Inspection Group (ISIG) into operation. Even though it seems that such an inspection group would be a new social institution that might go a long ways toward eliminating most of the fears of the military implications of the SPS system, the inherent "newness" of the ISIG concept is a barrier to its acceptance. And there are fears that participation in any international treaty concerning an ISIG—and it would take an international treaty to implement it completely—might seriously jeopardize a nation's sovereignty.

National sovereignty is a strange animal which has its deep roots in national security—or insecurity, as the case may be—and a natural desire for self-defense. It also has its roots in the Atilla Syndrome which historically has caused many a stable, peace-loving, secure nation to suddenly begin reaching out to take the lands, property, and people of its neighbors. Often the Atilla Syndrome results from hard times at home—a shortage of land, food, raw materials, etc.

But just as often the Atilla Syndrome results from good times. The Harvard mathematician and satirical songster Tom Lehrer once spotted the reason why in his song, "In Old Mexico," a parody recorded in 1959. In it, he sings that the crowd at the bull fight was "hoping that death would brighten an otherwise dull afternoon." When times are good and life is easy, people become bored. When people become bored, they go looking for excitement, and what is more exciting than a rousing war that starts the adrenalin flowing and promises the fun of unrestrained looting and raping?

National sovereignty was a relatively innocuous principle to which national groups held firmly because they *knew* that their next door neighbors would someday come pouring across the border again in spite of the fact that the king's daughter had married the prince amidst the pomp and ceremony of finalizing a solemn peace treaty between the two nations. Forever is a long time, and the neighbors had broken treaties before when it suited them. The old story tellers sitting around the marketplace still spun horror tales of what had happened and how the neighbors had committed unforgivable and unforgettable crimes. *Lest we forget* was a basis as well for national sovereignty.

The principle of national sovereignty was discarded among the thirteen United States of America upon adoption of the Constitution on September 17, 1787 and its final ratification on September 13, 1788. To "form a more perfect union, establish justice, insure domestic tranquility, provide for the common defense, promote the general welfare, and secure the blessings of liberty," the former separate British colonies did something unprecedented in the annals of history: they gave up a major portion of their sovereign state powers. Mind you, the individual States still maintain their own military forces in the form of the state militias. Many of them, even in 1981, have sealed their borders; try to get into Arizona with an orange or grapefruit grown in Florida. Many of the trappings of national sovereignty so jealously grasped by other nations in the world are still retained, albeit often in atrophied form, by the individual States. In spite of it all, the relinquishment of a portion of the individual States' sovereignty to the federal government did accomplish the goals set forth in the Preamble to the Constitution. The idea of North Dakota going to war with South Dakota over *anything* simply doesn't occur to the state governments. And it isn't because the federal government is constantly looking over their shoulders. This is not to say that there aren't serious problems between many states, but they get solved without the impediment (to Americans) of sovereign rights of states getting in the way. Our forefathers fought a very bloody war to straighten that out, and even the War Between the States or the Civil War (depends on where you live as to what it's called) was not fought between the States, but between the United States of America and the Confederate States of America.

But the principle of national sovereignty became in reality a rather obsolete concept in August 1957, when both the United States and the Soviet Union possessed thermonuclear weapons and the means to deliver them anywhere in the world. National sovereignty *had* to be dumped, and the crippled United Nations was the only international institution in which such careful maneuvering and careful reduction of the principles of national sovereignty could take place.

Getting nations to sit down and give up a little more of their national sovereignty when it comes to a Solar Power Satellite system may be a difficult task, particularly when they hate each other with a passion bred from centuries of being at one another's throats in a world of scarcity. But it may be possible if approached correctly and if every nation is aware that there's more to be gained by doing it this way.

Obviously, although a beginning has been made in international law, there's a long way to go in order to achieve agreement and acceptance of such a new and potentially controversial abrogation of sovereignity as ISIG with its apolitical and pan-national organization.

The first step toward an ISIG has already been taken in the 1967 Outer Space Treaty. Article XII of that treaty states:

"All stations, installations, equipment, and space vehicles on the moon and other celestial bodies shall be open to representatives of other States Parties to the Treaty on a basis of reciprocity. Such representatives shall give reasonable advance notice of a projected visit, in order that appropriate consultations may be held and that maximum precautions may be taken to assure safety and to avoid interference with normal operations in the facility to be visited."

However, the 1967 Treaty says nothing about stations, installations, equipment, and space vehicles *in space*, only on a celestial body. Furthermore, advance notice is required.

The important aspect of the Article is the reciprocity statement. If Lower Slobbovia doesn't have any space facilities, technically under the precise wording of the Treaty it cannot reciprocate and is therefore excluded from being able to request inspection rights. The question of the *ability* of Lower Slobbovia to make such a space inspection is also left up in the air because, until space travel becomes commonplace, they may have to use another nation's spacefaring capability to make their inspection.

And if the concept of inspection isn't internationally controversial, it's certainly controversial in the United States! The recent UN Moon Treaty (known also by its full title, "Agreement Governing Activities of States on the Moon and Other Celestial Bodies") is not only controversial because of the possiblity it will restrict the activities of private enterprise in space, but is also drawing fire because of the provisions that would expand beyond the scope of the 1967 Outer Space Treaty the rights of foreign governments to inspect US space facilities. The draft position paper of the Los Angeles Section of the American Institute of Aeronautics and Astronautics, the primary US professional aerospace society and the US representative to the International Astronautical Federation, attacked this inspection provision harshly:

"In the interest of verification, the treaty allows any State Party to inspect all facilities in space, whether the facilities are owned by a nation, corporation or individual. While some form of verification is desirable, this provision makes legal the unrestricted searches of private residences as well as government facilities. These are intolerable infringements of human rights."

So is a war.

Others have pointed out that unrestricted inspection is contrary to the basic principles of freedom ingrained in American political philosophy as a result of the United States Constitution.

There is practically nothing in international law that relates to a supra-national organization entrusted with inspection of domestic operations. There is no *precedent*. And when there is no precedent, lawyers, legislators, and diplomats proceed with great trepidation and concern over the consequences of their decisions and actions.

However, assuming that the United States undertakes the unilateral construction and operation of the SPS system, some manner of workable inspection activity *must* be arrvied at in order to reduce the risk of the SPS military threat and thereby reduce the military vulnerability and the risk. Otherwise, the bankers and financiers won't back it. And no insurance company or consortium would touch it. Even the federal government couldn't cover the risk by insuring it as it does for savings accounts and home mortgages through quasi-corporate government organizations such as FDIC, FSLIC, and FHA. And the government can't provide insurance in the form of military defense because other nations would look up such an action as proof of the military threat of the SPS system.

It looks like a "catch-22" activity.

If the SPS system construction and operation is undertaken by any sort of international consortium, the same logic holds true.

If the USA waffles, stalls, and eventually opts out of the SPS program in favor of development of other renewable energy sources—and there are very few of them with the potential of the SPS—and if another nation or group of nations undertakes the program, the United States is certainly going to want some sort of inspection arrangement to reassure its own military and political leaders . . . especially if the USSR or the PRC is involved in the system.

One way or another, ISIG or something like it appears to be the way to go. We must try to work out the knotty problems associated with it. An internationally trustworthy inspection arrangement is necessary, and the trustworthiness of the institution involved rests on the inclusion of personnel from every nation desiring such an inspection program. If the SPS system is perceived as a military threat—and it definitely possesses that perception today among most people and many Third World nations—the motivation to develop ISIG may be strong enough to overcome the many obstacles standing in its path.

Military space power is too dangerous to the health and welfare of people everywhere to proceed into it without some strong and reliable safeguards above and beyond international conventions, treaties, and other agreements which may or may not work. We must have something with a higher reliability than the historic record of treaties reveals.

And if we construct and operate an SPS system under the inspecting eye of ISIG, we obtain *all* of the enormous advantages of the SPS system—a large space transportation system that opens the Solar System for science, industrial use, habitation, and development of extraterrestial resources; an end to use of non-renewable terrestrial energy sources, abundant energy available on a worldwide basis for building new social institutions and permitting have-not nations to pull themselves up with the excess energy; a relocation of heavy, high-pollution industries into space and a subsequent start toward completely rebuilding the terrestrial environment to our liking; and creation of new jobs and hope for the future around the world.

We also have the potential for ending the MAD doctrine of mutual military terror and instituting the first true worldwide arms control measures that we've ever had.

We mentioned earlier that one of the military implications of the SPS system would be its ability to provide copious amounts of power for space-based directed energy weapons, primarily high-energy lasers.

The SPS system will be in geosynchronous orbit where almost half the Earth can be viewed. Anything that is launched off the Earth below at the bottom of that deep gravity well will be detectable from GEO.

ICBM's launched from *anywhere* on Earth to targets anywhere else on Earth are readily detectable even today by the infra-red and radio frequency signatures as they're launched and as they rise above the upper limits of the Earth's sensible atmosphere in their trajectories. This ICBM detection is carried out by unmanned satellites carrying sensors of great sensitivity.

We have seen that directed energy weapons such as HEL's are not particularly effective against Earth targets when activated from GEO.

But according to some of the latest unclassified literature, it would be possible to target, hit, and destroy ICBM's in extra-atmospheric phases of their flight with HEL's at geosynchronous orbital altitudes provided there was adequate power for such HEL's.

Therefore, the best place to deploy an effective anti-ballistic missile (ABM) defense would be in orbit.

However, a unilateral national ABM defense system in space would not be tolerated by other nations. The ABM defense system would become an immediate military target of ASAT missiles launched from the ground and of killer satellites orbiting with the ABM defense system.

A space-based ABM defense system becomes feasible *only* if (a) both sides deploy their systems at the same time, or (b) both sides permit an international ABM defense system to be deployed. At first glance the latter appears to be a totally impossible achievement.

It isn't necessarily impossible.

If, under international agreement, the pan-national ISIG were given control over both a self-defense capability mounted on the SPS units *and* modifications of that self-defense capability which would amount to an effective ABM defense, it could become possible.

The scenario would proceed as follows:

First, the SPS system is constructed and put into operation with ISIG monitoring all construction and operations to insure that there is no weapon capability associated with the power satellites. Thus, the SPS system itself is constructed and deployed without the stigma of military threat and the associated military vulnerability issues. The capital risk would be reduced to the point where it involved only minor hazard risk since technological risk would have been practically eliminated during the earlier R&D phase.

This would be followed by the controlled installation of HEL weapon systems not only for self-defense of the SPS system but also for ABM purposes. The HEL weapon system would be installed by ISIG but would not be under the control of ISIG. Controlled installation means that the HEL weaponry cannot be activated unilaterally. ISIG could not use the ABM system until the rest of the arrangement is carried through. The HEL weapons system isn't active until multiple switches are thrown at several locations at mutually agreed upon times and conditions by national interests involved. This means that any ABM capability cannot go into action unless all concerned on the Earth below agree at the same time to turn the ABM capability over to the ISIG.

Once activated, even the ABM capability is subject to multiple switch controls within ISIG itself. This means multiple switching on the SPS satellites themselves with two-person isolated weapon crews, each person with their own switch and operating under the "no lone zone" philosophy that's been developed in the United States for effective strategic weapon control.

It doesn't take much ABM beam weapon capability in GEO to counter the most massive ICBM strike and thermonuclear exchange anticpated in the next fity years: that between the USA and the USSR. The USSR has three major missile launch fields. The USA has three. This means that the simultaneous launch of 1000 ICBM's from, say, the USSR toward targets in the USA must, by the very nature of ICBM's and their need to follow the rules of celestial mechanics, cause 1000 ICBM's to pass through three "windows" or "key holes" in space on their way to their targets. Since each warhead will probably be MIRV'ed with five to ten smaller warheads, this means 5000 to 10,000 entry bodies passing through three key holes almost simultaneously. This turns them into beautiful targets for ABM beam weapons whose energy beams travel at the speed of light.

Submarine-launched ICBM's are not subject to this key hole in the sky restraint, but they must still pass through space on their way to definite targets; they can be detected and hit with HEL beams in space.

Any ICBM exchange between any two nations can be detected and the ISIG ABM defense system activated because ISIG will have personnel and equipment installed in every SPS unit . . . and the SPS units will eventually ring the Earth in geosynchronous orbit.

Once ISIG has international ABM capability in the SPS system, negotiations can begin on Earth between the major powers concerning true strategic arms and weapons control: the dismantling of the ICBM forces which pose the most serious international military threat and the most difficult arms control problem.

Many people will react by claiming this scenario is totally impossible, that no nation would give up the sovereign right of its own defense by dismantling the only defense it has against ICBM attack: ICBM counter-strike. True, it's possible *only* if all nations with ICBM strike capabilities agree to the activation of an ABM defense *at the same instant of time* so there is no possibility of open ICBM attack during an interim period.

Many people will also react negatively against such an international group as ISIG exercising ABM control as well as operation of the self-defense weapon system of the SPS system.

But what control does the ISIG have?

What threat does the ISIG pose that is greater than the threats its presence eliminates?

And does ISIG control of a space-based ABM defense system really mean that any nation must give up any real measure of national sovereignty?

No matter how powerful the directed energy weapons mounted on SPS units in GEO are, they are ineffective against Earth targets. Review Table VI where the various space-to-Earth military threats are listed in detail.

HEL(CW) weapons are impractical when based in GEO. It

would take a *very* large HEL(CW) to be effective against terrestrial targets from geosynchronous orbit. The range is too great for any HEL weapon that can be imagined or forecast under the principles of physics. Technology has nothing to do with it, but the physical limitations of the universe do. Any HEL weapon in geosynchronous orbit capable of producing any extensive destruction on the Earth's surface would be very large, require the output of several SPS units, take a long time to build, be very expensive, and be very, very obvious to everyone. There are simpler and cheaper weapons systems and military actions that could do the same job, all of them Earth-based and using conventional weapons technology.

In any event, if ISIG is under the umbrella of the insurance consortium, any actions taken by ISIG to increase the military vulnerability of the SPS system would be subject to leverage from those who stand to lose a great deal if the SPS system becomes involved in military actions.

Other direct energy weapons are subject to the same restraints of the universe. HEL(P) weapons are most probably infeasible when deployed in GEO because of the distances involved. Particle beam weapons using neutral hydrogen, H+, electron, neutron, or gamma ray beams cannot be used in the space-to-Earth mode because the interaction of the beams with the Earth's atmosphere destroys any possibility of the beams being destructive in nature by the time they reach the Earth's surface.

Other space weapons systems such as projectiles and entry bodies are not under control of ISIG. Only the directed energy weapons mounted directly on the SPS units are controlled by ISIG and used for self defense and ABM counter-force.

There is no military threat to Earth targets from directed energy weapons in the hands of ISIG on the SPS units in geosynchronous orbit.

There remains, however, the space military potential of using projectile weapons against Earth targets. But if those projectiles do not carry thermonuclear warheads, they will have strictly limited destructive power. At this time, no nation can deploy weapons of mass destruction—nuclear or thermonuclear weapons—in space under the provisions of the United Nations treaties. The capability of ISIG and national military forces in space to detect, track, and monitor projectile weapons and their launch facilities is something beyond the consideration of the military capabilities of the SPS system.

What about a scenario in which ISIG leaders attempt to take over the world by seizing SPS units, denying power, and threatening to destroy space vehicles? The counter to this is twofold: (a) proper personnel selection, screening, training, and constant re-screening, and (b) to put ISIG headquarters perhaps at several places on Earth where it becomes vulnerable to conventional military action.

In this basic concept, something such as ISIG—unarmed except for multiple switch control of directed beam weapons on the SPS units for self defense and ABM defense, and with a purpose to reduce the military implications of the SPS system—should pose no inherent threat to the sovereignty of any nation or group of nations whose basic interests involve peace.

Only the Atillas of the world, the men on horseback, those who are interested in the classic, historic power over people, only those types will oppose such a concept.

ISIG or the control of the space power of an SPS-mounted ABM defense sytem destroys no national sovereignty. It does not take a nation's defense out of its own hands. It merely destroys the military counterstrike doctrine of defense, the MAD philosophy.

If nobody can successfully bring off an ICBM strike because of international ABM defense in space, nobody need worry about an ICBM strike any more.

Bomber forces, cruise missiles, naval forces, and all other military forces on the ground and in the air are left intact for national defense. All passive military space systems used for reconnaissance, surveillance, communications, command, control, and intelligence gathering are left intact for national defense.

But we will have removed a fifty-year threat that could lead to enormous levels of destruction and mass murder measured in megadeaths.

Robert A. Heinlein once put the following words into the mouth of his fictional space entrepreneur, Delos D. Harriman ("The Man Who Sold the Moon," Shasta Publishers, Chicago, 1950, page 189): "Damnation, nationalism should stop at the stratosphere."

Unfortunately, it hasn't. Military systems have already been deployed in space. To date there has been no serious concern because these have been passive military systems incapable of offensive activities.

Constructing and operating a solar power satellite system in space opens up the real potential for building an offensive military capability in space, especially in terms of the capability for building and providing power for high-energy laser weapons in near-Earth orbit for attacking specific ground targets (thereby dodging the provisions of the UN treaties prohibiting the deployment of weapons of mass destruction in orbit and on celestial bodies).

Down the line as the SPS system develops and expands to use extraterrestrial materials for its construction, and as heavy industry begins to move into space to use these extraterrestrial raw materials, there is the even greater military threat of utilization of mass drivers and space catapults to discharge projectiles as weapons against Earth targets.

To counter these basic military threats from space and to eliminate the ICBM strike as the dilemma it now is, we must consider in advance not only realistic international agreements to nullify the immediate military implications of the SPS system during its critical period of construction and initial operation, but we must also put into action some manner of pan-national guardian force, a human safeguard, in the form of something like the proposed ISIG.

The consequences are manifold. It will eliminate most of

the perceived and real military threats and vulnerabilities of the SPS system. It will permit financial investment without concern that the capital equipment will be blown out of the sky because it's thought to be a weapon system. It will both instill international confidence in the SPS system and permit a greater degree of international participation in both the benefits of the expanded system that results as well as the safeguards that are put into the system. It will confine nationalism to the Earth and permit us to expand into the Solar System without many of the political and ideological limitations that result from nationalism. It will allow us to eliminate the terror of an ICBM strike and give us a way to dismantle the ICBM systems, which will have become as obsolete in modern warfare as the mounted and armed knight became on the field of Agincourt. We will have, in effect, developed a stirrup that not only gives us an easier way to get into the saddle of space but also permits us to change the course of warfare, perhaps eliminating the doctrines of mass destruction long enough to allow us to survive and to mature as a species.

CHAPTER SIXTEEN

"A half-million years of experience in outwitting beasts on mountains and plains, in heat and cold, in light and darkness, gave our ancestors the equipment that we still desperately need if we are to slay the dragon that roams the earth today, marry the princess of outer space, and live happily ever after in the deer-filled glades of a world in which everyone is young and beautiful forever."

So said Dr. Carleton S. Coon, an anthropologist and author who was perhaps the first man to understand energy and its relationship to our history and our everyday lives.

We have seen what space power really is and how it can work to further the course of human civilization not only on Planet Earth but also throughout the Solar System.

We have seen the encouraging and awesome future that awaits us if we opt for the development of space power. We have also seen—as we see in our daily lives—what a shambles and an eventual holocaust will result from "conservation" and "sacrifice" in our energy future if we do not work out an alternative with at least the energy potential of space power.

We have also seen that space power is a concept with many facets, not all of which are totally consistent at this time because it is so new. Not the least among these facets is an energy rich future in which our high tech culture has the opportunity to expand into a new and endless frontier: space. And a future in which the low tech cultures of the world can find some hope of bettering themselves by a greater availability of energy to satisfy their survival needs with surplus energy left over to permit them to grow.

But if we don't handle space power properly with knowledge of its possible pitfalls before we attempt to gain it, we may be in trouble.

There are admittedly enormous dangers inherent in obtaining space power.

But there are probably greater dangers that are certain to face us if we do not.

There are no scientific barriers standing in the way of obtaining and using space power. All the scientific principles are well known. No great scientific breakthroughs are needed. Scientific breakthroughs would help if they would point to a way to increase the efficiency in any individual element of the proposed SPS system. But they're not needed. Space power can be obtained with the scientific knowledge we have today.

There are no insoluble technical probems involved with obtaining space power. There are some technical questions having to do with efficiencies which affect the final economic realities of space power. There are some technical questions regarding *how* to do some things and *how best* to do others. These questions require solutions that can be obtained in the 1980 decade with the space systems now in existence. We can get the answers. We can determine the best choice among technical options.

There are no untenable biological or environmental risks relating to space power that are known or even suspected. We have been living with high energy radio transmissions for three generations of human beings, no changes in the germ plasm attributable to radio waves have shown up . . . and they *would* show up in three generations if they were real. The biological and environmental risks of *not* opting for space power are far greater if we continue to send carbon-14 and other emissions up the stacks and continue to use fossil fuels whose mining does indeed disturb the local environment.

There is no way to obtain future energy requirements without opting for space power. No matter how long it takes—decades or centuries, depending upon your favorite forecast—the well is going to run dry and there is *no other place in the Solar System* where we know or suspect we will find fossil fuels or anything comparable to them. There is no other energy technology we know of today save fusion power that can supply the amount of energy we need—and we don't know how to build a fusion reactor. We *do* know how to *use* the fusion reactor we've already got, the Sun. And the place to go to use it best is space.

There is a large up-front capital requirement demanded by space power. This is accompanied by very high technical risk in the eyes of potential investors who may believe they can find less-risky technical ventures. Perhaps they can. But, in the long run, it will be those who have the sheer guts to back space power who will be those who profit in the 21st century *or sooner*. The capital resources exist. A mere $80 billion to $100 billion invested over the next twenty years is a drop in the bucket to the normal, every-day capital investment that goes on around us all the time. *Companies in the United States spent that much money in 1979 for pollution control.* We're talking only the gross sales of Exxon Corporation for 1979. Or about 10% of the 1981 federal budget and an even smaller percentage of the USA's Gross National Product. In 1980, there are 568 offshore oil drilling platforms either under construction or planned; the average cost of these units runs approximately $60-million *each* for a total capital investment of over $28-billion. There are currently 461 off shore oil rigs in operation, a capital investment of approximately $25-billion, and the fleet is growing at a rate of 9.8% per year. *Losses* due to accidents amounted to about $550-million. In *one* energy industry alone there is therefore a capital requirement base of $53-billion with a loss risk of better than 1%.

So when we talk about capital investments and risks and losses, we should keep in mind the magnitude of what's already going on around us every day. The large sums of money required to supply energy to the world seem staggering to the individual who has to balance his checkbook and pay bills every month.

A hundred billion dollars *or more* will have to be spent over the next twenty years in any event to provide the additional electrical energy sources to meet projected demand.

The plain fact of the matter is that we gain nothing but a few decades of time if we opt to spend that money solely for the construction of new fossil fuel and nuclear generating plants on Earth.

If we opt for the Solar Power Satellite system, that same capital investment not only buys us energy from a renewable source and eliminates the need to burn valuable, irreplaceable fossil fuels, but it also buys us *space power* with all that space power entails: a large space transportation system, space industrialization, new products from space, raw materials from the Solar System rather than from Mother Earth's bosom, space science and knowledge that is unavailable today, and a whole new frontier for mankind with all that such a thing means in terms of a philosophic outlook on the future.

Furthermore, since space power not only includes power and energy in the strict scientific and technical meaning, but also power in the social meaning, there are realistic scenarios that hold the promise of eliminating the current thermonuclear stalemate, the suicidal philosophy of Mutually Assured Destruction, the strike-counter-strike doctrine.

New international institutions will arise that can help us solve the real problems that keep us from getting along together around the world today.

Space power also permits the Third World to have some hope for the future by giving them the opportunity to participate. *Energy* is what they need to put themselves on the track toward a hopeful future. The SPS is the only way to get that energy to some of them. It will pay off by making the whole world a more secure place for the human race to live.

It can be done.

We can achieve space power with all that it promises.

We are as aware of the problems as of the benefits. We can act in advance to work on the problems to keep them under control.

The United States of America—including its corporations, labor unions, banks, insurance companies, small businesses, credit unions, and other private enterprise institutions—has the capability in terms of the capital resources, the technology, the people, the material resources, the energy, and the historic philosophies and policies to achieve space power.

If it is done by Americans, we have a much better chance of getting space power without the problems associated with its military implications. We are the nation of the Marshall Plan, the country that has provided billions of dollars in foreign aid, assistance, and grants to other less fortunate nations. For over a century, we have never been involved in a war for the purpose of expanding our boundaries or subjugating people to our government. Few people remember that we took Cuba from Spain and gave it back to the Cubans, that we told the Filipinos we would turn their islands back to them and did so, or that we have no military forces stationed today in any foreign land as occupation forces or as colonial peace-keeping units. This cannot be said of other nations in the world at this time.

If others undertake the task, we may not be so fortunate as to be able to solve the military problems of space power.

If the SPS system *can* be achieved on an international level, it would indeed solve many problems. But this possibility appears to be remote today. Where American firms have engaged in international ventures and expended capital and effort, these fruits of money and work have often been seized, appropriated, or nationalized by the Attilas of those lands. American capital and American management tend to be a bit shy about continuing to do this, regardless of the possibilities of short-term payoff.

The only thing that can prevent Americans from achieving space power is other Americans.

There are those in America today whose openly announced goal is to destroy the present economic and political system of the United States.

There are others whose goal—covert or overt—is to take political and economic power into their own hands by destroying or weakening the present system.

There are those who do not understand the culture in which they have been born and raised—a high technology civilization—and who would replace it with a romantic vision of a non-technical utopia in which they would force their philosophy of "small is beautiful" decentralization upon everyone else, whether such a philosophical approach would indeed work or not with technology—they haven't run the economic analyses to find out; they're too lazy or don't know how.

None of them realize the extent and inherent strength of the economic and political power they oppose. And not a one of them understands the ultimate consequences if, by some fluke, they should happen to win.

This doesn't keep them from trying, and they're trying very hard right now.

There is a concerted attack being made against the Solar Power Satellite concept even as you read this.

This attack is being carried out by taking the data you have seen herein and using it against the SPS system by distorting it, using only parts of it, falsifying it, placing it in negative semantic context, misquoting expert sources, quoting it out of context, partial quoting, and all the other tricks of Orwellian propaganda. The prepetrators of this intellectual and technical fraud are counting on the fact that other people are ignorant of science and technology and will not bother to dig up the real facts. And if some people manage to see through this fraud, these Nature-fakers will try to keep it from being published or attempt to hoot it down by heckling techniques.

In some cases, they are being aided and abetted by the Department of Energy of the United States of America which has used tax money to print and distribute the semantically negative falsehoods of these "citizens' energy groups." This claim would not be made here unless it could be documented, and it can.

They will ignore this book, as they have ignored others like it. To attack it or to write unfavorable reviews about it would bring it to people's attention. That isn't what they want to do. They are intellectual guerrillas. They fight only on their terms, and they choose their own time and place to attack. They wish to bury scientific honesty and hard data where it won't be noticed. They are the Modern Technological Inquisition.

Happily for our future, we're on to their game. And so are you at this point.

Lest I be charged as a non-thinking, knee-jerk reacting super-advocate of the SPS and space power, it is only fair to point out that I have in the past ignored the potential of the SPS. In 1976 testimony before the Senate Committee on Aeronautical and Space Sciences, I did not consider it the important part of the exploitation of space that I have since learned it to be. The SPS wasn't mentioned to any great length in *The Third Industrial Revolution* originally written in 1974. It was only after several years of reading, working with study groups on various aspects of the SPS concept, and thinking about the whole proposal that I became convinced of the importance of the SPS as a factor in our future because of its energy potential as well as its international potential to solve many problems of today. I was perhaps cautious because, as a long-term optimist for the future of the human race and as one who has firmly believed in the hopeful advantages of the endless frontier of space for over thirty years and worked in the aerospace profession to bring it about, I did not want to weaken my position by backing a possibly losing proposition. I don't have to worry about that now. The SPS is not wishful thinking on the part of space advocates. I must believe the data and the evidence because it is solid. In spite of problems which exist—and which can be solved—the Solar Power Satellite concept is a valid solution to an overall program which offers us realistic and achievable solutions to many if not most of the world problems today.

Mind you, this does not amount to apology because none is required. It's an admission of oversight because the benefits inherent in the total system weren't perceived for lack of data.

In this book, the discussion has tried to bring out and discuss a large number of salient issues having to do with the possibility of achieving space power. There is bright promise in a Solar Power Satellite program whose technology we now understand to a greater degree than any other large engineering and technical program undertaken thus far in history. But the discussion has also concerned the manifold problems. An attempt has been made to present the realities of the social, economic, political, and environmental problems. To some extent, it hasn't been possible to treat all of these with the rigor and thoroughness I would have preferred because of the problems of keeping this book down to an affordable size. But the problems in these areas have received attention in the volumes of study reports from the Department of Energy, the National Aeronautics and Space Administration, private companies, think tanks, and individuals.

And one must always leave something for someone else to do, someone with greater professional expertise and experience in certain specialized fields.

This sort of legacy was handed to me as a young man, and I suspect that I have to hand something of the sort along to the next generation as well. There were prophetic books in my youth, such volumes as "Victory Through Air Power" by Seversky and "The Conquest of Space" by Ley and Bonestell. A generation of scientists and engineers worked to bring those books from the printed page to reality. It's presumptuous on my part to believe that this book can or would do the same sort of thing, but perhaps it will start people *thinking*, which is the first step in the real solution of any problem. Once people begin to think about the problem rather than to wallow in it and look for a lucky break in their situation, the first step has been made and the rest becomes a foregone conclusion.

Perhaps the SPS isn't the solution after all. If not, we still will have started people thinking about audacious solutions to our problems.

Theodore Roosevelt said on 10 April, 1899, on the eve of the twentieth century, "Far better it is to dare mighty things, to win glorious triumphs, even though checkered by failure, than to take rank with those poor spirits who neither enjoy nor suffer much because they live in the gray twilight that knows not victory or defeat."

And sometimes it only takes a few people. "It is because nations tend to stupidity and baseness that mankind moves so slowly; it is because individuals have a capacity for better things that it moves at all," said George Gissing.

We are in state of transition, the greatest transition in human affairs to take place in the last 10,000 years. For the first time in all our long history, we have the knowledge and the intellectual tools to take a grip on our collective destiny as well as our individual lives. Equipped with trained and educated minds free of superstition and capable of compassionately solving complex problems, we are far ahead of our cowering ancestors who believed they were at the mercy of the gods and could influence their future only by mystic chanting, genuflections, and pleadings, supplicating their childish gods through sacrifice, human and animal.

To them, our earth power must seem like god power.

But it will be as nothing to the space power we are just beginning to realize lies within our grasp, if we can only fend off those who would rather we were still living in caves so that they could lead the mystic chantings to gods who behaved like spoiled children. We've grown beyond that. We can and will achieve the final frontier of space with the power of the gods in our hands and under control.

The pessimism that seems to grip our age is unfounded. It is not the first time in history that this spirit has taken hold of us. But now we know what to do about it. Ernest Temple Hargrove: "The gloom of the world is but a shadow. Behind it yet within our reach is joy. There is a radiance and glory in the darkness, could we but see; and to see, we have only to look."

Space power is that radiance and glory, the gleaming power of the Sun on the panels of the photovoltaic array of a Solar Power Satellite.

We can worry it to death, study it to death, and talk it to death.

It's time to stop worrying; the benefits far outweigh any disadvantages.

It's time to stop studying it; the studies have been done and it is time to start building hardware and getting it to work right.

It is time to stop talking about it.

It is time to start making it happen.

It is time for space power.

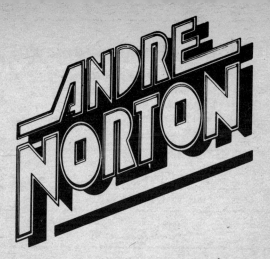

ANDRE NORTON

Classic stories by America's most distinguished and successful author of science fiction and fantasy.

145